MR

PRAISE FOR
BESTSELLING AUTHORS

JANE SULLIVAN

"Jane Sullivan has a gift for making outrageously comic situations seem plausible, and her likable characters shine."
—*Romantic Times*

"Ms. Sullivan gives us a well-written story, one with credibility, realism and sparkling characters that make it a joy to read."
—*The Romance Reader*

ISABEL SHARPE

"Isabel Sharpe pens a fresh tale with solid characterization and snappy dialogue."
—*Romantic Times*

"...a story full of unforgettable moments and a plot that simply delights."
—*The Best Reviews*

JULIE KISTLER

"Backing humor with a substantial plot, Kistler creates a memorable romance that will keep both giggles and heat on high."
—*WordWeaving.com*

"Julie Kistler holds the patent on romantic comedy. Follow your bliss to a sassy, sizzling read!"
—Bestselling and award-winning author
Vicki Lewis Thompson

Jane Sullivan earned a degree in professional writing from the University of Oklahoma, but several years passed before she pursued publication. Then a friend introduced her to romance novels, and after reading five of them in as many days, she knew she wanted to write romance! Jane was a finalist for Romance Writers of America's Golden Heart Award in 1999, which led to her first sale to the Harlequin Duets line. Several more sales followed, and now this award-winning author writes for Harlequin Duets and Harlequin Temptation lines, as well as single-title contemporary romances under the name Jane Graves. She lives in Richardson, Texas, with her husband, her teenage daughter and a beautiful but brainless cat who keeps her company while she's hard at work on her next book.

Isabel Sharpe was not born with a pen in her hand like many of her fellow authors. Instead of starting a writing career early on in life, she earned her B.A. in music from Yale in 1983 and a master's in vocal performance from Boston University in 1990. In 1994, motherhood happily interrupted a fledgling career in fund-raising for which she was vastly unsuited. Searching for something to keep herself stimulated while at home full-time with a demanding infant, she took the plunge into writing romance. Since then she has sold fourteen books to Harlequin. Isabel lives in Wisconsin with her two sons and a paunchy cat named Sinbad.

A former lawyer, **Julie Kistler** left the legal world in 1985 to start a full-time writing career. She wrote over fifteen American Romance books before moving on to write for the Love & Laughter, Duets and Temptation lines, for a total of over twenty-five books to date. A two-time Golden Heart finalist who has been nominated for a RITA® Award for *Black Jack Brogan,* Julie has received awards from both *Romantic Times* and *Affaire de Coeur.* Her style has always been romantic comedy, often inspired by old movies. She loves plots and characters that are funny, contemporary, sexy and a little off-kilter.

Always a Bridesmaid

Jane Sullivan

Isabel Sharpe

Julie Kistler

HARLEQUIN®

TORONTO • NEW YORK • LONDON
AMSTERDAM • PARIS • SYDNEY • HAMBURG
STOCKHOLM • ATHENS • TOKYO • MILAN • MADRID
PRAGUE • WARSAW • BUDAPEST • AUCKLAND

ISBN 0-373-83612-0

ALWAYS A BRIDESMAID

Copyright © 2004 by Harlequin Books S.A.

The publisher acknowledges the copyright holders of the individual works as follows:

BACKSEAT BRIDEGROOM
Copyright © 2004 by Jane Graves

LOVE IS A BEACH
Copyright © 2004 by Muna Sill

FAIR GAME?
Copyright © 2004 by Julie Kistler

www.eHarlequin.com

Printed in U.S.A.

CONTENTS

BACKSEAT BRIDEGROOM

Jane Sullivan

CHAPTER ONE

WHEN SERENA STAFFORD heard her doorbell ring, followed by a flurry of knocks, followed by more frantic ringing and more knocks, she was sure that something had to be terribly wrong. Maybe her condo complex was on fire. Maybe EPA officials were canvassing the neighborhood, warning of a sudden biohazard. Maybe her pregnant next-door neighbor had gone into premature labor while her husband was out of town.

Serena reached the door, looked out the peephole, and breathed a sigh of relief. It was only Chloe.

Wait a minute. What was she saying? It was never "only Chloe." Since they'd been kids disaster had followed her sister wherever she went. And as persistently as Chloe was knocking right now, Serena had a feeling that news of a biohazard would be a relief compared with what she was going to hear.

She opened the door. "Chloe? What is it?"

Her sister burst through the door, her short, spiky blond hair frozen in place even as the rest of her bounced with excitement. "The most wonderful thing has happened! You'll never guess what!"

"What?"

"I'm getting married!"

Serena closed the door. She couldn't have heard what she thought she heard. Her sister was getting married?

Again?

"Hold on, Chloe. Last time I checked, you and David had broken up. And none too nicely."

"Not David!" she said with a dismissive swipe of her hand. "His name is Bobby. Bobby Erickson. You remember. The blind date Kristi set me up with."

"Chloe. That was only three days ago."

Chloe gave her a big smile. "Yeah. I know."

"He asked you to marry him?"

"That's right."

"And you said *yes?*"

Chloe held up her palm. "Now, I know what you're thinking. But there's no doubt about it. Bobby's the one."

"That's what you said the last two times!"

Her sister rolled her eyes. "Will you stop being such a pessimist?"

"I'm being a realist. You cannot fall in love in three days."

"Sure you can. If you find the right man. And Bobby is the right man for me. I just know he is."

"Sit down, Chloe."

"But—"

"*Sit.*"

Chloe sighed and sat down on the sofa, right on the edge of the cushion, which didn't surprise Serena at all. Chloe spent every waking moment poised on the edge of life, ready to shift directions the instant the next outrageous possibility caught her attention.

Serena sat down beside her. Slowly. Reasonably. Trying to remain calm at the same time that she was on the verge of locking her sister in a room until the urge to ruin her life went away.

"What do you actually know about this guy?" Serena asked. "What kind of job does he have?"

"Something with computers."

"Does he make a decent living?"

"He drives a nice car. Lives in a nice apartment. I saw it today."

"How's his credit?"

"He seems responsible enough."

"Investments?"

Chloe shrugged.

Serena rubbed her temples. Okay. There was somebody out there for everybody, right? This guy had to be every bit as wild and impulsive as Chloe, so maybe it really was a match made in heaven.

Though how the two of them would ever function in daily life, Serena didn't know.

"And of course I want you to be my maid of honor," Chloe said.

Oh, God. Not again.

For Chloe's first wedding, Serena had stood barefoot on a beach, heavy morning mist flattening her hair as sand crabs crawled across her toes. During wedding number two, performed on the roof of a Phoenix skyscraper, a gust of wind had blown Serena's dress right up over her head. One of Chloe's close friends, a wild-eyed Woodstock throwback who Chloe swore wasn't as crazy as he looked, had snapped a picture of Serena's backside in nothing but a pair of flesh-toned panties. She'd had to threaten him with legal action to get the picture back, which meant the guy really had been as crazy as he looked, which meant Chloe really was a lousy judge of character.

"So where are you planning to get married this time?" Serena asked.

"Vegas. I've never tried that before. I found this cute place on the Internet. Cupid's Little Chapel of Love."

Serena winced. Just the thought of a tacky, hurry-up Vegas wedding made her crazy, and one taking place at Cupid's Little Chapel of Love had to be the worst of the worst. A wedding was the most wonderful day of a woman's life, a day that required months of planning after years of dreaming. But at least this time the ceremony would be indoors on ground level and she could probably wear shoes.

"Have you set a date?"

"Uh…yeah. August 22."

Okay. That was good. A year from tomorrow. Maybe her sister was finally growing up. A year-long engagement would allow Chloe plenty of time to get to know her fiancé and, if need be, give Serena plenty of time to talk her out of getting married.

"Okay," she told Chloe. "I'll be your maid of honor."

"Oh! I knew I could count on you!" Chloe gave Serena a big hug, then leaned away. "Well, don't just sit there!"

"What?"

"Bobby's waiting in the car!"

"*What?*"

"It's only a six-hour drive. We'll be there before you know it."

"But you said August 22. That's a year from—"

Then the truth struck Serena, and she nearly choked. "No," she said, shaking her head wildly. "No way. You are *not* getting married tomorrow to a man you've known only three days!"

Chloe's expression surged into pure rapture.

"Come on, Serena. Don't you ever feel the rush? That overwhelming, beautiful, wild, exciting feeling of being in love and not wanting to spend one second without that person?"

"That's lust, Chloe. Not love."

"Whatever it is, it's the most wonderful feeling in the world. Someday you'll find just the right guy, and you'll know what I'm talking about. Sometimes lightning just...strikes."

Lightning? That was what she intended to base a marriage on?

Marriage was something that came about after a long enough engagement period revealed the kind of compatibility that could sustain a relationship over a lifetime. It had nothing to do with a burst of electrical energy that rendered a person brainless. But if history was any indicator, telling Chloe that was an exercise in futility.

"Have you at least considered having a real wedding?" Serena said. "You know—one you actually plan?"

"Hey, I planned the last one!"

"In a week."

"Well, yeah..."

"Which was longer than the marriage lasted."

"Okay. That was a mistake. But this isn't. You'll see. I'm older now. Smarter."

Older? Definitely. But smarter? Serena would

have to take issue with that. "Have you considered just living with him?"

"Come on. You know Mom would freak out if I moved in with a guy."

"And she's not going to freak about this?"

"I think she's kind of used to it by now."

"How long were you planning on being gone?"

"We thought we'd drive six hours to Vegas, stay the night, get married, then drive back home tomorrow. That's all."

"But you need a marriage license."

"The marriage license bureau stays open until midnight. It's only four o'clock now, so there'll be plenty of time to get one as soon as we reach Vegas. Then we'll go to the chapel the next morning." Chloe took Serena's hands. "Please tell me you'll come. I wouldn't feel married unless you were my maid of honor."

This was insane. The last thing Serena wanted to do was take a road trip to Vegas so she could watch her sister screw up her life one more time. After all, it was Saturday, and she had errands to run. Bills to pay. Her car's inspection sticker expired in eleven days, so the clock was ticking on that. She'd brought a briefcase full of work home from the bank. Those things were on her schedule, and they had to be done.

But then again, if she didn't go, by this time tomorrow, Chloe would be married. If Serena took the trip with her from Tucson to Vegas, at least she'd have six hours to try to talk some sense into her.

She let out a sigh of resignation. "Okay. Let me go pack a bag."

"Oh, thank you!" Chloe said. "This is going to be such fun!"

Fun. As if that was all one had to consider when one got married.

Serena started for her bedroom. Chloe headed for the front door, then spun back around.

"Oh! Serena! I almost forgot! There's one more thing—"

"Not now, Chloe. I can take only so much good news at once."

"But—"

"Later. Tell me later."

"Okay, then. I'll be outside. Hurry!"

Serena went into her bedroom, where she packed a weekend's worth of necessities. She put her lights on a timer, watered her plants, made sure the back door was locked, grabbed her briefcase, then left her condo.

An SUV was parked at the curb. A man leaned against the fender, but it was hard to make out much about him when Chloe was attached to him from the lips down like a barnacle on the hull of a ship.

Serena cleared her throat, and Chloe spun

around. "Serena! This is Bobby. Bobby, my sister, Serena."

"Serena," Bobby greeted her. "Chloe's told me such wonderful things about you. She said we just had to bring you with us. Thanks so much for coming."

Okay. At least he seemed like a nice guy. And if physical attraction were the only criterion, she could see why Chloe had fallen for him. He was tall and well-built, with a flashy smile and the kind of facial features rarely seen outside the pages of a fashion magazine. Of course, his shaggy hair, T-shirt, baggy denim shorts and flip-flops kind of blasted away at the *GQ* image.

"Let me take your bag," Bobby said. He popped the trunk lid and tossed it inside, and then he and Chloe got into the front seat. Serena took her briefcase and slid into the backseat. But just as she was getting ready to close the door behind her, she came to a startling conclusion.

The backseat was already occupied.

"Serena," Chloe said, "this is Tom Erickson. Bobby's brother. He's going to be Bobby's best man. Tom, this is my sister, Serena."

The man turned to face her, and she felt a start of surprise. *This* was Bobby's brother?

Not that he wasn't a match for Bobby in the looks department. Sandy-brown hair, green eyes, attractive features, nice build—in those ways he was almost a mirror of his brother. But unlike Bobby, he wore a neatly pressed polo shirt tucked into a nice pair of jeans, his hair was cut conservatively short, and he wore wire-rimmed glasses. Bobby was congenial and flamboyant—the kind of guy you'd see at a frat party, tapping a keg and chatting up sorority girls. Tom was the controlled, orderly, academic kind of guy the sorority girls passed right by in college, then got to their thirties and wished to God they'd married.

He turned to Serena with a sharp, assessing gaze, then checked her out with a single up-and-down flick of those vibrant green eyes. Serena's heart started to pound. She'd never had much interest in tapping kegs, but she'd always had that thirty-something mentality, even when she was in college.

He folded his arms across his chest and cocked his head slightly. The faintest of smiles played across his lips. "Hello, Serena. When Bobby and Chloe picked me up, I had no idea I was going to be sharing a backseat."

Serena turned to look at her sister. "Neither did I."

"Well," Chloe said a little sheepishly, "I *did* tell you there was one more thing."

Serena couldn't believe this. The whole situation was completely insane. Unfortunately, by the time she opened her mouth to have another word with

Chloe, Bobby had already pounced on the lull in the conversation to engage her in a lip lock that Serena would have needed a crowbar to pry her loose from.

With a sigh of resignation, Serena shut the door and buckled herself in. If she went along with this now, at least she had the next six hours to talk her sister out of this insanity. If she didn't, by this time tomorrow, her sister would be married and that would be that.

A few seconds later the lovebirds came up for air. Bobby started the car and hit the gas, and the road trip from hell had begun.

THEY HAD JUST LEFT the Tucson city limits with nothing but open road ahead, when Bobby announced that it might be a good idea if they found a gas station.

Pronto.

Serena shook her head in disbelief. What kind of person would start a six-hour road trip with an empty gas tank?

Wait a minute. What was she saying? The kind who would marry a woman he'd known only three days.

A few minutes later, Bobby got lucky and found one of those big gas station/truck stop/convenience stores that sold everything from Arizona souvenirs to dirty bumper stickers to peanut patties. He drove over to one of the gas pumps and killed the engine.

"Hey, Tom," he said, pulling his credit card out of his wallet. "Chloe and I are going inside to get something to drink. Will you put gas in the car while we're gone? It'll get us back on the road faster."

"Sure," Tom said.

"You guys want anything?"

When Tom and Serena shook their heads, Bobby and Chloe got out of the car and walked into the store practically joined at the hip. As Tom got out and started the pay-at-the-pump procedures, Serena noticed a gigantic bug splat on the windshield.

No way could she look at that for the next three-hundred-and-fifty miles.

She got out of the car and circled around to the island where the gas pumps stood. She pulled the squeegee out of the bucket, slung off the excess water and turned to scrub the windshield. Tom took the nozzle from the pump and put it into the tank, then walked over. He turned to lean against the driver's door.

"Well," he said. "Lovely day for a road trip to Sin City, isn't it?"

Serena could dance around this and make nice, or she could cut to the chase. She opted for number two.

"Actually," she said, "there's nothing lovely

about it. The car is uncomfortable, it's hotter than hell, and my sister and your brother are getting ready to make the biggest mistake of their lives.''

A tiny smile crossed his lips. "Imagine that. And here I thought I was the only sane person in the car."

"So you don't think they should get married, either?"

"Of course not. Not that I don't believe in true love, but finding it in only three days is a stretch."

"So why did you come along?"

"How else was I going to get the opportunity to talk Bobby out of it?"

Serena felt a flood of relief. "That's why I came along, too. To talk Chloe out of it. I mean, I'm sure your brother's very nice—"

"And your sister, too. But they've known each other only three days, they're too impulsive, and neither one of them should be getting anywhere near a wedding chapel."

"Exactly. I tried to talk Chloe out of it as soon as I found out. And I might as well have been trying to tune in Mars. Did you have a word with Bobby?"

"Several words. None of which he paid the least bit of attention to."

"Don't get the wrong idea," Serena said. "I love my sister a lot. But when it comes to common sense—"

"I hear you. Bobby's got a lot of great qualities. But common sense isn't one of his strong suits, either."

Then Serena happened to glance toward the convenience store. "Will you look at them? They're making out in the potato-chip aisle!"

Tom peered over the top of the car and sighed. "I'm afraid Bobby's never really understood the concept of there being a time and a place for everything."

"Neither has Chloe. She's very proud of her mile-high club membership."

Tom turned back around. "So what are we going to do to break them up?"

Serena felt a rush of hope. She had a partner in crime. Maybe if the two of them joined forces, Bobby and Chloe would actually listen.

"I don't know," Serena said. "It's impossible to reason with Chloe when she's in a state like this."

"She's just like Bobby. They're both in love with being in love."

"What?"

"I read an article about it in *Time*. They referenced a Harvard study on the issue. For some people, when they get that endorphin high, it's like a drug addiction. Suddenly they can't think straight. They do stupid things. When they start to get comfortable with each other, it wears off. Then they split and go looking for it again with somebody else. The cycle never ends.''

"In other words, they're slaves to their hormones.''

"Exactly.''

"I can't imagine being that out of control.''

Tom smiled. "Well. It's nice to know there really are level-headed women out there. Gives me hope.''

"Hope?''

"Yes. Unfortunately, the world is filled with women who want nothing more out of life than to hop from one bar to the next, then hit the mall and run up their credit cards.''

"Sounds like Chloe. I once suggested that she might want to think about a retirement account, and she told me she intended to live it up until she was sixty-five and then die in her sleep.''

"Bobby just spent thirty thousand dollars on this SUV. Fine, if you have thirty thousand dollars to spend. Bobby doesn't.''

Serena cringed. The very notion of pouring that kind of money into a depreciating asset made her a little sick to her stomach. To meet a man who felt the same way she did about that was downright astonishing.

"Does he have any idea how much interest he could earn on that money over time?'' Serena asked.

"That was what I told him. Buy a nice used car and invest the rest. But try explaining compound interest to a guy who spends most of his time compounding his debt."

"Yeah, I know what you mean. Chloe thinks 'compound interest' means you're admiring two guys' butts at the same time."

"So we're in this together?" Tom said. "We'll do whatever we have to do to make sure they don't get married?"

"Yes. Absolutely."

"Okay, then. Here's plan A. There's no sense trying to talk to them when we're in the car and their backs are to us. It'd be too easy for them to blow us off. It's almost four-thirty now. In an hour or so, I'll tell Bobby to stop so we can get a bite to eat. During dinner we should have a solid half hour to make our case."

Serena nodded. "Sounds good to me."

A few moments later, Bobby and Chloe returned to the car. Bobby had a soda cup and a smear of lipstick on the shoulder of his T-shirt. Chloe had a soda cup and a hickey on her neck. And neither one seemed the least bit disturbed by either of those things.

Serena quickly ran the squeegee over the rest of the windshield while Tom returned the nozzle to the pump. As they all got back into the car, Serena was still marveling over the fact that Tom and

Bobby were related. Tom seemed logical and reasonable and down-to-earth—qualities men ought to have but rarely did. Qualities inherent in the kind of man she looked for but never found.

The kind of man she just couldn't take her eyes off.

You're staring, Serena. Cut it out.

But before she could look away, Tom gave her a furtive wink, sealing their pact as co-conspirators, and she felt the strangest little sizzle right down her spine.

She told herself she was just feeling gratitude. A sense of relief because she wasn't swimming upstream against the raging current of her sister's goofy whims all by herself.

Yes. That was it.

As Bobby started the car and pulled back onto the interstate, Serena reached into her briefcase to take out a few file folders, thinking she might as well get some work done. She opened one. Stared at it. It could have been printed in Mandarin Chinese and she wouldn't have known the difference, because all she could think about was the man in the seat beside her.

She let out a silent sigh. This was going to be a *very* long trip.

CHAPTER TWO

As THE MILES sped away beneath them, Tom tried to concentrate on the reports he'd pulled out of his briefcase to read, but he was failing miserably. It wasn't the music Bobby was playing—some weird hip-hop stuff that was more noise than music. It wasn't the fact that even though the air conditioner was blasting, it was still hot in the car.

It was Serena.

For the past hour, the woman in the seat next to him had occupied every one of his thoughts. At thirty-one, he had enough experience to know that women like Serena didn't come along every day. She was smart, she was pretty, and she was sane enough to realize that Bobby and Chloe were out of their minds. Three qualities he admired very much.

He'd once had a girlfriend who spent a hundred and fifty bucks every month getting her hair and nails done. He'd told her once that if she skipped all the flashy stuff, she could invest that money and be a millionaire by age sixty-five. She'd broken up with him the next week and started dating her yoga instructor.

In contrast, Serena had warm brown hair that looked as if it was the color God gave her. She had nice brown eyes he could see clearly because he wasn't looking through layers of mascara. Her nails were close-clipped and natural without those weird fake ones stuck to them. Some men liked the idea of bloody scratches on their backs from a woman's razor-sharp nails. He wasn't one of them.

She wore denim shorts. A white cotton shirt. Low-heeled shoes that looked comfortable enough to do some real walking in. She was a woman who radiated substance over symbolism. Though he never would have admitted it, there wasn't anything sexier to him than a woman who might actually be able to balance a checkbook. Of course, that didn't stop him from picturing her wearing a garter belt and black silk stockings as she accomplished that task. After all, unadorned didn't mean unattractive. Intelligence, a sensible nature and fiscal responsibility all wrapped up in a very pretty package. Did it get any better than that?

He glanced at her out of the corner of his eye. A strand of her hair had fallen along her cheek, and in one smooth, sensual move, she reached her index finger up and slowly tucked it behind her ear. As if she sensed him looking at her, she turned and their eyes met. Her lips eased into a warm smile. He smiled back, and they held each other's gazes several seconds past the point that mere acquaintances might.

She's interested.

That realization jump-started Tom's heart into a quick, erratic rhythm. The backseat of this car suddenly felt much smaller than before, because he swore he could hear every breath Serena took, even over the noise of the car engine. As she returned her attention to the papers she was reading, outrageous thoughts came to mind, not the least of which was grabbing her, pulling her right up next to him and making what Bobby and Chloe had done in the potato-chip aisle look tame.

Okay. So it was a completely irrational act that would make a rational woman turn and run. But that didn't stop him from thinking about it.

Fixating on it.

Obsessing about it.

He had to stop this. No matter how attractive Serena was, any interest he showed in her would only sabotage his mission, which was to get Bobby back on track again. Only after he'd accomplished that could he move on to more selfish ventures.

With that thought in mind, he dragged his attention away from Serena and issued himself a set of marching orders: *Think about her all you want to. Look when you can.*

But no matter what happens, do not touch.

FOR THE PAST HOUR, Bobby had held on to Chloe with one hand while he drove with the other. In Serena's book that was unsafe enough, but now he was slipping his arm around her, and even with the console between them, he pulled her so close that a lettuce leaf couldn't have separated them. In that position, he couldn't possibly have his full attention devoted to driving. To top it all off, every once in a while he'd lean over and give Chloe a kiss, during which time *none* of his attention was devoted to driving.

Tom looked up from what he was reading, and by the way his eyes narrowed, Serena could tell he didn't approve any more than she did.

Moments later, Bobby dove in for another kiss, only this time the car swung to the right. The longer his lips stayed glued to Chloe's, the more the car veered.

"Hey!" Tom said, smacking his brother on the shoulder. "Will you cut that out? Watch where you're—"

Bobby spun around to face the road again. He immediately swore and swerved hard to the left, but not before the car collided with something on the shoulder of the road. And as Bobby hit the brake, Serena felt the telltale *thunk-thunk-thunk* of a blown-out tire.

Bobby pulled over and brought the car to a halt.

He killed the engine, then spun around to face Tom. "Why did you do that?"

"Why did I do *what?*"

"Hit me like that and make me drive off the road!"

"You were already *off* the road!"

Tom threw open his door and got out. Bobby did the same, with Serena and Chloe close behind. Tom circled around to the right front fender and stared down at the tire. It was flat as the Arizona desert.

"Uh-oh," Chloe said, a little nervously. "That tire's pretty messed up."

"Hey, no sweat," Bobby told her. "I'll just put on the spare."

"Bobby," Tom said, his voice a low growl, "you don't know how to change a tire."

"Oh, yeah." Bobby gave Tom a sheepish look, then held out his keys. "Do you mind?"

With his teeth gritted so hard Serena was sure his jaw was going to crack, Tom took the keys and unlocked the rear of the SUV, pulled the luggage out, and flipped up the lid to the spare tire compartment. He froze for a moment, then slowly turned around.

"Bobby?"

"Yeah?"

"When's the last time you checked your spare?"

Bobby and Chloe walked to the back of the vehicle.

"Bobby!" Chloe cried. "Why are you carrying around a flat tire?"

"Uh...I guess I forgot to get it fixed after the last flat I had."

Chloe put her fists on her hips. "You started a six-hour road trip without even considering the fact that you might need a spare tire, and now we're stranded?"

Bobby opened his mouth, but nothing came out.

"How are we supposed to get to Vegas now?"

Serena felt a rush of hope. In spite of Chloe's generally cheerful nature, she did have a bit of a temper. Right now that could create some solid discord. Which could lead to a first-class argument. Which could escalate into a whole lot of trouble in paradise.

"But, baby," Bobby said, "I couldn't help it. I'd have checked before we left, but with you standing there looking so beautiful, how was I supposed to think about anything else?"

Oh, pu-leeze.

Serena felt sure that even Chloe would smack Bobby for that nonsensical explanation. Instead, her anger melted away, and she wrapped her arms around his neck and gave him a peck on the lips.

"That's okay, sweetie. It's just a little setback. We can call for help, right?"

Chloe reached into her purse, fumbled around for a minute, then turned to Bobby with a sheepish expression. "I think my phone's still at home hooked up to the charger."

"No problem." Bobby reached into his pocket, extracted his cell phone, and hit the button to turn it on. He hit it again.

"Uh-oh," he said.

"What?" Chloe asked.

"At least yours is charging. Mine's out of juice."

Tom rolled his eyes and reached into his pocket at the same time that Serena reached into her purse. They both pulled out cell phones. Tom held up his palm. "Don't worry. I've got it handled."

Looking at Tom's phone, Serena realized she'd seen one like it in last Sunday's paper.

"That's a Syntronic, isn't it?" she asked.

"Yeah."

"What model?"

"Sixty-six-twenty."

"That's state of the art."

"Yeah. I just upgraded."

Bobby let out a sigh of exasperation. "God, you are *such* a geek."

"Maybe so," Tom said. "But I'm a geek with a functioning cell phone who's gonna save the ass of the guy who doesn't have a spare tire."

Serena smiled furtively. Bobby might be movie-star handsome with a line of bull that would make the average woman swoon, but there was nothing more attractive to Serena than a smart, organized, take-charge kind of man she could turn to in a crisis.

In the distance, Tom spied a road sign pointing to a town named Windsor that was two miles down the state highway that intersected the interstate. He phoned directory assistance and found the numbers of the only three service stations there. He dialed one of them, and in a matter of minutes he'd arranged to have Bobby's car towed and his tire replaced.

Twenty minutes later, the tow truck arrived and hooked up the car, and they all managed to pile into the oversized cab to ride into town with the driver. He dropped them off at a local diner, telling Tom that he'd have the guy at the service station phone Tom when the work was done.

When they went inside the diner, Serena discovered that the 1960s were alive and well in Windsor, Arizona. The tables were Formica and the vinyl booths a screaming shade of aqua. The vintage jukebox in the corner belted out a scratchy version of "All My Loving." A long lunch counter was populated by a few men sipping coffee and reading the paper, and the aroma of fried everything filled the air.

Bobby and Chloe slid into one side of a booth,

leaving Tom and Serena to slide in the other. They ordered dinner from a tired-looking waitress named Lorena, who'd strolled straight out of central casting. She wore a Pepto-Bismol pink uniform, support hose, and an updo that looked like a mound of red-orange cotton candy. After promising Chloe extra cheese on her bacon cheeseburger and bacon just this side of burned, she rolled her eyes a little and headed for the kitchen.

"You know," Bobby said, "we needed to stop for dinner anyway, so this really isn't a setback at all, is it?"

"Of course it isn't, sweetie." Chloe gave him a kiss. "Everything's going to turn out just fine."

"Yes," Tom said. "We'll be on our way soon, which means that by tomorrow morning, you two will be married."

Bobby grinned. "That's right."

"Serena and I want to talk to you about that."

Bobby slumped with disgust. "Oh, great. You're gonna double-team us."

"No," Serena said. "We just think there might be a few things concerning marriage that you two haven't considered."

"Stop right there." Bobby held up his palm. "Look, I know you two don't get this because of the kind of people you are. But if you ever, just once, felt what we're feeling now, you'd never say another word to us again. Sometimes lightning strikes, and you know it's meant to be.''

"That's exactly what it's like," Chloe said. "Lightning."

Lightning. If Serena heard that nonsense one more time, she was going to stuff her sister in a box and ship her home UPS. And she might think twice about air holes.

"See, the moment I walked into that bar and saw Chloe," Bobby explained, "I knew she was the one." He dragged a fingertip down her cheek, and she looked at him adoringly. "We drank. We talked. We danced. It was the most incredible feeling, knowing that I'd found the woman of my dreams."

"Let's assume that's true," Serena said. "You've found the woman of your dreams. But to make a marriage work, there are other things you need to consider."

Chloe tried to interrupt, but Serena persisted, asking them about a few domestic issues, such as where they had decided to live, whether they were going to have kids, how they were going to split up housework. They merely smiled and said those were things they could work out later. Tom jumped in and made a very clear-cut argument about the need for a prenuptial agreement and asked them what plans they intended to make for their retirement. And they both continued to remain deaf to all of it, wearing smug expressions intended to tell her and Tom that they were deluded little fools who wouldn't know true love if it bit them on the nose.

"Why don't you come back to Tucson?" Serena said. "You can plan a really nice wedding. Get married by an actual minister. Invite guests. Have a reception."

"That's your wedding, Serena. Not mine." Chloe turned to Bobby. "She's been planning it since she was six years old."

Serena felt a twinge of embarrassment. "I have not."

"Oh, yeah? Get this, guys. She used to go to the prize machine in the grocery store and beg our mother to plug quarters into it until a ring popped out. Then she'd play bride. White towel on her head, flowers from the garden for a bouquet, the plastic ring on her finger—"

"Chloe—"

"And when we were teenagers, she had stacks of *Modern Bride* magazines. I think she still subscribes."

"Maybe you should take a hint," Serena said. "A wedding is something you *plan*."

"Before you've even got a fiancé?"

"All right," Tom said. "Just listen. We're not saying that you shouldn't get married. Just that you should have a little bit of an engagement period first.''

"But if we know where we're going," Bobby objected, "why would we want to waste time getting there?"

"Because it would be the rational thing to do."

"Rational." Bobby rolled his eyes. "That's you, Tom. Not me."

"It's Serena, too," Chloe told him. "She's always been that way. Can you imagine?" She gave a little shudder, as if behaving in a rational manner was worse than having a communicable disease.

"Don't worry, baby," Bobby assured her. "There's nothing they can do to stop us. Come tomorrow morning, we're going to be Mr. and Mrs. Bobby Erickson."

"Let's see," Serena said. "If she'd kept all her married names, that would make her Chloe Elizabeth Stafford Reese Schuler Erickson. Has a nice ring to it, doesn't it?"

Chloe winced. "Uh…Bobby?"

"Yeah?"

"Well…I took my maiden name back last time, and I was thinking maybe I'd just keep it."

Bobby's face fell. "But, sweetheart—"

"It's just so much simpler. I hate having to change my driver's license, my social security card. And then there's all that human resources stuff at work—"

"But I just assumed we'd have the same last name."

"I know. But really, sweetie. It's such a pain."

"This is exactly the kind of thing Serena and I are talking about," Tom pointed out. "Have you worked out *anything* ahead of time? What do you really know about each other?"

"All I need to know," Bobby said, his smile returning, "is that Chloe is the sweetest, most beautiful woman I've ever met. And you know what? I don't care if she wants to keep her maiden name. What does it really matter, anyway?" He dipped in to kiss Chloe, whispering against her lips. "A rose by any other name..."

Tom and Serena looked at each other, simultaneously shaking their heads.

"Hey, baby!" Bobby said suddenly. "Do you hear that jukebox? It's playing our song!"

"Our song?" Chloe asked.

"Every song is our song," he said as he slid out of the booth and held out his hand to Chloe. He led her to an open space in the diner and pulled her close. They began moving to the music.

"Oh, God," Serena said. "Are they actually dancing?"

"Looks that way," Tom told her.

"This is a diner. What's the *matter* with them?"

"It's part of the syndrome. They're totally self-absorbed, as if no one else is even in the room."

Lorena the waitress swept by and sloshed more water into their glasses. She nodded toward Bobby and Chloe. "What's up with them?"

"They're in *love*," Serena said.

"Nope," the waitress muttered. "They're just nuts."

As Lorena walked away, Tom sighed. "Well, it looks as if it's time to go to plan B."

"Plan B? What's that?"

"You'll have to give me a minute. I hadn't counted on plan A being such a bust."

"They're never going to listen to us. This is hopeless."

"No," Tom said, holding up his palm. "Don't give up yet. There has to be a way to get through to them."

Serena wasn't so sure. At the moment, Bobby seemed to have sprouted two additional hands, and Chloe didn't seem to mind where he was putting all four of them. He drew her so tightly against him that it looked as if they were on the verge of having sex standing up, and all the while he stared down at her with an adoring smile, as if no other woman on the planet existed.

As inappropriate as it was, Serena was surprised to feel the funniest twinge of envy, followed by a strange shiver of longing. What would it be like to have a man look at her like that?

Then she brushed off the feeling, telling herself

that if it came at the price of losing her mind, she could do without it.

"So what does Bobby do for a living?" Serena asked.

"He sells computers. He can talk the socks right off a customer, and he works on commission. If only he paired that with a little motivation and actually showed up to work on time, he could be pretty successful."

"Chloe sells cosmetics. Same song, second verse."

"And what do you do for a living?" Tom asked.

"I'm a loan officer."

His face brightened. "Oh, yeah? Consumer loans or mortgages?"

"Mortgages."

"Ahh," he said. "Real estate."

The appreciative tone of his voice sent an unexpected feeling of euphoria flowing through Serena.

"And what do you do?" she asked.

"I'm a financial planner."

Financial planner? Just those words conjured up a sense of stability and permanence and foresight, and Serena breathed a silent sigh of admiration.

"That's an interesting career," she told him.

"Not to most women. They want to spend money. I'm a reminder that they need to invest it."

"Hey, men don't find my profession terribly interesting, either. They're all looking for underwear models.''

''Underwear models? Now, I have to admit there *is* some appeal to that.''

Serena felt a swell of disappointment.

''For about fifteen minutes,'' Tom went on. ''I'm afraid I like women with a little more substance.'' He smiled. ''Believe me, Serena. You're interesting.''

You're interesting. How many men in her life had ever uttered those words to her? Like, zero?

Then it dawned on her. He was flirting with her.

Her heart did a little flip-flop at the realization. She'd always thought she'd been born without the kind of wit and charm and charisma that other women used to attract men. But as they talked, she tilted her head and gave Tom what she hoped was a series of tempting smiles at appropriate places in the conversation, and he acted as if she was positively scintillating.

Soon the song ended, and Bobby and Chloe headed over to the jukebox to play another one. As they began to dance again, Tom and Serena talked about the song, which they both liked, and the music Bobby had been playing in the car, which they didn't. They talked about the fact that Lorena the waitress was a little on the surly side. They laughed over a few of the dirty bumper stickers for sale near the counter. Soon Serena's attention had tunneled down to nothing but this tiny space where she was sitting alone with Tom, and she barely remembered that Bobby and Chloe were in the diner.

To her surprise, Tom turned a little and moved his elbow to the top of the booth, only inches away from her. "Genetics is a funny thing, isn't it?"

"What do you mean?"

"Who'd have thought that a woman like Chloe would have a sister like you?"

His expression was warm and inviting, and Serena felt a connection between them that was almost tangible. That was exactly what she'd been thinking about him and Bobby. How could two men so radically different from each other share the same gene pool?

"I think the stork must have screwed up a delivery at your house, too," she said.

Tom laughed. "That would explain a lot."

A dimple popped up in his left cheek, and little crinkles formed at the corners of his mouth and eyes, which made him appear open and friendly and just about as sexy as she could imagine a man looking. At first she'd admired his profession, his organizational skills, and his obvious focus on the important things in life, but now there was something more.

Much more.

Serena was vaguely aware that the music had

died away. Everything else in the diner seemed to fade away right along with it, until there was nothing on earth but this man sitting beside her. With the air quivering between them, Tom's gaze dropped to her lips. It lingered there a few seconds, then rose to meet her eyes again. Serena couldn't believe it. She'd dated only a handful of men in her life, but still she was pretty sure she knew male body language for *I'm thinking about kissing you.*

No. Stop it. That's impossible.

But if he wasn't thinking about kissing her, then why did he seem to be leaning closer to her with every second that passed? And why did she feel that exhilarating little buzz in her head, the one that made her heart beat like crazy and her mouth go dry as dust? And why, as she found herself looking at *his* lips, did she feel so unsteady and unstable and full of anticipation—

"What are you two doing?"

Serena spun around to see Chloe standing behind her.

CHAPTER THREE

SERENA JERKED AWAY from Tom, her mouth hanging open. Her sister stared down at her with a very baffled expression.

Shut your mouth, Serena. You look guilty as hell.

"What do you mean, what are we doing?" Tom said.

Chloe's brow furrowed with confusion. "It was so weird. For a minute there, I thought you were…" She shook her head. "Never mind."

"What?" Bobby said.

She laughed a little. "It looked like they were going to kiss each other."

"*Kiss* each other?" Tom's voice was full of surprise. "We were just talking. That was all."

"Yeah," Serena said, her heart beating wildly. "Talking."

Chloe turned to Bobby. "I knew I had to be seeing things. I mean, Serena usually makes a man wait until they've been on two or three dates before she lets him kiss her good night at the door. *After* she insists he disinfect his lips."

Serena shot a furtive glance at Tom, wishing

Chloe hadn't made her out to be the biggest prude in the state of Arizona. But at least it made her point, which was that getting up close and personal with men you barely knew was the wrong thing to do.

"So there you are," Serena said. "You know I'd never do anything as outrageous as kiss a man I hardly know, so I can't imagine what you think you saw."

"I can't either," Tom said, then made a scoffing noise. "A kiss? When we've known each other…what, Serena? Two hours?"

"That's right. Two hours."

"So you can see how ridiculous that is," Tom said.

"For you, maybe," Bobby remarked. "I'd known Chloe only fifteen minutes when I kissed her for the first time."

Tom frowned. "Like I said. Ridiculous."

Bobby turned to Chloe. "You'll have to forgive Tom. He's not exactly Mr. Spontaneity. This is a guy who has his ties arranged alphabetically by background color."

"That's nothing," Chloe said. "Serena has all the jars in her refrigerator door lined up according to height."

"Tom has never missed an oil change."

"Serena reads the newspaper in order. Page one, page two, page three…"

As their siblings prattled on, Tom took another sip of his water, and Serena sat feeling as dumb as she ever had in her life. How could she have thought that he'd been on the verge of kissing her?

Wait. Chloe had thought that, too.

No. Chloe had seen what she wanted to see: two people falling for each other at the drop of a hat, which would justify her own outrageous behavior. On the other hand, nothing outrageous was in the process of happening between her and Tom. In fact, if his unconcerned expression was any indication, he wasn't even aware that a storm had rolled in, much less that lightning had struck.

You've been without a man for too long. That's your problem.

Serena took a deep, furtive breath and let it out slowly. There. She felt better. She'd returned to her rational, reasonable self, in total control again. To play it safe, though, she excused herself to go to the bathroom, thinking that a little cold water splashed on her face might insure she stayed that way.

OUT OF the corner of his eye, Tom watched Serena walk away, his gaze falling on the rounded curve of her backside. And what a beautiful sight it was.

As she disappeared around the corner, he downed half a glass of cold water, then tried taking some deep breaths on the sly. It didn't help. He told himself to visualize something calm and serene, but that turned into "Serena," and he was lost all over again.

He couldn't believe Chloe had accused him of almost kissing Serena. He couldn't believe how right she'd been. And he couldn't believe that, if not for the fact that Chloe had walked up in the nick of time, he might actually have done it.

What was *wrong* with him?

He had no business having these thoughts, because they sure as hell muddied the waters. If Bobby had any clue where his brother's brain was right now, Tom would never get him back on the straight and narrow.

So get that grip, and do it now.

Instead, a tiny smile tugged involuntarily at the corners of his mouth. He wasn't an expert on the subject, but he thought maybe Serena had actually been flirting with him. And if that were true, then she was interested in him, too, which meant...

Which meant he was flirting with *danger,* and he needed to stop it.

Damn. He wanted this mess over with, and he wanted it over with now, because until that happened, he had to keep his hands off Serena. What he needed was to come up with a plan to prevent Bobby and Chloe from making a very big mistake. Unfortunately, in five hours they'd be in Vegas, so stopping their momentum at that point would be like arresting an avalanche once the first rumblings had begun.

Wait a minute. Five hours?

Maybe that was the problem. Maybe they just needed more time.

All at once it came to him.

He turned the plan over in his mind, looking for flaws, but all he saw was a way to provide them with the delay they needed.

"I'll be back in a minute," he told Bobby and Chloe, but they were so wrapped up in each other that he wasn't sure they heard him. He slid out of the booth, crossed the diner and headed down the long hall toward the bathrooms. He was just in time to catch Serena coming out of the ladies' room. He grabbed her by the arm and led her around the corner.

"Tom? What is it?"

He froze. With his hand still against Serena's arm and her dark eyes staring up at him, his brain took an instantaneous freefall right into his pants.

Man, feel that soft skin. Look at those long, long eyelashes. And the curve of her lips. And that smooth, perfect skin at her throat that leads to her collarbone, and then to her chest, and right down to her—

"Tom?"

Slowly he released her arm, giving his brain

time to head back home where it belonged. "Uh...I think I've got it."

"Got what?"

"I know how to keep Bobby and Chloe from going to Vegas." He glanced over his shoulder, then leaned in just close enough to Serena to keep his voice from being heard by those who didn't need to hear.

Or maybe a little closer than that.

"Did you see how Bobby started to lose it a little over the maiden-name thing?" he asked.

"Yeah. He didn't much like that, did he?"

"And Chloe was pretty miffed about Bobby not having a spare tire," Tom added.

"Right."

"If only we could keep them unmarried long enough to get into a decent-sized argument, they might just forget all about Vegas."

"That makes sense," Serena said. "But time isn't on our side. We'll be in Vegas in less than five hours."

"What if we stayed here longer? That'd buy us some time."

"But they're going to want to get back on the road as soon as possible. How do you propose we delay them?"

"Bobby doesn't know anything about cars. What if I have the guy at the service station tell him there's something else wrong besides just a blown tire? Something it'll take until tomorrow to fix?''

''You're going to make Bobby pay for nonexistent car repairs?''

''I'll make up something really cheap to repair but hard to get a part for. He won't know the difference.''

''How are you going to get the service-station guy to lie for you?''

''I'll ask him.''

''And if that doesn't work?''

''I'll bribe him.''

''You'd do that?''

''In this case, the end justifies the means. And we don't actually have to drive them apart. We just need to manufacture a car problem so we can delay them and create some stress. Then maybe they'll skip Vegas, go back to Tucson and have a nice, long engagement.''

''That's not a bad plan.''

''This could mean that we might not get home until Monday. Do you have any problem being away another day?''

Serena pulled her electronic planner out of her purse and tapped the screen a few times. ''Hmm. I'll have to make a few phone calls and shift some things around, but it'll be okay.''

She tucked the planner back into her purse and gave him one of those warm smiles that lit up her whole face. "Thanks for coming up with a plan. I don't know what I'd have done if you hadn't come along."

Tom laughed a little. "I gotta tell you, when I got up this morning, this was the last place I expected to end up."

"I know what you mean."

"But it hasn't all been bad, has it?"

Her warm smile heated up a degree or two. "No. It hasn't."

Tom could feel it. Something between them. Something physical and earthy that he could almost reach out and touch—the feeling of heightened alert that came when two people were humming along on the same frequency—and he had the most compulsive urge to lean closer to her and finish what he'd so foolishly started in the diner a few minutes ago.

Then his cell phone rang.

He grabbed the phone out of his pocket. It was Wally, the guy at the service station. Bobby's car was ready. Tom had a quick word with him about their plan, and he said he'd go along with it. They agreed on a problem to give Bobby's car, and Tom hung up.

"Okay, Serena. We're all set. Bobby's car will be out of commission for twenty-four hours. The guy told me there are two motels in town, but one's undergoing renovations. Fortunately, the other one is only about a quarter mile down the road from here. We can stay the night there."

"What about our luggage?"

"Wally said he'd bring it to the motel for us."

"Do you really think this will work?"

"It's our only shot," Tom said. "We have to make it work."

"Okay, then. I guess we'd better go break the news to Bobby and Chloe."

Yes. It was definitely going to work, no matter what he had to do, Tom thought. Then he could wrap this mess up and get back to the real business he wanted to attend to, which was getting to first base with Serena. Then he'd move to second. And eventually third. And by the time he crossed home plate...

Oh, *man*. He could only imagine what a beautiful day at the ballpark that was going to be.

THE SUN was sinking into the horizon as they walked toward the motel, but the heat of the day still hung heavily in the air. Serena swiped a sticky strand of hair off her forehead and wondered if the Sahara Desert would be a relief after Arizona heat.

"I still don't get it," Bobby said as he walked next to Tom. "My *what* is broken?"

Tom sighed with frustration. "Okay, Bobby. For the third time, your CV boot is broken because your differential is corroded."

"But what caused that? The car is only a year old."

"Well, if I had to guess, it's because you didn't maintain the manifold regurgitator."

"Hey, I had the car in for an oil change just last month! Shouldn't they have serviced that, too? How was I supposed to know they didn't?"

"It's your responsibility to know about these things."

"Okay. Fine. I'll learn someday. But for right now, it's only going to cost me twenty bucks, right?"

"Right."

"But the guy can't get the part until tomorrow afternoon."

Tom kept walking. "Right."

"So we're checking into a motel and staying overnight."

"Right."

"I can't believe we're stuck here," Chloe grumbled. "We were supposed to be getting married first thing in the morning."

Bobby dropped back and wrapped his arm around Chloe's shoulders. She shrugged away from him.

"Come on, Chloe. It's no big deal. I called the chapel and rescheduled for tomorrow night."

Chloe kept walking.

Bobby stopped, his palms turned up in a plead-
ing posture. "Baby! It's just one little setback!"

Chloe spun around, her fists on her hips. "Two
setbacks. First the spare tire, and now this."

"But what's one day compared to forever?
Huh?"

"Forever? Well, if this is what forever is going
to be like—"

Chloe stopped short, and Serena held her breath.
Maybe a twenty-four-hour delay might not be necessary. Could it be that they might start rethinking
their misguided little adventure right here and
now?

To her dismay, though, the anger melted away
from Chloe's face. "I'm sorry, sweetie. I didn't
mean that. Of course you're right. It's really no big
deal."

She gave him a make-up kiss, and they turned
and walked arm-in-arm toward the motel again.
Tom eased up next to Serena.

"It looks as if our plan is working," he whispered.

"I don't know. She forgave him pretty
quickly."

"Yeah, but it was a chink in the armor at least.
Between now and the time we pick up his car tomorrow, a lot can happen."

"And what was the problem with the car
again?" she whispered. "The manifold regurgita-

tor? I don't believe I've ever heard of one of those.''

"I'd be a little scared if you had. Since Bobby can't even point out a spark plug, one made-up car part is as good as another."

They reached the Windsor Motor Lodge and went inside the office, where the clerk informed them that there were only two rooms available. Chloe gave the woman a look of utter distress, then turned to Serena. "You don't mind sharing a room with Tom, do you?"

Serena's eyes flew wide open. "What?"

"I want to stay with Bobby."

"No way. Girls with girls, guys with guys."

"But Bobby and I are practically married!"

"Even if you were married, you couldn't expect Tom and me to share a room."

"What's the big deal? The room has two beds."

"Please tell me I don't actually have to explain that to you."

As Chloe continued to sulk, Serena felt a twinge of foreboding. This was a battle she absolutely had to win. The very idea of sharing a room with Tom when she'd already pictured him naked would be torture beyond words.

She gave Chloe her very best no-nonsense look, the one that usually intimidated her sister when nothing else worked. Finally Chloe rolled her eyes.

"Oh, all *right*." She folded her arms with a huff. "Now I know what Juliet felt like."

They checked in, then left the office and went down the sidewalk to their rooms. Bobby stopped at number twelve. Chloe continued on to room fourteen, and he looked longingly after her. Tom tapped him on the shoulder. "Hey, Romeo. We're in here."

Bobby dumped his luggage in their room and Chloe did the same, then they met back on the sidewalk.

"So what do we do now?" Serena heard Bobby say. "It's only seven o'clock."

Serena stuck her head out the door. "I vote we get a good night's sleep."

"Oh, come on!" Chloe said. "Let's go play. There's bound to be something to do in this dinky little town."

Chloe grabbed Bobby by the hand and led him into her room. Tom followed. Chloe took a phone book out of the nightstand and thumbed through it.

"Hmm. There's not much around here…oh, wait! A movie theater."

She dialed the number of the theatre and asked what was playing. Her eyes lit up. "*Terminator 3* at seven thirty?"

"*Terminator 3?*" Bobby said happily. "I've only seen that one twice."

Chloe asked directions to the theater, then hung

up. "It's within walking distance, right down on the main drag." She turned to Tom and Serena. "You guys want to come along?"

"No, thank you," Serena replied.

"I don't know, Serena," Tom said. "Sounds like fun to me."

Serena gave him a look of total disbelief. "*Terminator 3* sounds like fun?"

"Hey, what can I say? I'm a guy. Guns and explosions do it for me every time."

"Then it's settled." A big smile lit Chloe's face. "We'll all go."

As Chloe took Bobby's hand and they walked out of the room, Serena turned to Tom with a look of exasperation. "*Terminator 3?* Do you actually want to see that?"

"Not really," he said quietly. "But is it wise to turn them loose in a movie theater by themselves? They're liable to get naked in the fourteenth row."

It took only a few seconds of that horrifying image playing through her mind for Serena to realize just how right Tom was.

"On second thought," she said, "I never can get enough gratuitous violence." She grabbed her purse. "Let's go."

CHAPTER FOUR

THE DESERT ROSE was the archetypal small-town movie theater. One big screen, a couple hundred stained seats, and buttered popcorn guaranteed to clog any artery it came in contact with. A gum-cracking teenage girl with multicolored hair sold them five-dollar tickets. They stopped at the snack counter, then proceeded into the theater.

Bobby led Chloe down one of the rows, followed by Serena and then Tom. The place was so old that it didn't have cup holders in the arm rests, so after they sat down, Serena took a few sips of her soda and set it on the floor by her feet. Tom did the same.

Almost immediately, the lights dimmed and the room grew dark. The buzz of conversation quieted, and trailers for future releases began to play.

A few minutes later the movie started, but it could have been a blank screen for all Serena knew. A movie filled with bullets and body parts didn't interest her in the least.

But Tom certainly did.

She turned her eyes furtively in his direction.

There was something about sitting next to him in the dark that made her insides get all quivery, and if she kept looking at him on the sly like this, her eye muscles were going to be worn out before the movie was over.

"Ah," Tom whispered. "I see you're looking at my popcorn."

Serena flinched with surprise. His popcorn?

"There's nothing like movie popcorn," he went on. "I bet you wish you'd gotten some." He held out the bag. "Would you like to share?"

His words sent little tremors of excitement zinging right up Serena's spine. But why was she getting all hot and bothered about such a trivial question?

Because his attention was focused squarely on her. Because the tone of his voice was smooth and warm and very, very sexy.

And because maybe it wasn't just about the popcorn.

His eyes seemed to shimmer in the light from the movie screen, mesmerizing her, and he stared at her without blinking, waiting for her answer.

Say something. Anything.

"Uh...okay," she said. "Maybe I'll have a little."

"You can have all you want."

His words said one thing, but his eyes seemed

to say another: *If you think I'm talking about pop-corn, think again.*

"Thank you," she said, with a smile that said *No second thoughts necessary.*

She reached into the bag and pulled out a few pieces. She wasn't crazy about popcorn, but it didn't matter what this man offered her.

She wanted it.

Just that thought sent a surge of exhilaration racing through Serena. This couldn't be happening. Usually it took two or three dates for her to rationalize a little sexual interest in a man, but there was nothing rational about this. It was an all-consuming, cut-to-the-chase kind of attraction that made her body hum with anticipation.

But anticipation of what? Nothing could happen between them here and now. Absolutely nothing. Unfortunately, that didn't stop her body from waking to the possibilities.

Tom held the popcorn bag on his knee nearest her and rested his other hand on his thigh, his fingers spread. His hands were large and strong with neatly clipped nails and tapered fingers that looked as nimble as any she'd ever seen, and all at once her mind conjured up images of the miracles he might be able to accomplish with them. She saw his hands skimming over her, stroking her, caressing her, touching her in places that would make her body sing with pleasure.

Which she guessed would be just about any-where.

Serena jerked her gaze away, suddenly feeling a little shaky out on that limb. *You have to stop this. Wrong place, wrong time.*

But just as she'd pounded that edict home to herself, Tom reached for his soda cup, which was sitting on the floor between them. And as he rose again, the back of his hand brushed against her leg.

All…the way…*up*.

Serena held her breath, feeling as if he'd branded a streak from her ankle to her knee. She told herself he couldn't have actually *meant* to do it. It had to have been an accident. But when she glanced at him, he gave her a smile that seemed to say *You don't really think that was unintentional, do you?*

This was killing her.

For the next hour or so, Serena did not compre-hend one single shout, explosion or gun blast of the movie, and for every minute of that time, Tom might as well have had his hands all over her, given the way her body was reacting. Her breasts felt tingly, her nerves raw and her face hot, and she seriously considered holding her cold soda cup between her legs to cool herself down where she needed it the most. She was surprised Tom couldn't feel the heat radiating from her body in huge, undulating waves of pure sexual frustration.

Or maybe he could.

Good Lord. If he ever actually kissed her, she'd probably spontaneously combust.

Then Tom shifted in his chair. She tensed. Waiting. What was he doing?

As she held her breath, he stretched his hand over his head as if he was relieving stiffness from sitting too long. But when he brought it down again, it wasn't to his lap or to the armrest.

He draped it over the seat behind her head.

Serena's heart went crazy. Okay. No accident there. Yeah, he was touching the seat, not her, but still…

"Tom?" she whispered. "What are you doing?"

"Just getting comfortable. But if it's uncomfortable for you—"

"No," she said quickly. "No. Of course not. Not at all."

He gave her a smile. "Good."

Good. Now, what did he mean by that? Good that he was comfortable? Or good that he was closer to her and she didn't seem to mind?

All at once Serena thought about Chloe. Could she see what Tom was doing?

Serena glanced at her sister, only to realize that she and Bobby had stopped watching the action-fest on the screen and had started creating a little action of their own.

"Don't worry," Tom whispered. "They don't even know we're here."

Serena turned back to find an expression on Tom's face that seemed to say *This is as far as we can go for now. But once our mission is accomplished, watch out.*

Suddenly those hot, hazy images were swirling through her mind again—images of the kind of wild, sinful sex she'd never allowed herself to think about before, much less participate in.

But she sure was thinking about it now.

Serena kept her eyes glued to the screen, pretending to watch the movie, but the movie that was playing inside her head was far more entertaining. With Tom sitting so close to her, every second seemed to last an eternity, and by the time the movie was over, the two hours of unrelenting tension had just about worn her out.

Finally the credits rolled and the lights came up. Tom leaned away from her and picked up his popcorn sack and soda cup, his manner as unconcerned as if he'd sat through the entire movie by himself.

Maybe she was misreading every bit of this, Serena thought. Maybe he really had touched her leg by accident. Maybe he really was just getting comfortable with his arm draped behind her. And maybe his comment about Bobby and Chloe was just a generalized one, if you didn't take into account the look in his eyes when he'd said it.

Or had she imagined that, too?

As they left the theater to walk back to the motel, Serena was anticipating a drop in the temperature outside, hoping a blast of cool night air would quell her craving to hold on to Tom the way Chloe was holding on to Bobby. Unfortunately, the heat was just as powerful as it had been two hours ago, intensifying every sultry, sexual thought she was having.

Ten minutes later they reached the motel. Before going into their room, Chloe threw her arms around Bobby's neck and kissed him with the passion generally reserved for GIs heading off on a three-year tour of duty. The animosity that had popped up between them earlier seemed to be gone now. Serena could only hope that tomorrow might bring a little discord back into their lives.

Finally Chloe whispered one last thing in Bobby's ear, pried herself away from him and headed for her room.

"Good night, Serena," Tom said casually, then followed Bobby toward their room. At the last moment, though, he turned back and gave her a smile that practically melted her where she stood.

Thank God she'd insisted on sharing a room with her sister tonight. The last thing she needed was to be staying with a man she had an unprecedented case of the hots for, a man she couldn't stop thinking about, a man she should be staying at least a mile away from.

She went into their motel room to find Chloe peeling off her clothes and tossing them on a nearby chair. "I'm going to take a shower," she said, and disappeared into the bathroom.

Serena unpacked a few essentials and stuck them into a dresser drawer. She'd just filled the coffee pot with water and coffee so all she had to do was switch it on in the morning, when Chloe stuck her head out the bathroom door. She was dripping wet.

"Serena. Will you go get my loofah?"

"What?"

"My loofah. There wasn't room left in my suitcase, so I packed it in Bobby's. Will you get it from him?"

"It's only one night. Can't you go without it?"

"Come on, Serena! I have to exfoliate." She grinned. "After all, tomorrow's my wedding day."

Not if I can help it. "Sure, Chloe. I'll go get it."

She picked up her purse with the key in it and left the room, locking the door behind her. She was just getting ready to knock on room twelve, when she heard a noise. Turning back, she was surprised to see Bobby come around the corner and step up to room fourteen. He rapped twice. The door opened, and he slipped inside.

What was going on?

Serena went back down the sidewalk and tried

the door. It was locked. She unlocked it with her key, but when she attempted to open it, the door clanged against something.

The chain lock? What was going on here?

She knocked on the door. "Chloe! Unlock the door!"

Nothing.

She banged on it. *"Chloe!"*

All at once, Serena heard a giggle, followed by a "Shush."

Then she knew. They'd plotted to commandeer a motel room. And damn it, they'd succeeded.

"Chloe! Bobby!" Serena said, knocking wildly. "You open this door right now!"

Suddenly the room went dark. More giggles. More "Shush"-ing. Serena stood there for a moment, completely dumbfounded.

What the hell was she supposed to do now?

She pulled the door closed, walked back down to room twelve and knocked. Tom opened the door with a look of surprise.

"Serena? What are you doing here?"

Serena opened her mouth to rant, but one look at Tom made the words get all clogged up in her throat. He was wearing a pair of jeans. Nothing else. Bare feet, bare chest. And he'd removed his glasses, which made his green eyes even more enticing.

"Serena?" he said. "Is there a problem?"

She blinked back to reality. "Yeah. We've been had."

"What?"

"Chloe sent me to your room to get something from Bobby. He was waiting around the corner, and as soon as I left the room, Chloe let him in. Now they're holed up in there with the chain lock on and the lights off."

Tom ran his palm up the door frame and leaned against it, looking sexier than any man had a right to. A smile spread slowly across his face. "Are you telling me that we really are stuck together tonight?"

"No! You have to go down there and make Bobby come out of that room!"

"What am I supposed to do? Keep banging on the door until somebody calls the police to complain about the noise?"

"Yes! If that's what it takes!"

"Let's be realistic. What are the odds of us getting them out of that room with anything less than a SWAT team?"

Serena sagged with resignation. Tom was right. Trying to get Bobby and Chloe to do anything was like trying to teach a pig to sing. It only frustrated you and irritated the pig.

"All my luggage is in the other room," she said. "I don't even have a nightgown."

"You can borrow one of my shirts."

"A toothbrush."

"Not a big deal for one night."

"But—"

He held up his palm to quiet her, then took her hand, led her into the room and closed the door behind her.

"Tell you what. You can put on one of my shirts, and then we can sequester ourselves in separate beds, where we can fall asleep discussing the relative merits of 401K accounts and Roth IRAs. Or…"

He locked the door with a flick of his fingers, and just that tiny click shocked Serena's heart into a wild, erratic rhythm. He slid his hands along her shoulders, then laced his fingers through her hair, meeting her eyes with a hot, seductive stare.

"Or," he said, lowering his lips toward hers, "we can do this."

CHAPTER FIVE

THE MOMENT Tom's lips brushed Serena's, she yanked herself away. Backing against the wall, she pointed at him.

"No! You can't do that!"

"Can't do what?"

"Kiss me!"

Tom took a step closer. "Are you sure about that?"

"No! I'm not sure! That's why you have to stay away from me!"

That prompted a grin from Tom, and Serena felt as if she'd been struck by another blast of equatorial sunlight. When he smiled at her full force like that, it was impossible for her to think straight.

"Tell me you haven't been thinking about me, too," he said. "Go ahead. Tell me."

"I haven't been thinking about—" She blushed a little and turned away.

"Well, look at that," Tom said. "Who's crazy now?"

"Both of us!"

He smiled. "Well, at least we're in this to-gether."

"Bobby said you aren't spontaneous. What do you call this?"

"There's nothing spontaneous about it. I've been thinking about kissing you for quite some time now."

She stared at him incredulously. "So, when we were in the diner…"

"Yes."

"And the movie theater…"

"Uh-huh. And when we were in the back of Bobby's car, when we rode in the wrecker, when we walked to the diner, and when we checked into the motel. It's been pretty much nonstop."

So she'd been right? All that time when she'd been thinking about him, he couldn't keep his mind off *her?*

Serena felt a shot of pure, unadulterated lust, and it was all she could do not to throw her arms around Tom's neck and give him exactly what he wanted. What they both wanted. But she couldn't. Not now. If something happened between her and Tom, and Bobby and Chloe found out, their bar-gaining position would be shot.

Damn. How could the most perfect thing in the world be taking place at the worst possible time?

She had to be reasonable about this. She *had* to.

"Listen, Tom. I know the way Chloe thinks. If

she finds out we're doing *this,* she'll feel justified in doing *that.*"

"One has nothing to do with the other. Are we going to head to the altar three days from now?"

"Of course not."

"Well, there you are. They're crazy. We're not."

"I thought you were a rational man."

"Oh, yeah. I'm about as level-headed as a man can get. Boring, some say. I can't blame them for that, really, because I've built my career on reasonable and rational. But there's a third *R.*"

"What's that?"

A smile spread slowly across his face. "Risk."

Oh, Lord.

"But not a big one. Yes, eventually we need to set Bobby and Chloe straight. But since we can't do anything about them until tomorrow morning, and since we're safely alone, and since I'm getting the feeling that you want what I want…"

He leaned in closer. Serena pressed her palm against his chest.

Big mistake.

Unlike his unassuming appearance when he was clothed, his naked chest was to die for. And with her hand currently pressed against that chest, another thought raced wildly through her mind: *What must the rest of him feel like?*

And still he moved closer.

"Tom?" she murmured, her breath coming in shallow spurts. "What are you doing?"

"I believe we've identified that already."

"Okay. So I get what you're doing, but—"

"I just want to know one thing," he said.

"What?"

"Are you really going to make me disinfect my lips?"

Serena took a deep, unsteady breath. "Another one of my sister's faults. She exaggerates."

"Good thing," he said, moving closer still. "I never have liked the taste of disinfectant."

"Can't you see the problem this is going to cause?"

"Of course I can. If Bobby and Chloe find out what's on our minds after knowing each other only a few hours, it's going to make our job of breaking them up that much harder."

"Yes. It will."

"So we'd better make sure they don't find out."

With that, Tom circled his hand around her waist, pulled her up against him and dropped his lips against hers. And just like that, she slid headlong into a deep, blistering kiss that made anything she'd seen Bobby and Chloe do pale in comparison.

Her hand fluttered to Tom's shoulder. Grasped blindly. Slid around his neck. And before she knew it, she was pulling him closer, asking for more. He stroked his hand down her back, tilted his head to a new angle and kissed her deeper still, giving her exactly what she wanted. *This is wrong, wrong, wrong,* her mind was telling her, but it felt so *right* that she couldn't have stopped doing it if her life depended on it.

Finally his kiss softened and dissolved, and when his lips left hers, she leaned in automatically, following them for a few millimeters to brush against them one last time. She blinked her eyes open, feeling as if her bones had liquefied and wondering when she was going to be able to breathe again.

"I have a confession to make," Tom said.

"What's that?"

"I've been thinking about more than kissing. Much more."

Serena felt as if he'd zapped her with a stun gun. But before she could get her bearings, Tom was kissing her again, cupping his hand behind her neck and pulling her closer, threading his fingers through her hair as he plunged in deeply and stroked his tongue against hers. Then he backed off and teased her with softer, gentler kisses on her cheek, her jaw, her neck, before meeting her lips all over again.

She had to stop this. She had to. She wasn't the kind of woman who kissed men she barely knew, much less made love with them. In so many ways,

Chloe had been right. No, she had no intention of hauling out the disinfectant, but spontaneous she wasn't.

She pulled away suddenly. "Wait. Hold on. I've got to think about this."

Taking a deep, steadying breath, Tom lifted his hands away from her. "Okay," he said in a voice that said it wasn't okay at all. "Sure. Go ahead. Think about it."

Serena just stared at him.

"Are you thinking?" he asked.

"Yes."

"Um…can you think a little faster?"

"I'm working on it."

"What exactly are you thinking about?"

About how I'd like to make mad, passionate love with you on that lumpy motel room bed if only I could work up the nerve.

"About…consequences."

"Which are?"

"Bobby and Chloe—"

Tom held up his hand. "Now, wait a minute. You and I both know that they're far too wrapped up in themselves to pay any attention to us."

"But they may hear—"

"They're two doors down. But I promise not to scream, no matter how much I'm moved to. Any other potential consequences?"

"Well, yes. Possibly. I mean, not if I still

have…'' She grabbed her purse. "Hold on. Let me check."

She dug through her purse, relieved to see that her failsafe condom was indeed still there.

Tom smiled. "I should have known you'd be prepared."

"It's just one of those things I always have with me, like Band-Aids and moistened towelettes. It's not that I ever expected to use it."

"Never?"

"Well, maybe not *never*, but…"

"But you just like to be prepared."

"Yes. And don't worry. It's a good brand, and I change it every month so it's not old and brittle."

Tom reached into his wallet and extracted a condom. "I have a better one."

"Better?"

"Yeah. Mine glows in the dark."

She gave him a look of utter shock. "A glow-in-the-dark condom? Are you *serious?*"

"I never joke about sex toys."

Serena shook her head. "I don't understand this."

"Understand what?"

"You're every bit as methodical and reliable as I am. Then suddenly you pull out a condom that glows in the dark?"

"Serena. Just because you're a responsible adult doesn't mean you can't have fun."

For a moment, that didn't compute. Serena had assumed that those things were mutually exclusive. Sex had always been mundane, methodical, premeditated; worse, it had been so infrequent that the average healthy twenty-eight-year-old woman would have been clawing at her bedsheets, desperate for a man. Instead, Serena had pushed those feelings away and continued along her regimented course, making responsibility and good judgment number one and number two in her life. But now she realized that there had never really been a number three. Something had always been missing, but she'd never known exactly what.

Maybe this was it. This spark that made her feel alive. A *man* who made her feel alive. A man who was every bit as careful with his life as she was, but who seemed to have the missing piece of the puzzle she'd never been able to locate. And when the reality of that hit her, something gave way inside. A barrier broke. A paradigm shattered. She couldn't rationalize it, and she couldn't intellectualize it. All she could do was feel it slip inside her and steal her breath away.

She tossed the condom to the nightstand, wrapped her arms around Tom's neck, pulled him forward and whispered to him in a voice as hot as the Arizona desert.

"I can't wait to see you glow in the dark."

His start of surprise melted into a slow, devilish

grin. He tossed the condom he held to the bed, then kissed her hard and fast, slipping his hand up to hold the back of her head. She loved the feel of his mouth, all warm and moist and wanting, and she pressed herself against him and kissed him back with everything she had to give.

He ran his hand the length of her back in smooth, rapid strokes, then tugged her shirt from the waistband of her shorts. *Yes. Good.* That was what she wanted. She wanted to be naked, to feel her breasts pressed right up against his already-bare chest.

He pulled her shirt over her head and tossed it aside. Pausing a moment, he stared down at her, then pressed his open palms against her upper chest, fingers spread wide, his thumbs brushing her collarbone. He dragged his hands down, easing back as he went, so just his fingertips grazed the upper swell of her breasts above her bra. She closed her eyes with a gentle sigh, even as her heart was beating like crazy. Then he came forward with his hands again, reversing the process, this time sliding them all the way up the column of her neck to cradle her face.

As he bent to kiss her, she reached up quickly and flicked open the front clasp of her bra, shoved the cups aside and leaned into him, her nipples brushing against his chest. An inch from her lips, he murmured, ''Oh, yeah, that's *good*,'' and forgot all about the kiss, enveloping her in his arms instead. It felt wonderful—no barriers, skin-to-skin—and she did a slow shimmy against him. He groaned with satisfaction, and she could feel the vibration pass from his body to hers, along with enough heat to melt a glacier. She felt as if the spirit of some bold, brash, sex-starved woman had slipped inside her body and taken over, and she loved every minute of it.

With his arms still wrapped around her, Tom shuffled backward a couple of steps until he found the bed with the backs of his legs. He turned her around and laid her down, then quickly unzipped her shorts and pulled them off, her panties coming right along with them. He stretched out beside her, rested her head in the crook of his elbow and kissed her. At the same time he closed his hand over the curve of her waist and eased it up to the outer swell of her breast, then leaned in to flick her nipple with his tongue and suck it gently. Serena thought she'd die from the pleasure of it. He touched and teased her endlessly, until her mind grew foggy and her body pulsed with desire.

No matter where he touched her, sensation streaked right down between her legs, so when he moved his hand there, she was so hot and so ready that he met moist, slick flesh. He kissed her deeply as he circled his fingers around and around and back and forth, moving, always moving. She clutched his shoulders, every muscle in her body tensing and tightening as she lost herself to the feeling. Blood surged through her veins and pounded in her head, every molecule screaming for release.

With a sudden gasp, she grabbed his hand, stilling it, taking deep gulps of air to return oxygen to her brain.

"Tom?"

"Yes?"

"I admire your mind," she said breathlessly. "I truly do. But right now I really, *really* want your body."

"Any particular part you're interested in?"

"The part you have to take off your jeans to get to."

"Not a problem," he said, stroking her again. "I'll just finish up here, and then—"

She slapped her hand down on his. "Tom! *Now!*"

He drew back with surprise. "Why, Serena. I had no idea you were such a domineering woman." He grinned. "I like that."

"Then move it!"

"Yes, ma'am."

She was still breathing hard as he backed off the bed and stood up, and in record time he'd pulled off the rest of his clothes. He looked positively gorgeous—long limbs with an abundance of lean muscle, and that broad, beautiful chest with its soft sprinkling of golden hair that glinted in the lamplight.

"Where's a condom?" she said. "Get a condom."

Tom fumbled around on the bed and grabbed the packet he'd tossed there. Kneeling next to her, he tore it open and rolled it into place. Serena started to pull him right down on top of her, but then she noticed the strange milky tone of the condom.

She stopped. Stared at it. In spite of the urgency she felt, curiosity was getting the better of her. Had he really been telling her the truth?

"Turn out the lamp," she said.

Tom leaned over to the nightstand, and with a flick of the switch, he plunged the room into darkness. Serena looked down and got the shock of her life.

It really did glow in the dark.

She rose on one elbow, staring in awe. She started to smile. Then pretty soon the giggles began. Then more giggles. And before long, she fell to her back again, shaking with laughter.

Tom settled back on his heels with a sigh of mock disgust. "Okay. So it's bright enough to bring a 747 in for a landing."

"Tom," she said, talking through her laughter,

"it's bright enough to bring aliens in from other galaxies."

"You realize that you're laughing at my manhood," Tom said. "Most men would find that an ego-crushing experience."

"Can't help it. It's green." She clamped her hand over her mouth, but still her laughter bubbled out. "Now I know what it's like to have sex with the Incredible Hulk."

Tom sighed. "Well, I guess that beats Kermit the Frog."

That only made her laugh harder, causing her to get all teary-eyed. Tom moved between her legs, dropped a palm to the bed on either side of her and loomed over her.

"You're still laughing, Serena."

She wiped the tears from the corners of her eyes. "Sorry, Tom. If you want me to quit laughing, you're going to have to put it someplace where I can't—"

All at once he slid inside her. She gasped, her laughter coming to an abrupt halt.

"Oh, *yes,*" she said with a sigh of satisfaction. "That's the place."

Laughing so hard had left her deliciously weak, but when Tom began to move inside her, her body came to life all over again. With every thrust she arched against him, asking for more, and she couldn't have anticipated what he gave her in return. The rhythm they created, the heat they generated, the slow, sweet, maddening drive they shared to a breathtaking climax—all of it gave Serena the unmistakable feeling that she'd found a man who answered every need she'd ever had.

And as they lay together afterward in a tangle of pillows and sheets and arms and legs and total satisfaction, Tom wasn't the only one who was glowing.

DAZZLING MORNING SUN peeked through the blinds of room twelve of the Windsor Motor Lodge, casting brilliant fans of light on the blue shag carpet. Tom lounged on the bed, a pillow scrunched up behind him, watching as Serena poured two cups of coffee.

He'd pulled on a pair of jeans, and she wore one of his shirts. When she stood, it hung down almost to her knees, but as she sat down on the bed beside him, the tail of it rose on one leg, baring just enough thigh that he started to think about last night all over again.

He took a sip from the cup she handed him, then rested his free hand on her leg, stroking it gently, and suddenly he was getting hard all over again.

"Damn," he muttered.

"What?"

"Can't believe we're out of condoms."

"Hey, I gave you the option. It was your choice to use them both last night."

Tom sighed. "I usually like to save for a rainy day. Wonder what came over me?"

Then Serena kissed him, and he knew what had come over him.

When Bobby had talked him into this crazy road trip, he'd never imagined that he'd find such an incredible woman along the way, much less that he'd be waking up with her this morning. He had the most uncanny feeling that theirs had been a meeting not just of bodies, but of minds and souls, as well.

Watch it, Erickson. You're sliding right off the deep end.

It was true. He was starting to think like some kind of new-age nutcase who floated through life with his head in the clouds instead of a man grounded firmly in reality, but it felt so damned good that he wasn't willing to come back to earth just yet.

Serena shifted around and leaned against the headboard, cradling her coffee in both hands. She stared straight ahead, and slowly her face fell into a frown.

"Serena? What's the matter?"

"I don't know. I guess this feels a little strange."

"Strange?"

"What's happening between us." She sighed. "This really isn't like me. I don't do this kind of thing. Nothing even *close* to this kind of thing. *Ever.*"

"Are you sure? You seemed pretty good at it to me."

She closed her eyes. "You know what I mean."

He ran his hand along her thigh. "Yes, I do. I don't make a habit of it, either. But last night...I'm not going to apologize for it or say it was wrong. And I hope you're not going to, either."

"No. It's just that..."

Her voice trailed off, and Tom felt a twinge of apprehension. "Serena? Did I push too hard last night?"

"No," she said. "Of course not. I wanted it, Tom. Every bit as much as you did. But now I'm a fine one to tell Chloe that she shouldn't be doing what she's doing, when I'm doing—you know—what *I'm* doing."

"It's okay, Serena. She and Bobby will never know."

"I still feel like a hypocrite."

"It's like I told you last night. It isn't the making love that's wrong. It's the getting married in three days that's wrong."

Serena nodded. "We have to make sure they don't do that."

"We will."

Tom took her cup from her hands, set it down on the nightstand, and pulled her into his arms. She kissed his shoulder, then stroked her hand along his chest. Tom closed his eyes, loving the way she touched him, and it was all he could do not to make love to her all over again. From now on he wasn't leaving home without an entire box of condoms.

"You know what?" Serena said.

"What?"

"I think last night was the first time I ever laughed during sex."

"Why, thank you, Serena. That's just what a man wants to hear when he's with a woman for the first time."

"Oh, please. Your ego is perfectly intact. I wasn't laughing *at* you. I was laughing *with* you." She sighed contentedly. "And that was why I had such a good time."

He had, too. More than he ever could have imagined.

All at once there was a knock on the door. Tom got up and looked out the peephole. "It's Bobby," he whispered, then pointed across the room. "The other bed. Make it look slept in."

Serena ran to the bed, yanked down the covers, mussed up the sheets and smacked the pillow a time or two.

"Now, remember," Tom said. "We're supposed to be ticked off that they forced us to be roommates.''

Serena nodded. She sat down on the newly un-made bed and tucked her bare legs beneath the covers. Tom answered the door. Bobby came into the room carrying Serena's suitcase.

"I thought I'd better bring this over," he told her.

Tom took it from him and set it down on the floor. He shot his brother an angry glare. "That was a real dumb-ass stunt you pulled last night."

Bobby blinked. "What? Oh, yeah. The room. Sorry about that."

"Sorry? Is that all you can say?"

"Yeah. I guess it is." He turned to Serena, look-ing a little perplexed. "Can I ask you something?"

"What?"

"Does Chloe always talk in her sleep?"

"Yeah. She's been doing it since we were kids. She usually denies it."

Bobby's eyebrows shot up. "Denies it? She could be a 3:00 a.m. talk show host the way she goes at it."

"Just wake her up," Tom said.

"Nope. No way. I tried that."

Serena suppressed a smile. "Kinda like waking up a grizzly bear, isn't it?"

Bobby looked over his shoulder, then leaned toward them and whispered, "I thought she was going to bite my head right off my shoulders."

"Hmm," Tom said. "Amazing what you learn about people as time goes on, isn't it?"

"It's not a big thing, Tom. It just, you know… *is.*"

"And it will just *be* for the next sixty years."

Bobby's eyes widened. "Sixty years?"

"That's about how long you'll be married, isn't it?"

"Uh…well, yeah. I guess so."

"Hey, don't worry. It'll probably be no big deal once you get used to it. If not, there are always earplugs."

"Uh…yeah. That's right. It's no big deal." Bobby said the words, but he was clearly having a hard time making himself believe them. He glanced over his shoulder. "Well, I guess I'd better be getting back."

"Hey, bro," Tom said. "Serena and I thought we'd go to breakfast in a few minutes. You and Chloe want to join us?"

"Maybe in half an hour or so. Chloe's putting on her makeup." He sighed. "That's been known to take a while."

Tom clapped his brother on the shoulder. "No problem. Just phone us once you're ready and we'll head on over there."

Bobby walked away looking slightly baffled.

Tom closed the door and turned to Serena. "Well? What do you think?"

"I think," she said, "that a second thought is knocking around inside Bobby's brain."

"And we've got until this afternoon to toss kindling on the fire." Tom smiled. "And I know just how to fan the flames."

CHAPTER SIX

THEY CHECKED OUT of the motel, left their luggage at the front desk and went to the diner for a late breakfast. Lorena didn't seem particularly pleased to see them, but Tom noticed that she changed her tune in a hurry once he offered her twenty bucks on the sly to reject Bobby's credit card when he tried to pay for his and Chloe's half of the breakfast bill. Then things got even better than Tom had anticipated.

Bobby wasn't carrying enough cash to cover the amount, leaving Chloe holding the tab.

Even though Bobby assured Chloe there had to be some kind of mistake, from the way she behaved—tightening her jaw, folding her arms, speaking in clipped sentences—she seemed determined to make him pay for breakfast one way or the other. Tom was amused to see Serena add a little friction by giving Chloe a sympathetic look that said, *Oh, you poor thing. I know how embarrassing it must be when your man can't even pay for breakfast.*

After that, kindling wasn't necessary. Watching

Bobby and Chloe interact over the next several hours was like watching spontaneous combustion.

As the four of them were killing time walking along main street, Chloe stopped to pet a stray dog. Bobby muttered something about fleas and rabies, which annoyed Chloe, but not nearly as much as the fact that he didn't want to hold her hand after she'd touched the dog. She gave him a look of disgust and went into a rest room at an antique store so she could return to the level of cleanliness her fiancé demanded.

Later, after Bobby had found an ATM and loaded up on cash, he spied the Windsor Bowl-a-Rama and asked Chloe if she wanted to bowl a few games. Chloe declined, telling Bobby there wasn't anything more disgusting than wearing somebody else's shoes. He gave her a look that said *Except maybe petting a scroungy stray dog.*

When the one-thirty matinee at the Desert Rose rolled around, Bobby suggested they see *Terminator 3* again. Chloe said she didn't feel like it. Translation: *If you think you're making out with me in a movie theater again, you've got another think coming.*

Tom had been a good boy all day, walking sedately beside Serena as if he hadn't spent hours last night getting to know her in the most intimate way possible. But right now, as they were traipsing along the streets of Windsor, he knew if he had to pretend for much longer, he was going to drag her right back to that motel and lock himself in a room with her for about twenty-four hours straight.

Get out of the heat. Cool yourself off. Pretend she's your first cousin. Your sister. A nun. Your sister who's also a nun.

Down one of the streets that intersected the main drag, Tom spotted a strange little Starbucks knock-off and offered to spring for a round of iced coffees. They went inside to a welcoming blast of cool air, ordered coffee, then sat down and drank it and talked about nothing in particular. But Tom noticed that the interaction between the lovebirds had cooled considerably. They sat close, but not extremely so. They talked, but without much animation. They touched, but only if it was accidental.

The way Serena was touching him right now, though, was no accident. She'd slid her sandal off and was teasing her toe up and down his leg, all the while sipping her coffee as if she wasn't doing everything she could to make him crazy.

After a while, Chloe got up to look at the dessert case and Bobby headed to the bathroom. Tom leaned over and whispered to Serena, "You must want me to strip you naked right in the middle of this coffee shop."

"Now, Tom, you're forgetting our mission."

"Our mission," he said, "is to break up Bobby and Chloe."

"Right."

"So *then* I can strip you naked."

Serena sipped her coffee, looking straight ahead. "I could go for that."

"When all this is over with, we're spending three days in bed."

"I could go for that, too."

"Speaking of bed," Tom said, "it's as if Bobby and Chloe have never spent any time out of it. And now that they are, they're imploding."

"But it's small stuff they're arguing about."

"Doesn't matter. They just need to get angry enough to reconsider Vegas. That's all."

"I saw you and Bobby talking while Chloe and I were browsing in that antique store. How's he doing?"

"Slipping fast," Tom said. "He asked me if you'd told me anything about Chloe's ex-husbands. I said no. Then I said, as offhandedly as I could, 'Hmm. I wonder what those guys know that you're getting ready to find out.' No offense against Chloe, of course."

"None taken. It's a valid question, right? I imagine there are a few ex-girlfriends of Bobby's who could tell a tale or two."

"You don't know the half of it."

"Looks as if our plan is working," Serena agreed. "But we're going to be on the road to Vegas pretty soon now. I was hoping they'd cave before then."

"It's okay," Tom said. "They're probably going to have to go a little farther before they admit defeat, even if that means stepping right up to the altar. Don't worry. They'll eventually crack. We just have to go along for the ride until they do."

"I'd rather take a different ride."

Before he could wonder what she meant by that, she reached under the table, squeezed his thigh, then moved her hand up to tease her fingertips along his zipper, all the while keeping her eye on the dessert counter and the door to the men's room.

Tom let out a ragged sigh. "I'm going to get you for this."

A tiny smile played across her lips. "Is that a promise?"

A FEW MINUTES before five o'clock, Wally met them back at the hotel, loaded their luggage into his truck, and took them to his service station. Tom told Bobby to transfer the luggage to his car and he'd settle up with Wally. Bobby was surprised that Tom offered to pay for the repairs. Tom just told him to think of it as a wedding present, then went inside to give the impression that he was indeed paying for something.

While Bobby and Chloe were moving the luggage, Serena walked around the side of the building and went into the ladies' room. Just as she'd finished and was washing her hands, there was a knock on the door.

"Serena, it's Tom. Let me in."

She quickly dried her hands and opened the door. Tom slipped inside and locked the door behind him. He took Serena by the shoulders, backed her against the counter, then slid his hands up and cradled her face, his breath hot against her lips.

"You've been trying to drive me crazy all day, haven't you?" he asked.

"I haven't just been trying. I've been succeeding."

"You are *so* bad."

Bad. Serena had never been called that in her life. She'd always been the good girl. Head on straight. Ducks in a row.

Bad. She liked the sound of that.

She liked it a lot.

"I told you I'd get you back," Tom said.

"I think you're all talk. Where's the action?"

He jerked down the zipper of her shorts, and before she realized what was happening, he'd caught the waistband with his thumbs.

"Tom! I didn't mean—"

"Don't do the crime," he said, yanking her shorts and panties down around her thighs, "if you can't do the time."

"I thought you just dropped in for a kiss!" Serena whispered. "We don't have time for—"

"Sure we do."

"But Bobby and Chloe—"

"Sorry. We've got the ladies' room. They'll have to go to the men's."

"But aren't they ready to go?"

"Car needed gas. I gave Bobby my credit card and told him to fill it up on me. For some reason, I'm feeling very generous."

In seconds he had his jeans down, leaving them resting along his thighs. Serena looked down, and any lingering doubts about whether he was serious vanished.

"Wait a minute," she said. "We don't have a condom."

"Remember a few hours ago when I ducked into that drugstore to get some aspirin?"

"Yeah?"

"I didn't have a headache."

Tom lifted her to sit on the counter, then pulled a condom from his pocket, ripped the packet open and rolled it on. Serena's heart was beating madly. Even though they'd gone from zero to sixty in no time at all, she felt shockingly hot and unbelievably ready.

Tom pulled her legs up, forcing her to lean back against the mirror, then plunged inside her. She gasped at the sudden surge of pleasure, and he gripped her thighs, thrusting wildly. Even though it felt unbelievably good, he was moving fast— way too fast to bring her along with him this time. But the incredible feeling of him being inside her again was more than enough for her.

Then the strangest thing happened.

Inside her, something caught fire.

The heat of him, the pressure, the angle, the friction, the astonishing fact that she was having hot, exciting, forbidden sex that might even be against the law—all were catalysts that quickly coalesced into a focus of energy that grew exponentially with every second that passed.

She grabbed Tom's shoulders and pulled him to her, tilting her hips up, trying to increase the pressure, rocking against him, begging him to move faster, harder. Then all at once, he ducked his head and let out a groan—a long, harsh sound of satisfaction.

And it pushed her right over the edge.

With a sharp gasp, Serena clenched her muscles hard against him, pleasure washing over her in fierce, undulating waves, dragging her down like an undertow. A cry filled her throat, and she pulled him forward and pressed her mouth to his shoulder to drown it out.

After several long, shuddering breaths, Serena lifted her head and rested it against the mirror behind her, closing her eyes. "I can't believe it," she murmured, her words almost incomprehensible. "I can't believe it.... That was so incredible...."

Tom nodded wordlessly and dropped his head to her shoulder, his hot breath gushing over her. They paused together for several seconds, trying to come back to earth, trying to gather some semblance of rationality.

"We have to go," Serena said, still breathing hard. "But I'm not sure I can walk."

Tom lifted her off the counter and tugged her shorts back up over her hips. Her legs felt like noodles. As she was zipping her shorts, she glanced in the mirror and saw that her cheeks were flushed bright red.

"Oh, no! Look at my face!"

"They'll think it's the heat," Tom said, buckling his belt. "It is a hundred and five degrees out."

She put her hand on the doorknob. Tom pulled her back and kissed her, then fixed his gaze on hers. "I'm crazy about you," he told her.

Euphoria swept through her. She felt as if she was on a roller coaster, taking one exhilarating twist and turn after another, and she never wanted it to end.

She put her palm against his cheek. "I'm crazy about you, too."

He swept a stray strand of hair away from her forehead, then kissed her there. "Now, act nonchalant. We can't set a bad example for the children."

Serena laughed softly and opened the door. She stuck her head out, looked left and right, then motioned for Tom to follow. They walked along the side of the building. When they came around the corner, they ran headlong into Bobby and Chloe. Startled, Serena stopped short, wondering why they both looked angry.

Really angry.

Bobby folded his arms across his chest and skewered them with a glare so hot it could have melted steel.

"What in the hell have you two been up to?"

CHAPTER SEVEN

TOM FELT a shot of apprehension. This was it. They knew. They knew that he and Serena had just had hot, passionate sex in the gas station bathroom. But how?

Serena turned and gave him a very nervous *What do we do now?* look. But in Tom's estimation, there was only one thing they could do.

Come clean.

"Okay, Bobby," Tom said with resignation. "How did you know?"

"Because the pay-at-the-pump wasn't working."

Tom blinked. "What?"

"I had to go inside to pay. And what did I overhear? A couple of mechanics talking about how dumb I was that I didn't know that my brother had faked a car problem that kept me stuck here for twenty-four hours." He glared at Tom. "That was a really crappy thing to do."

Tom couldn't believe it. Bobby had found out what he'd been doing with his car, not what he'd been doing with Serena? He felt a momentary

twinge of relief, only to realize that the car reve-
lation might be far worse.

"This whole thing was a ploy to keep us from
getting to Vegas, wasn't it?" Bobby said. "What
did you hope to accomplish by that? Did you think
you could keep us here forever?"

Tom sighed. "We just thought if you had a little
more time to think about it, you might reconsider."

Chloe threw up her hands. "Is there anything
you two won't do to keep us from getting married?"

"Please try to understand," Serena said. "It was
for your own good."

"You know what? I'm getting really tired of
hearing that from you. From now on, *I'm* the only
one who's going to decide what's good for me, and
you are going to butt out."

"The same goes for you, Tom," Bobby said.
"And I've got news for you. We don't care what
you two think. We're getting married the minute
we hit Vegas, and there isn't a damned thing you
can do to stop us."

With that, he and Chloe spun around and
stormed back toward his car. Tom considered grabbing Bobby by the collar, hauling him back and
telling him one more time that he was behaving
like an idiot, but at this point would it do any
good?

"Oh, boy," Serena said. "What do we do now?

They're mad enough to get married just out of spite."

"Take it easy. We've got several more hours before we get to Vegas to try to calm them down."

"I don't know if that's possible. I don't think I've ever seen Chloe this angry."

"Bobby either. But they'll settle down, and as soon as they do, we can apologize. Then we can try to talk some sense into—"

"Tom? What is Bobby doing?"

Tom spun around to see Bobby depositing two suitcases and two briefcases on the pavement behind his car. Then he slammed his trunk lid and headed for the driver's door.

Oh, God. Surely not.

Tom took off running toward the SUV, but by the time he reached it, Bobby and Chloe had leaped inside and shut the doors. Tom reached for the handle on the driver's side, but he was a split second too late. Bobby had flicked the locks.

"Bobby!" Tom shouted. "What the hell do you think you're doing?"

Bobby cracked the window. "Going to get married, big brother. By ourselves. And if you're very, very lucky, maybe we'll pick you up on the way back home."

Before Tom could wedge his hand through the open window to take his brother by the throat, Bobby rolled it up again. He started the car and burned rubber out of the gas station, leaving Tom and Serena standing beside the pump, watching them disappear down the road.

"I don't believe this," Serena said. "They're actually leaving!"

Tom sighed. "Yeah. It looks that way."

"So what do we do now?"

"I think we've worked our way up to plan C."

"Which is?"

"We follow them to Vegas."

"How are we supposed to do that? We haven't got a car."

"Come with me."

Tom went into the service station, where Wally was sitting in a chair, feet propped up on the desk, drinking a soda. He grinned. "Hey, there. Looks like you two got yourself a little problem."

"Big problem, Wally. Any buses run from here to Vegas?"

"Yep. One's coming through here tomorrow morning."

"None before then?"

"Nope."

"Tom," Serena said, "they'll be married by tomorrow morning."

"Is there a rental car company anywhere around here?" Tom asked.

Wally looked baffled. "In Windsor? You kidding?"

"Do you have a car I can rent? I can have it back to you tomorrow."

"Nope, but I got a car you can buy."

"Buy?"

"Three hundred dollars cash."

"Does it run?"

"Sure. Don't look like much, and it burns a little oil, but it'll get you there."

Tom turned to Serena. "How much cash do you have on you?"

She fished through her purse as Tom tore into his wallet.

"Eighty-seven dollars," Serena said.

"I've got a hundred and ninety four." Tom turned to the man. "We'll give you two hundred and eighty-one dollars if you throw in a tank of gas."

Wally grinned. "You just bought yourself a car."

FIVE MINUTES LATER, Tom and Serena were chugging down state highway 87, heading for the Interstate, in their brand-new used car. The ancient hatchback had a dent in every fender and a color that was either red or rust, depending where you looked. The trunk was held shut with baling wire, and the head liner drooped to within an inch of Tom's head. But Wally had been true to his word. The car was ugly as hell, but it was showing every indication that it just might take them the rest of the way to Vegas.

"They were so close to reconsidering," Serena said. "I know they were. If they get married now, it'll only be because they're mad at us." She looked down at the speedometer. "Can you go any faster?"

"I'd better hold it steady. I'm ten miles over the limit already. Did Chloe tell you what time Bobby rescheduled for at the chapel?"

"No," Serena said. "He knew his car would be ready around five, and it's four hours into Vegas. But they still have to get a license, so they'll head to the marriage license bureau first. Should we go there?"

"No. They've got about a twenty-minute head start on us, and if Bobby is pissed, he'll put the pedal to the metal. If they're determined to do this, we'd better plan on intercepting them at the chapel instead." He checked his watch. "We should hit the city limits around nine o'clock."

Serena nodded. Then she got to thinking about how mad Bobby and Chloe had been, and she started to feel a little guilty.

"Maybe we shouldn't have been quite so devious about the car repairs," she said.

"Serena? Has anything really changed? Is it smart for Bobby and Chloe to get married after knowing each other only a matter of days?"

"No."

"Then we did the right thing."

"Only now we're having to chase them all the way to Vegas."

"Hey, that's your fault," Tom said.

"My fault?"

"If you weren't so damned irresistible, I never would have gone into that bathroom and Bobby might not have been any the wiser about his car." He sighed. "I guess that's the price I pay for meeting the woman of my dreams."

Serena froze. *The woman of my dreams.* Did he really mean that?

No. It was just something guys tossed off, like "Hey, beautiful," or something like that. He didn't mean it the way it sounded.

Then he reached over and took her hand. He gave it a squeeze, along with a knowing smile, and Serena had the most unbelievable feeling that maybe he really did.

CUPID'S LITTLE CHAPEL of Love was even more of a nuptial nightmare than Serena had expected. The clapboard structure was tropical-flower pink, with raspberry-red shutters and an arch of bright gold lightbulbs around the front door. Flanking the door was a pair of giant wooden cupid cutouts.

Tom pulled the car into a parking space and

stared up at the building with an expression of total astonishment.

"Chloe found it on the Internet," Serena said.

"It's…unique."

"Frightening is more like it." She looked around the parking lot. "I don't see Bobby's car. Could we be too late?"

"With luck, we're too early. But let's make sure."

They entered the chapel's reception area. It looked like a Victorian brothel. Red and pink fabric was draped everywhere, with chubby little cupids flying across the wallpaper, their bows and arrows poised to shoot. A few couples sat on red velvet benches, but none of them were Bobby and Chloe. Tom went to the desk to talk to the proprietor, a round little woman in her fifties with a nametag that read Myrna.

"I wonder if you could tell me if a couple has been here tonight?" Tom asked her. "Bobby Erickson and Chloe Stafford?"

The woman flipped through her register. "Nope. They never made it. Called and rescheduled."

"Rescheduled?"

"Yeah. Had three couples tonight like that. The computer at the courthouse is on the fritz. If they waited until tonight to get a license, they were out of luck." She looked back at the register. "They're coming in at 11:00 a.m. tomorrow."

Tom thanked Myrna, then pulled Serena aside. "Do you have any idea where they planned on staying tonight?"

"No. If they made reservations, Chloe never told me where."

"Okay, then. There's nothing we can do about it tonight. We'll just plan on being here at eleven o'clock in the morning to take one last stand."

"Okay," Serena said. "So what now?"

"I don't know. We *are* in Vegas."

"Yeah."

"Ever been here?" he asked.

"No."

"Neither have I." Tom raised his eyebrows. "Wanna check it out?"

SERENA HAD ALWAYS THOUGHT of Vegas as a place full of bright lights, gaudy decor, oppressive crowds, excessive drinking and casinos filled with people who were systematically throwing away their life savings, and any one of those things would have been reason enough never to step foot within the city limits.

But Las Vegas positively entranced her.

Of course, she did allow for the fact that it might be Tom who entranced her, not Vegas, and that as long as she was with him, anyplace from a New York subway car to a Louisiana swamp to a Texas trailer park would have delighted her.

They walked down the Strip, ducking into a few casinos to play nickel slots, even though Serena had never gambled in her life. Then they went over to the Bellagio to see the fountain show. And even though she wasn't a fan of heights, Tom talked her into riding the roller coaster at New York, New York, and going to the top of the Eiffel Tower at Paris Las Vegas.

And she loved every minute of it.

They had a late dinner at the restaurant on the eleventh floor of the Eiffel Tower, which had a spectacular view of the city. Serena heard about Tom's childhood, which mirrored her own to a remarkable degree. He'd been a little too regimented, a little too precocious, a little too smart for his own good. He'd graduated from college with honors, had gone to work in a field that had to do with finance, and had once taken a public-speaking course because it helped him relate to customers.

So had Serena.

Over dessert, she asked him where he lived. When he told her he owned a condo at Greenbriar, she recognized the name immediately.

"Nice place," she said. "Upscale. I've closed a lot of loans there. When did you buy?"

"Five years ago."

"Pre-construction?"

"Yeah."

"Five years ago there was nothing but empty acreage all around it."

"I know."

"Now that all those stores and restaurants have gone in, people who bought at those prices are making a killing when they sell."

"Yeah. They are."

She smiled. "You checked out the building permits that had been granted in the area ahead of time, didn't you?"

"Uh-huh."

"So you knew what was coming."

"Yep."

Serena blinked with delight. "Mmm. I love a financially responsible man. That is *so* sexy."

"Oh, yeah?" He leaned in and kissed her neck. "Want me to talk dirty to you?"

"By all means."

He lowered his voice to a steamy drawl. "I've got a fully funded retirement account and a credit score of 790."

Serena sighed blissfully. "I think I just had an orgasm."

"Not yet," he told her. "But as soon as we get a room you will."

Fifteen minutes later they'd checked into the hotel at Paris Las Vegas and were heading up the elevator. The minute they got to their room, Tom closed the door, tossed down their luggage, grabbed Serena by the arm and pulled her right up next to him. He started to kiss her, then stopped and just stared at her in the dim lamplight. Slowly he took her hand and kissed her fingertips, his eyes never leaving hers, and a thousand little shivers warmed her from head to toe.

"I've never felt like this before," he said softly. "I can't even put it into words."

She rested her hand against his arm, then leaned in and touched her lips to his. "I can't, either. But I feel it, too."

"I want to make love to you tonight. And a thousand more nights after that." He brushed his lips against hers. "Ten thousand."

Serena couldn't believe it. She couldn't believe that they were in this place tonight, saying these things to each other, and that nothing about it alarmed her in the least or made her want to back away. It simply seemed *right*.

And when Tom made love to her, she felt as if she was no longer anchored to earth, as if she was soaring in the outer atmosphere, where oxygen was sparse and it was nearly impossible to catch a breath. And afterward when they lay together, completely spent, it was a long time before either of them could breathe peacefully again.

One more thing we have in common. We leave each other breathless.

THE NEXT MORNING, Tom felt as if he'd woken up in heaven.

He and Serena got up, ordered a light breakfast from room service, then took a shower together. He was delighted to find that she was as fastidious about cleanliness as she was about everything else in her life, because she insisted on running that bar of soap over every inch of his body. Coincidentally, he felt the need to do the same to her, and they marveled once again at how much they had in common.

After they got out of the shower, Tom poured them another cup of coffee while Serena dried her hair. She came out a few minutes later wearing a pair of sky-blue panties and a matching bra. She reached for her clothes.

"Serena. Wait a minute."

She turned around. "What?"

"Walk over there. To the door."

"Huh?"

"Just do it," he said. "Slowly."

Serena looked confused, but she did as he asked.

"Now back again."

She did, then stopped and looked at him questioningly.

"Ahh," Tom said with a satisfied smile. "I've finally got the underwear model I've always wanted."

Serena's mouth dropped open. Then her surprise

turned to a glare of mock disgust. She strode to the bed and stood over him, her fists on her hips, looking ferociously beautiful. "I refuse to be the object of your adolescent fantasies!"

He gave her a disappointed look. "Does this mean you won't model your underwear for me?"

"That's right, buster. No more underwear for you." She unhooked her bra and flung it aside, then stepped out of her panties and tossed them on top of her bra with a dismissive swipe of her hand.

"There," she said, standing naked in front of him. "That'll teach you to use *me* as a sex object."

He grabbed her wrist, dropped to his back on the bed and pulled her down on top of him. She laughed wildly and tried to squirm away, but he flipped her over, pinned her to the mattress and kissed her until she became limp in his arms and the fight had melted right out of her. When she opened her eyes again, she was staring up at him in a way he'd never seen a woman look at him before—as if the sun rose and set with every breath he took—and a feeling of exhilaration hummed through every nerve in his body. He was crazy about this woman. Absolutely, completely, over-the-top *crazy*.

All at once, Tom felt the oddest *swoop* in his stomach, as if he was in a plane that had hit a pocket of turbulence. He sat up suddenly.

"Tom? What is it?"

He didn't know. He felt the most incredible sense of euphoria, but something seemed to be fogging his brain, until he couldn't put two consecutive thoughts together.

He turned to face Serena. "I was just thinking about…"

"What?"

"I don't know. Thinking about how much fun I've had in the past few days."

She smiled. "Yeah. It has been fun."

"From the moment I first thought about kissing you…" He traced his fingertips down her arm, then took her hand. "It has been incredible."

"Yes."

He'd always led his life in a systematic way, very structured, very controlled. While he'd flirted with a lot of boundaries in his life, he'd never been one to cross them, but suddenly all those boundaries seemed to be falling away and something was beckoning him, tempting him to a place he'd never been before.

"But it's not just the fun," he said. "It's the two of us. Together."

"What do you mean?"

"There's some kind of…I don't know. Some kind of connection between us. A bond. It's been so short a time, but still…"

A strange sensation crept inside him, one that was both invigorating and unsettling at the same time. He couldn't categorize it. He couldn't quantify it. He couldn't put it into any of the carefully constructed niches of his life. A silly phrase circled through his mind—*a place for everything and everything in its place*—but what he felt right now was so unfamiliar that he had no idea where to put it.

"We like the same things," he went on. "We look at life the same way. We speak each other's thoughts. When I look at you, in a way it's like..." He paused. "It's like I'm looking in a mirror and seeing part of myself. And when I make love to you..."

Tom couldn't remember a time in his life when words had come hard to him, but suddenly his thoughts were scrambled and he couldn't make sense of any of them.

"I can't explain it. Making love with you is like...I don't know. It's that feeling of making love because..."

"Because?"

Serena blinked her beautiful brown eyes and gave him a soft smile, and all at once understanding settled over him and the words flowed out like warm honey.

"Because I'm *in* love."

CHAPTER EIGHT

FOR SEVERAL SECONDS, Serena stared at Tom, her entire body numb. Did he actually say he was in love with her?

"No," she said, turning away. "That's impossible."

"Look me in the eye and say that."

Slowly she turned back to find Tom staring at her, his expression unwavering, and the look in his eyes said it all. *Three days. Three hundred days. It doesn't matter. I love you.*

And suddenly it wasn't impossible. A sense of total clarity spilled through her, revealing something deep in her heart that she'd never felt for a man before.

Love.

But in three days? How could it happen so fast?

Soul mate.

The term popped into Serena's head, and it seemed so outrageous that she almost dismissed it outright. She'd never allowed for the fact that there might be something about love she didn't understand. Something she couldn't quantify. She'd never believed that there was one person out there she'd been born to love, who had been born to love her.

Now she did.

She looked back at Tom. "It's not impossible," she said, her voice filled with awe. "After so short a time, in the middle of this strange situation, it shouldn't be possible. But…" She slid into his arms. "I love you, too."

Tom tightened his arms around her and held her close, and in that moment, Serena felt a fundamental shift, as if her life had taken a drastic turn. As if something had come out of the blue and shot her straight in the heart. As if…

Come on, Serena! Chloe had said. *Don't you ever feel the rush? That overwhelming, beautiful, wild, exciting feeling of being in love and not wanting to spend one second without that person?*

"My God," she said.

"What?"

She whispered, so softly it was barely audible. "Lightning."

Tom blinked. "What?"

"Chloe tried to tell me, but I wouldn't listen. And Bobby said it, too. Remember in the diner? He said that if we could feel what they were feeling, then we'd never say another word to them again. He said that sometimes lightning strikes, and you know it's meant to be. And he was right."

Tom leaned back against the headboard and gathered Serena in his arms. She rested her head against his shoulder, feeling something that she'd sworn couldn't possibly exist racing through her.

"You know," Tom said, "I've never seen Bobby look at a woman the way he looks at Chloe."

Serena tilted her head up at him. "And when Chloe talks about Bobby, she positively glows."

They both froze, staring at each other. For a long time neither one of them spoke, but the truth hovered between them.

"Maybe we've been trying to break up two people who really are meant to be together," Tom suggested.

Serena felt a surge of guilt. Was that what they'd been doing? "But, Tom, they were fighting. Remember?"

"Yes, but mostly because we instigated it."

He was right. She and Tom had spent a good portion of the past two days setting Bobby and Chloe up to fail by telling them how dumb and deluded they were. Telling them they didn't know what was best for them.

Telling them that nobody fell in love in three days.

"At least we didn't break them up," Serena said. "They're still getting married."

"Yeah." Tom stroked his hand up and down

Serena's arm. "And if they feel about each other the way we do, I want them to make it together."

Serena did, too. She wanted Chloe and Bobby to get married and stay married for sixty or seventy years. To love each other. To grow old together. And she wanted them to look back on this with fondness for her and Tom, not anger.

"So no more trying to break them up?" she said.

"No. As a matter of fact, I think we should be doing everything we can to help them stay together."

Serena smiled. "I knew there was a reason I fell in love with you."

"Only one?"

"A thousand and one."

She sat up, wrapped her arms around Tom's neck and kissed him, so lost in love that she almost didn't hear her cell phone ring. She grabbed it out of her purse, hit the button and put the phone to her ear.

"Hello?"

"Serena. It's me."

"Chloe! Hey! How are you?"

Silence.

"Serena?"

"Yes! Of course it's me! Where are you?"

"At a hotel in Vegas. Listen, Serena. Bobby and I got to feeling bad about leaving you and Tom in that crummy little town, so I wanted to let you know that we'll be back through there this afternoon. And of course we'll pick you up.''

"Don't worry, Chloe. We're not in Windsor. We're in Vegas, too.''

"You're here? But how did you—''

"Never mind. It doesn't matter. Look, we know about the computer glitch at the courthouse last night. That you couldn't get a marriage license and you had to reschedule at the chapel for this morning at eleven o'clock. Tom and I are glad we're here, because—''

"Wait a minute. If you're going to try to stop us from getting married—''

"No! I was going to tell you that we'll meet you at the chapel. We came along on this trip to be your maid of honor and best man, and that's exactly what we're going to do.''

"You are?''

"Yes. Tom and I want you and Bobby to know how sorry we are for trying to break you up. We were the cause of some of the arguments you were having, and we're sorry about that, too. We were wrong for telling you that you couldn't possibly be in love. That lightning can't strike. Because the truth is…'' She glanced at Tom and smiled. "It can.''

Another silence.

"Are you sure this is Serena?'' Chloe said.

"What?"

"My sister, Serena? Serena Stafford? Loan officer? From Tucson, Arizona?"

Serena laughed. "Yeah, Chloe. It's me." She took Tom's hand. "The new improved version."

"I don't get it."

"I know. We have a lot to talk about. But this is your day. We'll talk after you're married. You and Bobby go to the courthouse and then meet us at the chapel, okay?"

"Yeah. Okay."

"Eleven o'clock," Serena said. "We'll see you then."

AT TEN FORTY-FIVE, Serena and Tom were driving toward the chapel. Tom had put on a pair of slacks and a sport coat he'd brought with him, and Serena had slipped into a skirt and blouse. Tom liked the skirt so much that he almost dragged her back to bed to make love to her all over again, but Serena gave him a rain check and managed to get him out the door.

As they neared the chapel, Serena spotted a grocery store.

"Tom. Hold on. I've got an idea."

"What?"

"We have a little time. Let's stop and get flowers for Chloe. Every bride needs flowers, right?"

He smiled. "Good idea. Let's do it."

Tom pulled into the parking lot and they walked into the grocery store hand-in-hand. *I love this man,* Serena thought, *and he loves me.* She felt as if she was floating a foot above the ground, pure exhilaration flooding every molecule in her body.

By now, without interference from her and Tom, Bobby and Chloe must be feeling the same way. They'd kissed and made up and had great sex and slept curled in each other's arms, and now they were on their way to the chapel to get married.

"I'm going to get white roses if they have them," Serena said. "If not, I'll get white carnations. I can buy some scissors and clip the stems, and get some ribbon to tie them into a bouquet."

"Hey, how about champagne, too?" Tom said.

"Yes! Champagne! You get a bottle of that, and I'll get all the other stuff. I'll meet you back at the cash register."

They went on their respective missions. Several minutes later, Serena headed for the cash register with the goods in hand. Tom was already there, carrying a bottle of champagne. He wrapped his arm around Serena, pulled her right up next to him and kissed her, forcing her to hold the flowers out to keep them from getting squashed. The scissors slipped from her hand, followed by the ribbon, but she didn't hear them hit the floor. *Yes!* It had been too long. Five minutes was too long to go without a kiss from this man.

Then she did hear a noise. What was that?

She opened her eyes and leaned away from Tom. The clerk was clearing his throat. A long time must have passed, because the customer who'd been checking out in front of them was long gone.

Tom picked up the scissors and ribbon, and they put their purchases on the counter. She leaned close to him and whispered, "We were making out in public."

He smiled. "Do you care?"

"Absolutely not. You can kiss me wherever you want to."

"Sweetheart, if I kissed you where I wanted to right now, I'd be arrested."

Serena laughed, feeling silly and giddy and absolutely wonderful.

"I think Bobby and Chloe are planning on driving back to Tucson after the ceremony," she said. "But what do you say we spring for another night in Vegas for the four of us?"

Tom grinned. "I think that's a great idea."

TOM HAD NEVER VISITED cloud nine before, but if they ever built condos there, he was going to be the first in line to buy. He'd buy every last unit, charge a premium price for them and make a killing.

No. Better plan. He'd buy them and give them

away as a service to mankind, so a couple hundred other people could feel the way he felt right now, which was head over heels in love. Yes, that was a cliché. But clichés got to be clichés for a reason.

He pulled into a parking space at Cupid's Little Chapel of Love and killed the engine. Serena had put together the bouquet on the way there, and it looked beautiful.

So did Serena.

"They're not here yet," Tom said. "Let's wait inside where it's cool. We don't want the flowers to wilt and the champagne to get hot."

They went inside and sat down on a bench. Evidently it was a slow morning, because there was only one other couple in the reception area. Tom looked around at the flying cupids on the wallpaper, surprised to see that they didn't look nearly as ugly as they had last night. Maybe it was because it was daytime and sunlight filled the room.

Or maybe it was because one of them had shot him squarely in the heart.

Myrna came out and escorted the other couple into the chapel, leaving Tom and Serena alone in the reception area. Serena checked her watch, then rose and went to the window to look for Bobby and Chloe.

"Oh, look! They're here!"

Tom came up behind her, peered through the blinds and saw Chloe and Bobby sitting in his car talking. As they watched, Bobby gave Chloe a kiss and a hug.

"Look at them," Serena said with a smile. "They can't keep their hands off each other."

But Tom didn't want to look at them. He wanted to look at Serena. She was holding that bouquet and looking as gorgeous as any bride on her wedding day. Muted sunlight filtered through the blinds, making her golden-brown hair glint like a new penny. He looked at that skin he'd touched. Those lips he'd kissed. And all he could think about was how they'd talked and laughed and made love and found more in common in three days than he would have found with any other woman over a lifetime.

He took a deep, steadying breath. Even though he'd thought about it, and seriously considered it, he hadn't really *planned* on it. But now...

Could he actually do it?

"Serena?"

She turned and gave him a soft, beautiful smile, and in that instant, his indecision vanished. He loved this woman, and he wanted to be with her forever. Suddenly the words he couldn't have fathomed saying even an hour ago spilled right out of his mouth.

"Marry me."

She froze. "What did you say?"

Now that he'd said it, the idea seemed to gain

momentum, every nerve in his body waking to the possibilities.

"I want you to marry me, Serena. Today."

Serena was so stunned that for a moment she couldn't speak. "Marry you?" she repeated. *"Today?"*

"Yes. Do you love me?"

"You know I do. But—"

"No buts. Both of us have spent our whole lives being careful. Following the rules. Walking the straight and narrow. Planning our lives to death. Maybe for once we need to follow our hearts instead of our heads."

"But I can't...we can't..."

"Yes, it's crazy. I know that. But, Serena..." He edged closer to her, taking her face in his hands. "Somehow I know it's *right*. Don't you?"

Tom's expression was steady and unwavering, and in his eyes Serena saw the truth: She could look the world over for the next twenty years, maybe a lifetime, and never find a man like him.

"Yes," she said, "I do."

"Then marry me. We can make an appointment for later in the day. After Bobby and Chloe are married, we can run to the marriage license bureau and get a license, then come back."

Serena had a fleeting thought about her dream wedding, a fantasy she'd held since she was six years old. But that was all it was. A fantasy. Tom was reality. A perfect reality that she never could have imagined finding. And he wanted to marry her right now. What were doves and candles and rice bags compared with that? Why mess with all that trouble and expense when her married life with the man she loved could begin at this moment?

Tom was right. It was time to go with her heart and not her head. Being with him was like floating into uncharted waters and coming upon a lush desert island where they could revel in each other forever. That was just what she wanted to do. And she wanted to do it *now*.

"Yes, Tom," she said. "I'll marry you."

"Yes!" He gave her a quick kiss, then picked her up and spun her around, and when he set her back on her feet again, he flashed her one of those thousand-watt smiles that had made her fall in love with him in the first place. She felt so giddy she could barely keep from giggling, and her heart was about to burst with happiness.

"But let's let Chloe and Bobby have their moment," she said. "Then we'll tell them what we're going to do."

"You're right." Tom grinned. "And I think we'd better be prepared for a lot of 'I told you so's.'"

"I don't care," Serena said. "I don't care at all.

They can say I told you so from now on, because they were right. And I can't wait to tell them so."

"So this is it?" Tom asked, his face filled with excitement. "We're actually getting married?"

"Yes. Oh, *yes.*"

She kissed him. Then she kissed him again. And she didn't stop kissing him until she heard a car door slam outside. A few seconds later, the door opened and Bobby and Chloe came in.

"There you are!" Serena said. "Oh! I'm so glad you're finally here!" She gave Chloe a big hug, almost squashing the bouquet. Then she smiled and held it out to her. "This is for you."

Chloe took it, blinking with surprise.

"Do you like it?" Serena asked. "I wanted white roses, but all they had at the grocery store were carnations."

Chloe touched one of the blooms. "Yeah. It's really pretty."

"And this is for after the ceremony," Tom said, holding up the champagne. "I imagine they have some champagne glasses around here somewhere."

All at once the door to the chapel itself burst open and the couple who had gone in earlier came out. Serena couldn't help smiling. The bride looked so beautiful, so happy, so glowing. In a few hours, Serena knew she'd be feeling the same way.

Right now, though, it was Chloe's turn.

Serena smiled at her sister and nodded toward the chapel. "Well, I guess this is it, isn't it?"

But neither Bobby nor Chloe moved. Chloe opened her mouth to speak, but nothing came out, and she was gripping the bouquet so tightly her fingers had turned white. Suddenly, Serena realized that the bridal glow that should have been emanating from her sister was strangely absent. In fact, she was frowning. Why was she frowning?

"Chloe? What's the matter?"

"Thanks for the bouquet, Serena. And the champagne. I mean, we really do appreciate it, but…"

"But what?"

"But Bobby and I aren't getting married."

CHAPTER NINE

FOR AT LEAST ten seconds, Serena stared at her sister, certain that she couldn't have heard her right. "What did you say?"

"Bobby and I have decided that we've both got a lot of things to work out in our own lives, and it's best if we do it apart."

"But...but I saw you just a moment ago in the parking lot. You were hugging each other...kissing..."

Chloe gave Bobby a bittersweet smile. "We were saying goodbye."

Serena just stood there, stunned.

"You and Tom were right," Bobby said. "Driving to Vegas to get married was stupid. And after knowing each other for only three days? *Really* stupid. What the hell were we thinking?"

Serena felt as if somebody had pulled the ugly red rug right out from under her feet.

"We know that the only reason you're here supporting us now is because you thought you couldn't stop us," Chloe said. "And we appreciate that. But the truth is we really don't get along that well. I mean, Bobby's a nice guy and everything, but..."

"And Chloe. Gorgeous. And fun. But when it comes to the two of us together someplace besides bed...well, it's pretty much a disaster."

"No," Serena said, a twinge of desperation in her voice. "It wasn't a disaster. You just had a few little disagreements, that was all."

"It was more than that," Bobby said. "When it gets right down to it, we just aren't right together. And if only we'd slowed down long enough to see that, we wouldn't have made such a mess of things."

"We're really sorry for dragging you along on this trip," Chloe said. "And for leaving you in Windsor. We were so mad at you for what you did with Bobby's car, but then after we got the license and were driving over here, we got to thinking that if you'd do all that to try to stop us from getting married, then maybe we really were making a mistake. So we talked about it. And we decided you were right."

Serena knew she should say something, but she just didn't know what. She glanced at Tom, who appeared to be as speechless as she was.

"I've always admired you, Serena," Chloe said. "I've never told you that before, but I do. You've got your head on straight. Maybe if I'd listened to you the last two times, I wouldn't have made those mistakes. And here I was getting ready to do it again. Even thinking about getting married like this…'' She rolled her eyes. ''God, I feel like such an *idiot*.''

''No,'' Serena said. ''You weren't an idiot. Really. You weren't.''

''Yes, I was. A really big one. But I swear there'll be no more spur-of-the-moment road trips. No more flash engagements. From now on, I'm going to be more like you.'' She gave Serena a heartfelt hug. ''Thanks. I don't know what I'd do without you.''

Bobby swallowed hard, then looked at Tom. ''Ditto what she said, man. I owe you one.'' He gave Tom an awkward hug. Tom flicked his gaze to Serena, looking totally shell-shocked.

''So,'' Bobby said with a sigh of finality, ''I guess it's time to get back on the road to go home.'' He and Chloe started for the door, but Serena couldn't move. Tom's feet seemed equally stuck to the floor.

Chloe turned back. ''Hey, are you two coming?''

Tom looked at Serena. ''Uh…we'll be there in just a minute.''

Bobby and Chloe left the chapel. Tom and Serena sat down on a bench.

And Serena felt like an utter fool.

As she sat there next to the man she'd been ca-

vorting with like an infatuated teenager for the past
three days, her stomach churned with embarrassment. Suddenly all she wanted to do was crawl
under a table and hide her face in humiliation.

"My God," she whispered. "Do you know
what we almost did?"

"Oh, yeah." He blinked with surprise. "Wow.
Those endorphins are powerful things, aren't
they?"

That was it. Endorphins. Serena closed her eyes
painfully. "We knew better. We knew better, and
still—"

"And still we acted like a couple of lovestruck
idiots?"

"Yes. God, Tom, what were we thinking?"

Serena couldn't believe she'd behaved exactly
like Chloe, and now Chloe was being the voice of
reason. There were so many things wrong with that
scenario that Serena couldn't begin to count them.

"Serena?"

"Yes?"

"I have a confession to make."

"What's that?"

"I kind of liked acting like a lovestruck idiot."

"You *what?*"

He shrugged.

"Tom," she said, lowering her voice, "we had
sex in a gas-station bathroom!"

He smiled. "Yeah. I know."

Serena bowed her head. "This is *so* embarrassing."

"It didn't embarrass you while you were doing it."

"Yeah, and hindsight is twenty-twenty. I just hope the day comes when I can forget about all the crazy things I've done for the past three days."

Tom frowned. "Is that how you really feel? As if it's something you want to forget?"

She didn't know how she felt. Her mind was mush. During the whirlwind of the past few days, her emotions had been stretched, twisted, bent, wound into a pretzel and tied into a knot. But right now the only emotion she seemed to be able to feel was embarrassment.

"I don't know, Tom. I don't know how I feel. All I know is that when we're apart, we're perfectly sane and normal people. But put us together and—"

"And you get wild sex, public displays of affection and three-day marriage proposals?"

She groaned softly. *"Yes."* She leaned her head back against the wall, closing her eyes.

"Serena?" Tom asked.

"Yes?"

"Do you believe in signs?"

She opened her eyes. "Signs?"

"You know. Those things that happen out of the blue to point you in the direction you ought to go.

Metaphorical little road markers that pop up out of nowhere.''

"I guess I never really thought about it."

"Do you remember when we were in the grocery store, when you were picking out the flowers and I was getting the champagne?"

"Yes?"

"I passed by one of those prize machines. The ones you liked so much when you were a kid."

Serena's heart skipped. Prize machine?

"I noticed there were a few rings in it. So I stuck a quarter into the machine, telling myself that if a ring popped out, it would be a sign."

"A sign?"

"That I should ask you to marry me."

Tom reached into his pocket and drew out a small plastic container. He cracked it open and took out a ring—a silver plastic ring with a shiny fake diamond in the middle of it.

"There couldn't have been more than half a dozen of them in the machine," Tom said. "But sure enough, I twisted the handle, and look what fell right into my hand."

Serena stared down at the ring, surprised to see that it wasn't much different from the ones she'd worn as a child, the ones she'd built a dream on, and suddenly her heart was beating rapid-fire.

"But expecting us to get married three days after we met was a little insane," Tom said. "I'm afraid lovestruck idiots do things like that sometimes.''

"So you don't believe in signs?''

"Oh, no. The sign was exactly right. My timing was just a little off.'' He took her hand. "Serena?''

"Yes?''

"Will you marry me?''

For the umpteenth time that day, Serena was stunned. "But you just said that getting married after three days was insane!''

Tom drew back. "Of course it is. A Vegas wedding? What do you think I am? Crazy or something?''

"But you just asked me to marry you!''

"It's like I've said all along. We're only crazy if we get married in Vegas.'' He smiled. "That's why we're getting married in Tucson.''

"What?''

"One year from today. In Tucson. I want you to marry me.''

It took Serena several seconds to comprehend what he was saying, and when she did, it was as if the last piece of a puzzle had fallen into place.

"A year from now?'' she said.

"Yeah. See, it's not the falling in love in three days that's crazy. It's the getting married in three days.''

Serena looked at him with surprise, only to realize that he was absolutely right.

"The past few days have been incredible," he went on. "And more to the point, they've felt *right*. I don't care how it came about. I meant it when I said I loved you. Did you mean it when you said it to me?"

She couldn't lie. Didn't want to lie. "Yes. Of course I meant it."

Tom took her face in his hands and traced his thumbs over her cheeks. "Then say it. Say you'll marry me."

She wanted to answer, but she was still so shocked by everything that had happened that her voice had completely deserted her.

"Come on, Serena. You've said yes once today already, and this is a much better offer. A nice long engagement with plenty of time to plan the perfect wedding." He smiled and held up the ring. "Say yes, and this lovely piece of jewelry is yours."

For several moments, the only thing Serena could do was look at the ring, then at Tom, and suddenly her emotions twisted all over again. It was nothing but a silly little token of childhood, but its meaning had suddenly magnified tenfold, bringing tears to her eyes.

She thought about that era of make-believe, about the first time in her life when she could remember dreaming of a moment like this. As she'd grown older, those childhood dreams had become adult ones, flashing through her mind at odd times—in business meetings, in the shower, while she was driving, in those nebulous moments between waking and sleep. And now those bits and pieces were moving out of her imagination into reality, finally allowing her to see clearly the man she'd dreamed about for all those years.

And he looked just like Tom Erickson.

"Yes, Tom. I'll marry you. One year from today." She smiled. "I can't wait."

Tom slipped the ring on her finger, then turned her hand left and right, letting the light glint dully through the huge plastic gem. "You'll have the real thing as soon as we get back home and I can investigate the diamond market. An engagement ring is a real investment, you know."

She slid into his arms. "Right now, symbolism works for me."

"If we wait a year," Tom said, "that's plenty of time to be absolutely sure we belong together."

"I'm already sure."

"So am I. But after everything that's happened, I thought I should do the responsible thing and at least say it."

"Now, we still have issues to work out," Serena said. "Compromises to make. And a lot of things to learn about each other."

"Some of those things might take a lifetime."

Serena smiled. "That's what I'm hoping for."

Tom glanced toward the door. "Well, Bobby

and Chloe are waiting for us. I guess we'd better go.''

"Do you think maybe we should wait until we get back to Tucson to tell them? Let the dust settle a little first?''

"Yeah. That's a good idea.'' Then a look of distress came over Tom's face. "Wait a minute. Does this mean I'm going to have to ride in the backseat of a car with you for six hours and I can't touch you?''

"That's right. Unless you'd like to drive our lovely new car all the way back to Tucson.''

He sighed with resignation. "Remind me to call somebody before we leave town to haul that sucker off.''

Serena started for the door, but Tom stopped her. "One more thing. You don't talk in your sleep, do you?''

"Would it matter if I did?''

"Of course not. As you said, compromise. I'll just sleep in the other room.''

"No way, buster. You're sleeping with me.''

"Okay. On one condition.''

"What's that?''

"You'll model your underwear for me.''

Serena smiled. "Just say the word.''

They walked hand-in-hand to the door, sharing one last kiss before stepping outside beneath the blazing summer sun of Las Vegas. They walked a discreet two feet apart on the way to Bobby's car. And for the next six hours, they discovered that it was possible to play a remarkably exciting game of footsie in the backseat of an SUV.

LOVE IS
A BEACH

Isabel Sharpe

CHAPTER ONE

EMILY WAKEFIELD stuffed rolled-up panty hose into her black dress sandals and tucked the shoes in the bottom of her suitcase, wedged against the side. She was the champion of efficient packing. Five days in the Caribbean—one afternoon tea, one cocktail event, one dinner, one wedding, one small suitcase.

Next, walking shoes, stuffed with socks, underpants and her deodorant. She needed those for hikes along the trails and sandy beaches of Lilia Island, her childhood friend Sally Graham's family treasure, and for clambering up the beautiful green hills on the island's western end, which overlooked endless miles of the sparkling Caribbean Sea.

Paradise.

Her visits to the Virgin Islands were a bright spot every year, especially since her own family couldn't afford so much as a blade of grass in the tropics. She and Sally always stayed in the main house, Gloryside, but whenever possible they'd row Sally's rickety boat over to Daim Island, which her family also owned—a glorified rock

barely big enough for the one-room cabin perched
on its high end. As teenagers, they had spent the
day, and often the night, giggling over fanzines,
sipping sneaked-in beer and fantasizing about the
future. Now that they were adults, their activities
tended more toward reading, relaxing and reflect-
ing.

Emily hadn't been to the island since she'd
started business school. And the last visit—two
years ago—she'd spent most of the time sobbing
over her broken engagement to Loring Mackenzie.

Not this time. This time Emily would be maid
of honor to Sally, who was marrying John Mackenzie, handsome, charming and successful—her
perfect match...and Loring's brother.

Emily squelched a cold stab of nerves with
warm genuine happiness for her friend and metic-
ulously filled the space in the suitcase not occupied
by shoes with casual tops and shorts and appropriate underwear for each outfit, until the surface
was totally flat and she could fold her good dresses
on top.

Of course Loring would be there this week.
She'd have to see him for the first time since she'd
given him back his ring. Though *given* might be
too gentle a word. *Flung* was a little too harsh.
Tossed? That worked.

But she was a different woman now, no longer
working for starvation-wage non-profit causes,

much as she'd loved her job counseling teenaged moms. She had a business degree from Harvard, and this morning, a third interview with Borwyn and Company Management Consultants, her absolute dream job. No more Cinderella Emily, waiting for Prince Loring to take care of her.

Since she'd *tossed* back his ring, though, Loring had quit his high-powered trading job and moved to Paris for a year. Now, she heard, he was teaching school in North Carolina.

Nothing had been said, but she surmised he'd had some kind of mental breakdown. Why else would an obsessive and extremely successful Wall Street workaholic move to the South and teach high-school history? He was too careful and too talented to be blackballed in the industry. And pardon her for generalizing, but men like Loring didn't have spiritual epiphanies.

She carefully folded the rose silk dress she planned to wear to the wedding—bless Sally for letting her choose her own—so that enough space was left on the right side of the suitcase for her toiletry kit.

There. She left the kit open for her toothbrush in the morning, tucked two romance novels and sandals into her carry-on bag, and glanced at her watch: 10:00 p.m. Seven hours of sleep, then she'd get up, grab some breakfast and hop on the T to Logan International Airport. Boston to Atlanta, At-

lanta to St. Thomas. From there, a driver would
take her to Charlotte Amalie harbor, where the
Graham's boat waited to whisk her off to Lilia Island for her first sight of her ex-fiancé in two years.

LORING MACKENZIE tossed his socks, a couple of
undershirts, briefs, his good shoes for the ceremony and parties, and his tennis shoes into his
largest suitcase. He'd have to put his tennis racket
in another bag; no way would it fit here. His favorite shirt—oh, and his second favorite—and
might as well throw in a couple more. It was hot
in the Caribbean, and he'd have to change often.
Then maybe a couple of long-sleeved ones in case
it cooled down at night. Shorts, pants, formal
pants, jackets, ties, what else? He examined his
ravaged dresser drawers, hands on his hips, frowning.

Okay, maybe he'd lost his knack for efficient
packing. He used to go on business trips so often
he could pack in his sleep. But it had been a while
since he'd traveled—assistant principals didn't
tend to be globetrotters. And this wasn't business,
this was pleasure. On a lot of levels, he hoped.

His brother and Sally had been dating for nearly
three years; their wedding was excitedly anticipated by everyone. No question they were a perfect
match when it came to breeding, culture and in-

telligence, and both had a bone-deep sense of fun that kept them from being stuffy.

What else? He went over a mental checklist of the activities he'd be required to attend. His brain wasn't working quite up to par, and even though he'd already done his usual workout, his body felt twitchy and restless.

No-brainer why that was: he was on his way to see the woman who'd agreed to marry him then changed her mind, sending him into the beginnings of a tailspin that had ended with him rejecting corporate America, spending a year in his late mother's hometown of Paris, France, and coming to re-evaluate what was truly important in his life.

Two words: *Emily Wakefield.*

He frowned at his dresser again, then snapped his fingers. Cuff links. He'd need them for his formal shirt. He dug around in his drawers, then his closet, and finally found the box on the top shelf under a sweater.

It'd been forever since he'd had to wear cufflinks. Which ones should he bring? He opened the box and his heart stopped.

He'd forgotten it was in there, sparkling among the several pairs of cuff links and studs, like a sign from above that he was on the right track. The multi-carat diamond ring he'd given Emily, which she'd hurled back at him, more figuratively than literally. *I'm afraid this isn't going to work out.* It still hurt to remember her icy words, and her anger, which he had no way to comprehend at the time.

Impulsively, he snapped the lid shut on the box and dumped the entire thing into the overflowing suitcase. He'd done a lot of thinking over the last two years. A lot. And as he'd sorted painfully through the jumbled mess he'd made of his life, one fact remained unchanged, amid all the other shifting facts of his existence: he loved Emily. She was the one and only woman for him. And he was going to get her back this week.

No matter what it took.

EMILY STRETCHED and did a silly girlish twirl in the bedroom Sally had assigned her at Gloryside, dubbed the Lemon Drop Room because of the bright-yellow walls. Sweet of Sally to reserve Emily's favorite. Everything looked exactly as she remembered, except the traditional welcome glass of fresh-squeezed lemonade was missing. When the girls had arrived each winter, there was always a glass waiting for them in their rooms, on a silver tray with a linen napkin, iced and deliciously soursweet.

Not a problem. Bride Sally had plenty on her mind, like organizing guests and accommodations and activities—oh, and let's see…a wedding ceremony and a reception. Whew! Enough to make Sally forget her address, let alone lemonade, even though she'd hired an army of caterers and florists and consultants to help. And even though she'd been planning this ceremony practically from the day she and John had started going out.

Of course, back then Emily thought she'd be attending this wedding as Loring's wife.

Not.

She'd imagined seeing him again so many times, girded her mental armor so carefully that now she was here, it would be no big deal. Nothing could happen that would surprise her. Whether he was hostile, conciliatory, defensive, patronizing, amorous—oh God, she hoped not amorous—she'd imagined them all and had the appropriate reaction.

Who cared?

She shook out her dress for the wedding and hung it in the huge cedar-lined wardrobe, inhaling the warm salty Caribbean breeze that flowed unimpeded through the arched doorways and windows, over the king-sized wooden bed, across the potted palm in the corner, weaving around her blissfully bare legs like a hungry cat.

No matter what Loring threw at her, she was ready. She wasn't the same just-graduated doormat she'd been when he'd swept her off her feet and insisted she say yes to his mega-carat diamond. Looking back, she could see it all so clearly it made her wince. What she thought was love was simply an exchange—the safety of college for the safety of a man.

No more. She'd gotten herself through Harvard business school, gotten herself interviewed by Borwyn and Company, and gotten herself way, way over him.

She finished unpacking and waltzed into the enormous bathroom—her favorite—with the gold dolphin taps and the white tub big enough to bathe the Green Bay Packers. A bath would feel good, refresh her and wash off the plane smell. It would also relax her.

The tub gurgled full and Emily sank down into its warmth, taking deep even breaths. She could use the time before the party to meditate. Visualize the meeting with Loring, and decide now what emotions she would engage. She'd learned a lot about emotional control over the years. Learned how to turn off fear and turn on self-confidence instead.

She closed her eyes, cleared her mind until she was completely relaxed. Then allowed herself to imagine Loring at the party this afternoon, and created a serene version of Emily, able to greet him without fear or nerves, chat calmly, even summon some sisterly affection. See? It would all go just as she planned. She was in control.

One eye sprang open from her meditative state and peeked at the clock. Time to get ready. She rose reluctantly from the warm soothing water, then stiffened as she heard the room door open. Strange. Steps sounded across the floor, then something clinked on the wooden table. More steps. The door closing.

Of course. She smiled and finished drying herself, then hung the towel back on the gold rack. Sally hadn't forgotten after all. Emily must not have heard the knock while she was in the tub. A little lemonade would hit the spot.

Grinning a welcome for the tall icy glass, she pushed open the door, enjoying the rush of outdoor air on her skin.

And stopped with a horrified gasp.

Stifled a scream.

Shot back into the bathroom and slammed the door, hand to her chest, panting hard.

Not lemonade.

Loring.

In her room. Standing there. Right there. Just now. *Oh my God.*

Even though she didn't love him anymore, was a different person from the woman he'd known and was utterly ready for their first meeting, nothing, *nothing* had prepared her to deal with the fact that after two years, Loring Mackenzie's first sight of her would be entirely butt-naked.

CHAPTER TWO

LORING CLOSED his mouth. He thought he closed his mouth. Hadn't he just closed his mouth? He wasn't sure.

He wasn't even sure if what he thought had happened had actually happened. Had it?

Had Emily just walked out of his bathroom naked? Or had he conjured her up out of his fantasies?

Either way, it was a welcome he was unlikely to forget.

He walked to the door and knocked. "Emily?"

"Go away."

He grinned at the muffled mortification in her voice. As if he hadn't seen her naked hundreds of absolutely thrilling times. "What are you doing in my room?"

"What are *you* doing in *my* room?"

"It's *my* room. The Daffodil Room."

"This is the Lemon Drop Room. The Daffodil Room is across the hall."

"Oh, for—" He rolled his eyes. Why couldn't they have given the rooms normal names? Like

Five? And Six? "Sally told me to turn right so I turned right."

"Left. You should have turned left."

"Okay. Left. I'm sorry."

"It's okay."

He lingered by the door. He was supposed to leave now. Take his suitcases and lug them to his own room right across the hall, and didn't *that* immediately bring to mind images of nighttime wanderings? But Emily Wakefield was about three inches away on the other side of the door and she was naked. A man couldn't walk out on that and stay sane. Not that standing here was doing much to keep him that way, either.

"It's good to see you again, Emily."

The ceiling fan creaked above his head. Voices sounded coming up the hallway, then drifted past. Was she going to ignore him entirely?

"Uh…yeah…same here."

"You look terrific."

A strangled noise came through the door. "Um…thanks. You do, too."

"I mean you look *really* terrif—"

"Loring?"

"Yes?"

"Go away now."

He took a step back from the door, suppressing a chuckle. "I take it you want me to leave."

"Yes."

"You don't want to come out and chat some more?"

"No."

He sighed loudly. "No glad-to-see-me hug?"

"Loring. I am naked in this bathroom."

"Believe me, I know that."

The door made a sudden loud noise. As if a certain twenty-six-year-old naked woman had punched it. "Leave. Now."

He put his hand to the door, almost in a caress, imagining her on the other side, annoyed, embarrassed—maybe titillated? Just a little? He hoped so, because one-way titillation was a lonely and pathetic place to be. "See you at the party?"

"Yes."

"Oh, and Sally said not to bother dressing up. What you have on should be fine."

"Good-*bye,* Loring." He could hear the beginnings of laughter in her exasperation. Thank goodness.

"See you later?"

"Yes."

He turned away, grabbed his suitcases and hoisted them across the hall to a slightly more orangey yellow room. Okay, daffodil. Not as yellow as lemon drop. He got it. But he prided himself on his excellent memory and sense of direction, and Sally had definitely said to turn right.

He shrugged. No biggie. Brides had other more

important things on their minds than left and right. Coincidentally, so did he. And how embarrassing for a manly man to admit, but he had more on his mind than Emily's stunning naked body and how to reintroduce it to his own as soon as possible.

Besides the shock and lust, other more powerful emotions had come roaring back. *C'est toujours l'amour*— Literally, "It's always love." Madame Rabeaux had said it over and over again, a wrinkled lid collapsing into a sly wink, her cigarette smoke drifting into the Parisian breeze, blowing over whatever café they happened to be sitting at. His mother's best friend had taught him more than she knew.

Not that he'd stopped loving Emily in the years they'd been apart, but the sight of her had brought that amazing feeling on again in such force that he couldn't imagine how anything else had ever been important to him.

What had his first career given him but stomach acid, anxiety attacks and the loss of the love of his life? And somehow he'd thought that had been worth it?

Well, okay, it had brought him millions of dollars, he wasn't about to spit on those. But his current job as assistant principal, dean of students and occasional history teacher at Asheville Prep, brought him infinitely more satisfaction. Now he just needed Emily to give him a chance, so he could prove to her that his priorities had shifted. That if by some miracle he managed to convince her to let him back into her life, she would always be number one.

And if he couldn't make that happen this week, on this beautiful island paradise with romance filling the air, he had a feeling he never would.

EMILY ACCEPTED a glass of iced tea from a uniformed maid and smiled her thanks. Ahead of her, on the beautiful front lawn of Gloryside, wedding guests here for the week's festivities swarmed around tables set up with a fabulous assortment of tea sandwiches, cookies, tarts and tiny cakes. She recognized about half of the approximately two dozen people. Including, now that she looked harder, one dark, incredibly attractive man who had just seen her naked, chatting with an equally attractive redhead who didn't look familiar.

Okay. She could do this.

She marched resolutely ahead—in the opposite direction—and snagged Sally in a bear hug from behind.

"Hey! You made it!" Sally turned and squeezed her back, petite and bubbly, a Reese Witherspoon look-alike. "Did you find everything okay?"

"Yes. Everything. It's so good to be here."

"Now that you're out of school, you'll have to come every year again." Sally grabbed her arm and dragged her aside, beaming excuse-mes to the guests she'd been chatting with. "Have you talked to him yet?"

"Uh…" Emily's eyes glanced over at Loring at the exact moment his eyes glanced over at her. Immediately she de-glanced, before the little thrill that shot through her could take hold and grow into anything resembling a big thrill. "Sort of."

"Sort of?"

"He came into my room while I was taking a bath."

"No way." Sally gasped and squeezed her arm. "He wants you back, I know it."

Emily gazed up at the brilliant blue heavens to beg for patience. "Actually, no. You just gave him the wrong directions to his room."

"Did I?" The bride's blue eyes opened enormously wide.

"Sally…" The maid of honor's voice sounded a dire warning. "Don't start getting any matchmaking ideas."

"Moi?" The blue eyes opened wider. "Oh look, there's my sweetie. Have you talked to John yet? Come talk to John."

"I'd love to." Emily sighed in relief at having that topic over with and scanned the crowd for Sally's groom.

Goodbye relief. John had moved to chat with Loring and the redhead. Speaking to John would now involve speaking to Loring. And of course that wouldn't have occurred to the bride.

"Sa-a-lly..." Her protest bounced as Sally dragged her across the lawn. "Don't you dare try to—"

"Hey, Emily!" John shouted the greeting, moved the camera around his neck carefully over his shoulder and stretched out his arms for a welcoming hug.

Emily went into them, enjoying the affectionate moment until she locked eyes with Loring looming over John's broad shoulder.

Gulp. She needed to meditate, *now*. Or maybe medicate. Had his eyes always been that blue? Dark hair and blue eyes, sign of the Black Irish. God, he was gorgeous.

She became aware of John trying to disengage from the hug while she was still clinging like a shy four-year-old.

"Uh...John, it's great to see you." She managed to let him go. "Congratulations."

"Thanks." He beamed and had just introduced the redhead as Mimi, when Sally suddenly thought it tremendously important that Mimi try a shrimp sandwich and swept her off, and then John thought it tremendously important to take a picture of Emily and Loring before *he* swept off, leaving Emily and Loring not at all coincidentally alone.

"Well." Emily lifted her iced tea to him and

buried her face in it, wishing it was about a hundred proof. "Apparently we are supposed to talk."

"Apparently." He grinned and glanced over her simple flowered sundress. "By the way, I like what you're wearing now, too."

She nearly spit out her tea. "Can we forget about that?"

"Maybe *you* can."

A man pushed behind Loring to get at the petits fours and Loring took a step closer.

Very close. Much too close. Close enough that she could smell him.

Oh, no. That cologne...she'd forgotten it. *Oh no, oh, no.* She inhaled a huge, delicious, sexually evocative lungful.

Oh, yes. Did that ever bring back memories. She should have meditated the smell of him out of her system, too, if that was even possible. Maybe she and Loring had had a destructive relationship emotionally, but in the bedroom they'd done just fine.

She inhaled again. More than just fine. On a scale of one to five...

Nine.

Help.

"So..." She cast around desperately for a topic—any topic except the two of them heating sheets. "You're teaching school now."

"Yes, I'm teaching school now." His eyes twinkled at her desperate life-preserver grab for chit chat. "A small private school in Asheville, North Carolina, about as far away from the life you knew me in as I could get."

"Well." She tried not to feel sorry for him. Clearly the fall had been long and painful; the rumors she'd heard of his trouble at Clarkson Brothers were obviously true. "That must have been very hard on you."

"What must have been hard on me?"

"Losing your job. That life. It meant so much to you."

"Yes." His eyes stopped twinkling; his jaw tensed. "It did."

She took a deep breath to keep herself from empathizing. It was one of her greatest weaknesses, taking everyone else's problems on as her own. Correction: *had been* one of her greatest weaknesses. "Well, I'm sure if you work hard, you can climb back up to—"

"No, no, no. You don't understand. I *chose* the life I have now."

"Oh, I'm sure." She tried to keep the pity out of her smile and wasn't sure she succeeded. Loring G. Mackenzie III, choosing to teach school? In North Carolina? No way. Maybe his drinking had gotten worse, too.

"Emily." He used his listen-carefully-you-small-child voice and her body stiffened to instant rigor mortis. Oh, she was so well rid of this man.

"Yes, Loring?" The sweetly intoned words fought to escape from between her clenched teeth.

"I left that life deliberately. It wasn't what I wanted anymore. I went to Paris and I met this woman who—"

"A woman." Funny how when one clenched one's teeth as hard as one could, they still found ways to clench harder all on their own.

"Yes. Madame Rabeaux."

"Rambo?" She deliberately misspoke, while picturing a cross between Juliette Binoche and Isabella Rosselini. He'd loved this Madame Whatever desperately. Emily knew it. The woman had shown him a depth of love he hadn't thought possible, and had taught him sexual positions Emily couldn't begin to manage.

She hated her.

"Rabeaux. A classmate of my mother's at Wellesley."

Ah. Emily's teeth released and a puff of air exited her mouth loudly enough to be audible, which made his eyes screw up in that very sexy amused way all over again. *Oh, goody, Emily, advertise that you're relieved.*

Why should she be relieved? She shouldn't care either way. He could screw any woman he wanted. Not like they belonged to each other anymore. Heck, she could have any man she wanted, too. Just never mind that she hadn't really wanted any

of the ones she'd met in the last two years or so.
The men she'd been attracted to in business school
had reminded her of Loring—the drive, the ambi-
tion, the devotion to the dollar—but without his
charm and the intriguingly sexy contrast of down-
to-earth approachability and supremely sophisti-
cated.

She hadn't wanted to go near them. Wasn't
ready for that kind of man again. Ever.

"So what about this woman?"

"After I left Clarkson, I went to Paris and lived
with her. She showed me around the city, except
that's such an understatement. She imbued me with
the city, maybe that's closer."

"She imbued you." Call her stupid, but she
wasn't at all sure what he meant.

"She took me everywhere, introduced me to
everyone, even got me work at a bakery."

"A bakery?" Emily's mouth hung unattrac-
tively open, but she was unable to close it. She
couldn't begin to imagine Loring serving customers. Serving anyone. There were servers and there
were those who were served. She was—used to
be—the former. He would always be the latter.

"Yup." As if on cue, he selected a tea sandwich
from a silver platter *served* to him by one of the
circulating wait staff, a pretty brunette who smiled
a little less than professionally at Loring and then
entirely professionally at Emily. "I even learned

how to make the bread, though it's hard to recreate here because the flour is different.''

"You baked."

"I baked, Emily." He looked absolutely serious.

This was entirely too strange. The Loring she knew did things like take calls and schedule meetings, and take more calls, invariably in the middle of dinner, and strategize and take more calls, and then make about a hundred himself. He'd spent more time with his phone than he did with her. And now she was expected to believe he rose each morning before dawn and played with dough?

It made no sense.

"Well, that must have been…" *Humbling* was the word that came to her lips, but maybe she'd better leave that alone. Humility and Loring hadn't been close companions when she'd known him. "…nice."

"It was more than that. I'd love to tell you about that year, Emily."

She nodded politely, wishing he'd stop using her name so much. It sounded so intimate on his tongue. It also brought up an unwelcome image of the times he always said it. During sex, when he was least like the eternal employee and most like the man she'd loved. He always said her name right when he… She *had* to stop thinking about this. She needed to get away from him, from this gathering. Get back to the Lemon Drop Room and meditate, clear her mind, reprogram it away from this crazy vulnerability to him that she'd been so sure she wouldn't feel.

"I'd love to hear about it sometime, Loring." She used her super-polite voice, which he would understand meant she wasn't really sure she wanted to hear any of it, and maybe that kind of conversation should happen between him and someone who cared.

Except of course she did care, damn it. But not enough to want to spend any more time with him this week, smelling his amazing smell, looking into his unbelievably blue eyes, remembering how good they were together in that one, ahem, tiny arena—

Not any more time than she absolutely had to.

CHAPTER THREE

LORING LAY on his back in the supremely comfortable queen-sized bed in the Daffodil Room. A soft night breeze blew through his open window, bringing a floral seaside scent and the sound of frogs and insect life.

What a beautiful island. He hoped John and Sally would be inviting him down to visit often. And he hadn't even gotten much of a chance to explore yet. But John told him the ever-bubbly Sally had organized a treasure hunt and planned to pair guests off for the search. He'd get more of a chance to explore then. And Loring knew exactly who he wanted to explore…that is, explore with.

He inhaled, stretched and clasped his hands behind his head, shifting a few times to try and find a comfortable position. Of course, he'd changed radically from the manipulative person he used to be, or he would have demanded Sally pair him with a certain young woman who had once again taken center stage in his heart, not that she'd ever been far off in the wings. Seeing her again had doubled his motivation to get her back—now he needed opportunities. Lots of them. Long ones, preferably in private. The treasure hunt would be a great start.

However, since he was no longer that manipulative person, he'd had to content himself without even dropping a hint. Easy enough after he'd seen the sly looks between John and Sally when the subject of pairing the guests came up. After the tea this afternoon, when Sally had delivered Emily to him and swept that Mimi character away, he knew he had two powerful allies in his quest to get Emily back in his life. He just needed the time with her.

Across the hall her door opened. He brought his hands down and lifted himself on one elbow. Intriguing. Where was she going at this hour?

Immediately, he fantasized a soft knock on the door, Emily appearing in a cotton and lace nightgown—or no, an incredible clinging negligee, or a black silk teddy. Or how about a bustier and garters, with heels and black leather—

His fantasy evaporated wistfully as her steps went past his door and down the hall. Impulsively, he threw off the sheet and pulled on a T-shirt.

Maybe she was going downstairs for a snack? Though how she could eat after Sally and John had taken the gang to the Hook, Line and Sinker restaurant on St. Thomas and fed them to groaning, he hadn't a clue.

Maybe, just maybe, she was as stirred up and

restless as he was? Maybe, just maybe, for the same reason? She'd sat at the other end of the table at dinner, but he'd caught her eye several times, most notably when John had been toasting his bride. The lower the level in her wineglass, the more she'd glanced his way, and the longer their gazes held. She'd been gorgeous, flushed, laughing, enjoying herself, letting her new tight reserve slip. Two years ago she'd been one of the most open trusting people he knew.

He hated to think he'd done anything to change that part of her.

So…maybe, just maybe, she was heading outside for a walk in the balmy night air. And maybe the idea of him stumbling over her, purely by accident of course, in this romantic setting would appeal to her. More than that, maybe she was hoping it would happen.

Either way, he'd said he wanted opportunities, and fate could be about to hand him a helluva one. A tropical night, a lonely beach, the lingering effects of excellent wine and their still potent chemistry…

He opened his door and listened intently. Her footsteps sounded going downstairs, soft and light like a dancer's. He followed to the top of the landing and glanced down the elegant curving staircase, gripping the wrought-iron railing. Out of sight already.

More footsteps, heading to the back of the house. He crept noiselessly downstairs and waited before he turned the corner, listening again. Had she gone into the kitchen after all?

The back door opened, slid shut. He grinned and followed, peered through the window and waited until she'd disappeared down the narrow path to the cove before he went after her.

If he knew her as well as he thought he did, he'd find her on the beach, lost in contemplation. He'd loved sneaking up on her as she stood either deep in thought or mesmerized by a sight of particular beauty. She became so involved it was as if she'd exited this world for another one inside her own head. It was one of the things he loved about Emily—her imagination, her empathy. He'd creep up, slide his arms around her, surprising her, sometimes startling her, then pull her unresisting, laughing body back against his, burying his face in the soft skin of her neck....

Mmm. She wouldn't be able to help but remember some of the good times.

Yes. He had a history of being manipulative. Yes, it was one of the reasons she'd broken off their engagement. And yes, he had changed, had recognized the importance of taking other people on their own terms, not entirely on his.

But he had four more days here to prove to Emily he still loved her, that he knew now what it would take to make her happy and was more than willing to try.

With a time frame like that, he had to bend the rules.

EMILY WALKED along the strip of beach behind the house, luxuriating in the moonlight and the soft sand, still warm between her toes. She found a spot in the center of the cove and stood, letting herself become entranced by the familiar night noises, the chorusing of tree frogs, the breeze setting palm fronds rustling, the gentle lapping of the waves. In the last two years she hadn't had—or hadn't made—time to go to the beach. And frankly, when *beach* to her meant this uninhabited stretch on a private tropical island, she couldn't quite summon enthusiasm for the one-square-foot-of-sand-per-body experience in Massachusetts.

She'd been unable to relax enough to sleep. She'd tossed, turned, done yoga and meditation, but while her body had relaxed fairly completely, her brain wouldn't begin to turn off. *He* was right across the hall. How was she supposed to sleep, thinking of him in bed? Bare-chested—he slept that way in warm weather—with boxers or shorts hugging the firm flat line of his waist.

No wonder she couldn't sleep.

The tea party had been fine, they'd managed to be friendly, and she'd kept herself under pretty good control. But at dinner, the wine had gone to her head and let loose her memories and her imagination. Memories of how many times they'd gone out to eat at their favorite restaurants, split a bottle of wine and talked until the staff started sweeping up around them. Memories of their trips together, to London, to California, to the coast of Maine, when he'd actually hang up his phone and they could act like a real couple, sharing the same sense of adventure and fun.

At the Hook, Line and Sinker, when John had stood up and toasted Sally, Loring's eyes had zeroed in on hers at the same moment hers had zeroed in on his, and time had stood utterly still while her heart did an entire conga line all by itself. She'd probably lost ten years off her life.

She needed this time alone in the fresh warm night air to clear her head. Give herself a good talking to about how the rest of the week would go, and reign her libido in to some semblance of control. Loring was bad for her. She'd narrowly escaped being his little arm-candy wife; she had to remember what that life would have been like, compared with the grand adventure she was about to embark on now. An adventure of self-sufficiency, of—

Arms snaked around her waist. She reacted without thinking, grabbed the hand, stuck out her leg, twisted, and flipped the body behind her to land with a thud on the sand. A second later, her brain caught up and she covered her mouth with her hands.

"Loring! I'm so sorry, did I hurt—" She frowned. She sounded exactly like her old self. *Regroup.* "What part of sneaking up on me in the middle of the night struck you as a good idea?"

"In hindsight...none of it." He gasped the words out. "Where did you learn to do that?"

"Strong Women Studios, Somerville, Massachusetts."

He got to his feet, brushing off sand, and faced her. She hoped he could see the smirk on her face. "What, did you think I'd melt into your arms like old times?"

"I...no, of course not." He folded his arms and scowled.

She grinned. Score two. "These aren't old times anymore, Loring."

He glanced at the spot he'd landed and tightened his arms across his chest. "I'm well aware of that."

She lifted her chin higher. Oh, this was going so well. The only flaw, as far as she could see, was that if it hadn't gone well, *she'd* be wrapped in those big muscular arms instead of him.

But of course that would be bad. Wouldn't it.

"Want to walk?" He gestured down the beach, illuminated nearly to daylight by the moon, making

the colored lanterns strung out for the wedding festivities superfluous.

She bit her lip. Oh, that was such a bad idea.
He was so large and so solid and so male, and the
moonlight was doing all kinds of handsome and
mysterious things to his face, making him look
harder and then softer, depending on where the
shadows hit him.

And then there was that smells-good issue…

"I don't think…"

"Come on, Emily. I won't bite. Neither of us
can sleep, apparently, and a walk would probably
help relax us."

Right. Walking along a killer-romantic beach
with the man she once thought was the love of her
life would be right up there in the relaxation department with fleeing a swarm of killer bees.

"I should get back to the house."

"Why?"

"Because I'm…I'm…" Blanking out. Utterly
blanking out. "I need tampons."

"Not buying it." He shook his head. "Standard
freak-guy-out-with-mention-of-period trick."

A grin tried to fight its way onto her lips. "A
sudden need for aspirin?"

"'Not tonight, I've got a headache'?" He made
a sound of contempt. "Appalling cliché."

"Okay." She took a deep breath. "I don't want

to walk with you because I don't care to encourage any intimacy between us.''

That stopped him. He hadn't expected her to be so direct. Welcome to the new improved Emily Wakefield.

"Fair enough.''

In the midst of her triumph she experienced a traitorous stab of disappointment that he was giving in so uncharacteristically easily. Which meant deep down at least part of her did want to walk with him.

Damn.

"Compromise?'' He lifted both brows and unfolded his arms.

She narrowed her eyes, firmly squashing the giddy rush of hope. "Let's hear it.''

"Let me walk you back to the house.''

She glanced longingly at the pathway down the beach, wishing she hadn't said she needed to go in, and turned to him. "That would be fine.''

They set off toward the house at a leisurely pace. Extremely leisurely. Emily's hand bumped Loring's. Loring's bumped Emily's. The moon was perfect. Frogs accompanying. Beach. Balmy breeze. Their pace slackened further. God, she wanted him to kiss her.

Help.

"So I hear you made it through Harvard Business School.''

Made it through? "Didn't you think I would?"

"You're a very determined person. It doesn't surprise me at all. What surprised me is that you'd want to go in the first place."

"Why is that?"

He chuckled. "Why do I feel like no matter how I answer this, you're going to be insulted?"

"Because I know what you're going to say."

"Oh?" His hand bumped hers again. "What's that?"

"You're going to say that I was such a passive person, you didn't expect me to have the strength or the hunger to get through such a competitive program."

"Passive?" He turned and looked at her incredulously. "Is that how you thought I saw you?"

"Wasn't it?" Her heart gave a stupid leap of hope.

"No." He put his hands on his hips and stared at her as if she wasn't the person he thought he'd been strolling down the beach with. "Why on earth would I want someone passive in my life?"

"To support you. To take a back seat to you and your career, give you everything you needed and ask nothing in return."

Even in the dim moonlight she could see his jaw tighten. "I seem to remember this speech. As I recall, this is where the ring was hurled back at me—"

"Tossed. I tossed it."

"*Tossed* at me, followed by 'I'm afraid this isn't going to work out' and my office door slamming in my face."

Emily winced. "I guess it was a pretty…"

"Passive way to handle breaking up with me?"

She took a deep breath and looked down at her toes, wiggling them so they buried themselves under the sand. "Touché."

"Neither of us distinguished ourselves in that go-round of our relationship."

"I guess not." She wiggled her toes deeper. That go-round? Like there'd be others?

He took a step closer. She wanted to take a step back, but she'd dug her feet in so deep that—

Oh, okay, she didn't want to take a step back.

"Maybe we can try again."

"What?" She did take a step back then, spilling sand off the tops of her feet.

"I mean, maybe we can be friends."

She frowned at him suspiciously. It hadn't sounded as if he meant friends. And worse, her stinking traitor heart had bumped up to a lively island rhythm at the thought of them being more than friends.

No, no, no. Been there, decided not to marry that.

"Friends, of course. Friends is a good idea. We can do that."

"Good." He turned to go up the path.

She grimaced and followed. For one traitorous little second...oh, for heaven's sake, she'd been having traitorous little seconds ever since she'd first laid eyes on him this afternoon when she was butt-naked. So she was still attracted to him, so part of her would probably always be a little in love with him, that did not mean he was any more right for her now than he had been a few years ago.

Friends was a good idea. They could certainly do that. He lived in North Carolina, she lived in Boston. It wasn't as if they'd be tripping over each other all year long. And Sally had so many activities planned for her guests, they might not see much of each other even here.

In any case, for the next few days, she could manage to be friends with him. Good friends. They knew each other so well...or at least they used to...that they should be able to be very good friends.

That was it. All they could be. All they should be. All they would be.

Friends.

She stumbled glumly up the trail after him.

Her traitorous freaking heart would just have to learn to live with it.

CHAPTER FOUR

EMILY PUT ON royal-blue linen shorts and a sleeveless white linen top and frowned at herself in the full-length mirror inside the door of the Lemon Drop Room's armoire. Too casual? Too dressy? She'd spent the morning with Sally, getting a carefully controlled tan—SPF forty for her—and swimming in the glorious clear water. Loring had been off doing assorted manly things with his brother: boating, fishing, waterskiing, whatever, so she hadn't seen him since the night before.

Just as well. She needed this morning away from him to try to sort out her feelings. Was it possible to be just friends when the mere sight of him consumed her with totally unexpected lust?

She sighed and added the silver drop earrings she'd chosen for the outfit when she'd packed… day before yesterday? It seemed much longer. Then she slipped her cell phone into her pocket in case—oh please—Mr. Handel from Borwyn and Company called, though he'd said end of the week, and Wednesday didn't really count as the end.

In any case, she'd decided that while it was possible to be friends with Loring, it wasn't going to be particularly comfortable, and the best thing she could do was stay out of his way while they were both here. Last night some pretty powerful longings had nearly overtaken her common sense, and there was no point feeding the beast, so to speak.

Let him lie, napping, in his cave until she could get back home, removed from temptation.

Good.

She descended Gloryside's curving staircase and went out back to the series of terraces done in octagonal bricks that carved up the slope down to the fringe of palms and flowering shrubs bordering the beach and the brilliant expanse of ocean beyond.

The guests milled around, helping themselves to the incredible lunch buffet set in the shade of the colonnade leading from the house to the pool. Tables and chairs had been set on the terrace, but many people had taken their meals to eat on the chaises around the pool.

Emily smiled and greeted some guests, trying not to look for Loring and failing. Well, she needed to know where he was so she could avoid him, right?

Sure she did.

No sight of him. So she could relax now, though he'd doubtless be around soon enough.

She helped herself to the variety of salads and

meats, shrimp and conch and the homebaked breads, suddenly realizing how hungry she was. A tall glass of iced tea, silverware, napkin, and she was ready to scope out her seat. A chaise was available near the pool, next to a woman she vaguely knew named Bettina, who was extremely chatty so Emily could eat in peace and merely nod when required. Perfect.

Half an hour later, her plate was empty, stomach full, and head tired of nodding. She now knew everything that had ever happened to this woman. Minute by minute. Since birth.

Amazingly, Bettina let out a shriek, yoohooed to a suddenly panicked-looking man, grabbed her nearly untouched plate, excused herself and pounced on him.

Emily lay back in relief, holding her glass of tea, and closed her eyes, pleasantly drowsy in spite of the caffeine, enjoying the tickle of breeze on her bare legs and arms.

"This seat taken?"

Loring's deep voice shot her with adrenaline, effectively eliminating any lingering drowsiness. She should record his voice and use it for an alarm in the mornings.

"No." She sighed and struggled to sit up, feeling more in control of the situation if she wasn't lounging languidly. This might not be quite the avoiding-him technique she had envisioned, but since they were "friends" now, she couldn't be rude. "Be my guest."

"Thanks." He sat on the chaise Babbling Bettina had vacated, holding a loaded plate. He'd been swimming, his hair was still wet, his short-sleeved shirt unbuttoned and hanging loose over navy swimming trunks.

Which meant she could see his chest.

Damn. It was probably the finest chest she'd ever seen.

Now she got to see it again. And think of all the bouncy-fun time she'd had on it.

Groan.

"Did you have a nice morning?" Her voice came out unnaturally high and she made herself breathe deeply to calm down.

"Terrific. John and I played some tennis, then went for a swim down on the beach by the courts. The water is incredible. Did you go in?"

"Yes." She nodded. "It was amazing. Hard to believe it's February."

"You got that right." He began to eat and she watched him while trying to pretend she wasn't. He even ate sexily; she'd forgotten—or maybe suppressed the fact that absolutely everything about him had been such a turn-on. His teeth bore the perfection of early orthodontics, his strong throat did this cool slidy thing when he swallowed, his abdomen was flat and muscled—oh my goodness.

She really needed to remind herself that she wasn't little worshipping Emily anymore.

Her cell phone rang; she gasped, sat bolt upright and yanked it out of her pocket, praying it was Borwyn and Company offering her a job so she'd look Tremendously Important and smack Loring with exactly how not little-worshipping-Emily she was anymore.

She peered eagerly at the number and sighed. Nope. Her mother. Who would just want to know how it was seeing Loring again. Emily would call back later, if she ever figured out a way to describe it.

"What was that about?" Loring watched her curiously. His hair had begun to dry in stiff salty clumps and she wanted to run her hands through it to loosen the strands.

"I interviewed with Borwyn and Company before I left." She slipped the phone into her pocket and sat back. "I'm hoping for a job offer this week."

She tried to speak casually, but probably sounded smug. So there. Doormat Emily, who even used to worship the way Loring ate, was not only a Harvard Business School graduate, but a candidate at the top management consulting firm in Boston, arguably one of the top in the country.

He whistled admiration, but his eyes were grim. "That's quite a change from counseling teenaged moms."

She shifted in her seat. Okay, she still felt guilty for leaving that job. She'd loved everything about it but the paycheck, which had been fine while she was going to marry Loring. He made enough money for three couples to live comfortably. But if she was going to be the independent woman she vowed she would become, she needed to make a damn sight better than non-profit wage.

"Yes. It's going to be a change. But it's one I welcome. I'm ready for it and I'm qualified and I'll do well."

"No doubt." He went back to eating.

Emily frowned. He was thinking something and he wasn't telling her. That used to drive her crazy. She'd appear in an outfit for some function, he'd smile perfunctorily and say, "you look great." Then he'd clam up, avert his gaze—and she'd know she'd chosen the wrong outfit.

But if she asked him what to wear beforehand, he'd always say that she knew best. Worse, he'd never just *say*, "I don't like your outfit," he'd just start whistling. Then she'd spend ten minutes groveling until he deigned to tell her that yes, he thought so-and-so's wife wore something similar last time, and even though it didn't *matter*, if she *wanted* to change…

Then she'd scurry and do it. Yuck.

Granted, he couldn't whistle this time because he was eating, but it was the same old pattern. Only this time she wasn't going to play. Because what he thought of her or her life or her clothes or her choices didn't matter anymore.

She sipped her iced tea, feeling the tension rise as he continued to eat in silence. Fine. Let him. Didn't bother her.

Nope.

Not a bit.

She changed position, bouncing so hard the back of the chaise slipped and she found herself staring up at the sky.

Fine. She meant to do that. Even better, she couldn't see him from this position. Well, she could see his muscular thighs under the table, his muscular calves, his nicely shaped feet.

She used to massage his feet when he was feeling particularly tense. God, how pathetic. Kneeling in front of him while he, lord and master, sat in his armchair and complained about his work.

Ugh. She was never touching his feet again.

"You down there?" Loring's head appeared over the edge of the table. He was grinning and he had a piece of parsley stuck between his front teeth and she wasn't going to tell him.

"Yes. I'm here."

His grin faded; a look of concern replaced it.

Tender concern that went right through her pique and warmed...everything. "Emily?"

"Yes." She was whispering. Why was she whispering?

"Are you happy?"

A wave of angry panic invaded her stomach. "Happy?"

His eyes narrowed. "Happiness—an emotion, generally pleasurable."

She pulled herself up to a sitting position and lifted the arms of the chair so the back swung up straight again. "Yes, I'm happy. I'm very happy."

He watched her quietly, in that way he always did when he didn't believe her. *Grrrr.* It drove her crazy. Three years ago, Emily could have said, "My name is Emily" and if he gave her that look, she'd start to fret and wonder, "*Is* my name Emily? It is, isn't it?"

Not this time.

"Deliriously happy."

He opened his mouth and started to say something she was quite sure she didn't want to hear, when the noise of guests shushing each other interrupted.

Sally stood near the pool, beckoning the crowd around her.

"Hello, everyone. I hope you've had a good morning! This afternoon we're going to do something different. You know how I love party games…'' Chuckles and good-natured teasing from her friends. "We're going to have a treasure hunt, which will run until it's solved or until the wedding, whichever comes first. I'm going to pair off the twelve of you participating right now."

She waved a paper in the air, then began reading off names. Pair by pair.

One couple…two couples…three…four…

Neither Emily's nor Loring's name had been called yet.

"Mary Boering and Josh Campbell."

Emily's head snapped over to look at Loring. If he looked self-satisfied, even the tiniest bit self-satisfied, she was going to shoot him now. Right here in front of all the guests, even though she didn't have a gun. She'd find some way to do it, regardless.

He turned his head and looked back at her. She slumped in her chaise. He didn't look self-satisfied. Much worse. He looked…vulnerable. As if he was afraid she'd be upset getting stuck with him.

Well, she was upset. In fact, she wanted to stand up and scream that she couldn't, absolutely couldn't, spend that kind of time alone with him. But if she did that, everyone would want to know why. And if the only answer she had was that she didn't trust herself with him, then she wasn't the kind of woman she thought she had become.

"And that leaves our last couple, Emily Wakefield and Loring Mackenzie!'' Sally beamed at them. Those who knew them turned to look and murmur their hearts out. John snapped their picture. Emily smiled stiffly, feeling like a bug pinned down for an experiment.

''We'll start in an hour. Dessert's on—go stock up. You'll burn the calories later.''

The crowd headed over to the tables, trading gossip for sugar, and leaving a ghastly silence looming between two poolside chaises.

''Well.'' Loring looked warily at Emily. ''There's an amazing coincidence.''

''Amazing.'' She spoke through gritted teeth.

''I hope you're not too upset.''

''Upset? Why should I be upset? Just because my friend has this loopy idea that we can get back together if she throws us at each other enough?''

''I know.'' Loring smacked his forehead. ''Crazy idea.''

She put her iced tea on the table and leaned toward him. ''You didn't have anything to do with this, did you?''

''No.'' He shook his head, eyes direct and clear. ''I didn't.''

''Okay.'' She relaxed a little. ''Sorry. It was just—''

''I understand, believe me.'' He smiled and she was actually relieved that the parsley had gone from between his teeth because she didn't want to deal with the guilt of not saying anything.

"So." He gathered up his plate and glass and stood, tall and handsome and quite effective as a sunshade. "I'm going to check out the desserts and then take a shower and be ready for you in an hour. Okay?"

"It's a—" She was going to say "date," but that didn't seem an entirely good idea.

"Date?" He winked. "It will be fine, Emily. We'll have fun. Get to know each other again."

She nodded miserably. She already knew him. And the worst part was that even knowing him, she was still madly attracted to him. To the good parts—his strength, his humor, his intelligence, his charm, his killer bod....

Why did these kinds of feelings defy logic? If she ruled the universe, she'd make sure that people were only attracted to people they could be happy with for the rest of their lives. Save everyone a ton of heartbreak and bitterness and betrayal.

Loring's broad back became part of the crowd around the dessert table. Already two or three women had cornered him, were making him laugh.

So what? She was strong now. Strong enough to resist him and all these tempting jealous sexual feelings he brought back. Strong enough to stand spending an afternoon in his company. Or two. Or however long this damn hunt was supposed to go on.

She just wished she didn't have to put her strength to a test quite this hard.

CHAPTER FIVE

"PEOPLE DON'T remain the same here." Loring stared at the treasure hunt clue they'd been brainstorming leisurely for the better part of the afternoon. He couldn't say they'd made much progress. But they'd had so much fun wandering around the island, hoping for inspiration, that he couldn't say he cared. And by the way the other teams they'd come across were laughing over being equally clueless, they weren't alone.

Except physically, thank God. That part of the treasure hunt he definitely treasured.

He'd finally convinced Emily to take a break from exploring—though for Emily it was more like revisiting old haunts—and found them a spot in a tiny secluded cove, where a palm tree leaned toward the sea, defying the insistent force of the wind blowing from the opposite direction. A loner, fighting the natural, easy way of doing things. Was that more like him now? Or had he been like that back when he'd worshipped the false god of money, a god he'd sacrificed Emily to before he realized he cared nothing for money after all.

Deep symbolism aside, the tree cast a welcome shadow on the sand and allowed them a space to relax in without being fried by the sun. Even better, the shady spot wasn't that large and they needed to sit close together to take full advantage.

"People don't remain the same here." Emily repeated the words dreamily, as if she was working harder at enjoying the beach and the nearby surf than solving the clue.

Fine by him. Her long firm legs made an attractive triangle with the sand, which set off their waxes and wanes to advantage. He was dying to run his hand up the strong curve of her spine and tangle his fingers in her hair, turn her face toward him and—

"Do you think Sally's referring to how you leave a bit of your civilization behind when you come to the island?"

He grinned. "Is that what happens?"

"Oh, definitely, don't you feel it?" She tipped her head toward him, eyes glowing blue in her flushed face, making his lungs suddenly unsure how to function.

"So I can look forward to your gradual transformation into Zanna, tropical goddess of love?"

"Absolutely." She laughed and stretched both arms. "By nightfall I'll have shed most of my clothes and will be doing the dance of the male virgin sacrifice."

He opened his mouth for a witty reaction, but the mental picture of Emily in a low-riding grass skirt and nothing else, dancing around a fire looking fierce and savage, the way she did when she—

Oh, man. "Glad I'm not a virgin."

"You're not?" She blinked innocently and he started to get aroused. This was the Emily he hadn't seen since he'd been here. Playful, relaxed, gentle and full of spirit at the same time.

"Now that I think about it, maybe I qualify all over again. It's been a while." He said the words softly, with a hint of suggestiveness. Her expression grew wary; she grabbed the clue out of his hand and bent her head to stare at it, wavy hair swinging down to hide her face.

Too personal. Too soon. What had he expected her to say—*Oh, poor Loring, I'll straddle you right now, dear.*

Nice one. He couldn't push too hard, couldn't force her where she wasn't ready to go. But damn it, he had less than a week before he went back to his life and she went off to her new one. This was his only chance.

"People *don't* remain the same." He said the words with conviction and pushed back the curtain of her hair to see her looking too serious for his comfort—unless she was unearthing old feelings for him. Then she could be as serious as she wanted.

"No, they don't. Not always." She lifted her face, gazing out to sea, though she didn't flinch away from his hand on her hair. "I've changed a lot. I don't need the same things I used to need."

He tucked her hair behind her ear and followed the smooth clean strands down until his hand rested on her shoulder, bare in her sleeveless top, her skin as warm and soft as he remembered. "What don't you need anymore?"

"I don't need protecting. I don't need a relationship to function as a safety net because I don't know what else to do with my life."

He forced his hand to stay relaxed on her shoulder, though he wanted to grab hold and shake her. She'd twisted their past into something sordid, slid it into a neat little therapy box. She was completely discounting their similar views of the world, similar tastes, morals and politics. Not to mention the incredible passion between them, that mysterious pull that superseded intellectual needs and neurotic desires, that infinitely elusive element that drew two people together who were truly meant to be there.

But he wasn't going to be able to convince her of that here, not now, not yet. He hoped soon. Right now, all he could do was keep talking about the barest surface of their relationship, in the hopes that once they made the initial scratches, they could continue digging until they reconnected with the core of what brought them together. Physical attraction, sure, but it went way beyond that. If he simply pushed for sex, he'd be shut out forever.

"I've changed, too, Emily. I don't value my career above all things anymore. And I'm not looking for the woman who can help me make the most money."

"You're not?" She turned her head slightly toward him, though not enough to meet his eyes. Stroked one hand through the warm sand and let it pour through her fingers.

"I know what I was like." He squeezed her shoulder gently and let his fingers trail down her arm. She shivered, though he didn't think in revulsion. "But I also know what I'm like now."

"New and improved?" She sent him a sly glance and he grinned.

"It feels that way." He stroked up to her shoulder, pushed her hair back again, let his fingers linger this time at the back of her neck. "In Paris, at the bakery where I worked, they sold cookies, large ones, about the size of a saucer. Butter cookies that crumbled into nothing when you bit into them, sandwiched with raspberry jam, powdered sugar sprinkled over. The top cookie had a hole in the middle so you could see the jam. They were incredible. Better than sex."

Her eyebrows shot up in mock amazement. "Better than our sex?"

He froze rock-solid at the exact same time she did. Apparently her lips had let the comment out before her brain could stop it.

Excellent.

Except that Emily looked so mortified, instead of toppling her back on the sand and reminding her just how good they'd been, as a certain part of his body was urgently instructing him to do, he actually wanted to put her at ease. See? He *had* changed.

He'd turned into an idiot.

He grinned at his own joke and dropped his hand from the back of her neck. "Okay, not better than the sex we had. But every time I ate one of those cookies I thought of you. And not because of sex."

"Because I'm sweet and crumble easily?"

He made a sound of exasperation. "Because I knew you would love them. And I wanted to share them with you. And since I couldn't, no matter how delicious they were, they could never be perfect."

"Oh." She whispered the word, back to digging her hand in the sand, avoiding his eyes.

He wanted to move her hair again, see her face. He couldn't even count the other things he wanted to do, but he'd already pushed this topic farther than he probably should this afternoon. They had all day tomorrow to look for this treasure. In fact, if he got his way, they'd never solve a single clue and have to spend every free second until the wedding alone.

"So yes." He leaned back on his elbows, ready to enjoy another lazy hour or two in her company. "People do change."

"People change." Emily stiffened and stared at the clue in her fist. "'People don't remain the same here.' People *change* here."

She jumped to her feet, eyes glowing, and laughed triumphantly. "People change in the bathhouse. I've solved the first clue!"

THE MINUTE Emily went into the bathhouse, she knew it was a supreme colossal enormous mistake to have come with Loring. The second the familiar sight and smell of the building hit her, she remembered the last time she'd been in here.

Two years ago. She'd broken up with Loring a month earlier, had weathered the first weeks in staunch denial, letting the certainty that she was doing the right thing carry her through. Then she'd flown here, a spur-of-the-moment decision brought on by her manic need to avoid inactivity at all costs.

That night, she and Sally had overindulged in rum drinks and decided a midnight swim would sober them up. After a riotous splash session, they'd stepped into the bathhouse to change. Em-

ily's foot had slipped on a loose tile, and she'd
gone down hard on her tailbone.

In the midst of the jarring pain, an eerie out-of-
the-blue flash of dead certainty had hit her nearly
as hard as her butt had hit the floor: She'd done
the wrong thing breaking up with Loring. She
hadn't given him time to work through their problems, had spat on all the things that made them
such a good fit, had thrown away the greatest love
she'd ever known and would ever know, and
would wither into miserable spinsterhood and end
up having to pay men for sex.

The next morning she'd seen the moment for
what it was: the beginning of her next stage of
grief, brought on by alcohol and the vulnerability
of injury. She'd gritted her teeth, accepted the anger and depression stages and come out the other
side.

Until now, that moment, that seemingly incredible clarity of insight had been buried under the
messy emotional detachment process and rebuild-
ing of her new life. Now she was here and the
flashback hit her with a force that freaked her
nearly as much as it had two years earlier.

She whirled around and almost ran into Loring,
coming into the building right behind her.

He grabbed her upper arms, blue eyes warm
with concern. ''What is it?''

She blinked. The old Loring had hated her emotions. Whether she was bursting with ecstasy or crushed with sadness, he'd ask the same thing in that cool bland tone she detested: "Something up?"

"I…" She struggled to rid her brain of lingering ghosts, trying to forget how she'd sat on the floor, eyes screwed shut against the physical pain, praying with all her might that a miracle would happen and when she opened her eyes, Loring would be there, in the flesh, to let her take back her horrible ring-toss mistake.

Now here he was, warm and concerned and less than a foot away.

She managed a smile. "Just a weird memory."

He cocked his head, frowning quizzically. "Want to tell me?"

"No. Thanks." She laughed nervously. "It's too weird."

He opened his mouth and she stiffened, waiting. He couldn't stand it when she wanted to keep things private; he was always pressing, pushing, as if her private thoughts threatened him, as if he didn't feel he could control her adequately unless her every thought was his.

"Okay. But I'm here if you want to spill." He moved forward and pressed his lips to her forehead.

Shock made her jerk her head up to look at him. Was he serious?

Unfortunately, he hadn't yet drawn back from the kiss, and her tipped-up head brought their lips only centimeters apart. She'd better put her head back down and move away fast, because all that was going through her mind right now were other memories, memories of how Loring Mackenzie was the best kisser on planet earth.

"Emily." His voice came out low and slightly hoarse, which most likely meant he was thinking along the same lines as she was.

"Yes?" She didn't mean to say that. She meant to say something like, "Loring, this isn't the time or place we should be in such intimate contact."

"I think…we should look for the clue."

For a second she barely understood what he'd said, since her whole being was ready to hear, "I want to kiss you more than I want to go on living."

Then it registered what and where and who she was, and she finally had the good sense to step back out of his hold, literally and figuratively.

"Yes. We need to find the clue."

They searched in a kind of daze, checking the wooden cupboards where bathers hung their clothes, in the enormous flower arrangements, under the woven grass mats scattered on the floor, behind the picture frames created from tropical shells on the walls.

No luck.

"Maybe I wasn't right." Emily sighed. She felt

lonely and sad and peculiar, and she wanted to get out into the bright sunshine again, get away from Loring and indulge in meaningless chatter with strangers.

"Maybe." He took two steps toward the entrance, then frowned at the floor. "What's this?"

She glanced down and grimaced. One of the tiles was set in wrong. She knew that tile too well.

"It's loose. And there's something white showing. He pried a piece of paper out, unfolded it and grinned triumphantly. "It's the next clue. 'Time heals all wounds.'"

Emily's head began to spin. She and Loring paired together? People change? Time heals all wounds? Under the very tile she'd tripped over, making her realize she wanted him back?

She was going to have a serious chat with her friend Sally. A very long chat. With a weapon at her disposal.

"Terrific." She smiled wearily.

"I don't know about that." He frowned, looking at the clue as if it might be a phony.

"You don't think it's terrific?"

"No, not that." He folded the paper in his pocket and stared at her with a significance that made her nervous. "Some wounds are so deep even time won't help."

She swallowed. Was he talking about her? "You mean…"

"I mean, if you love someone and you lose them, I think that pain can go on forever."

She stopped breathing. Her heart gave a tremendous stab of agony. "Even if that person wasn't right for you?"

"You were always right for me, Emily."

She inhaled sharply and braced herself against the wave of gooey warmth threatening to suck her back in. Oh, he was so, so good. Of course she'd been right for him. She just had to remember that he hadn't been right for her. And now, two years later, she wasn't even that same person anymore.

Except he didn't seem to be the same person either. Not entirely.

God, this was confusing.

"I'm sorry, Loring," she whispered. "This is all a little much right now."

"You're right—we need a break." He smiled and offered his arm. "How about going to the bar and experimenting with rum drinks?"

Her head gave a nasty throb of remembrance at the same time she noticed his arm looked strong and tempting, and found herself thinking that since they were friends now, it wouldn't hurt to take it. Would it?

Who do you think you're fooling, Emily?

She took his arm anyway, because the situation was getting awkward with him holding it out to her and her staring stupidly, doing nothing. At the doorway he paused, and as she preceded him out of the bathhouse, that same arm managed to find its way around her shoulders.

Oh, this was dangerous, being close to him like this. She should beg off the rum drinks, go back to her room and cool off her body and her mind. She was having a hard enough time resisting him sober, and if history were to repeat itself, rum drinks would make her want him back again…

No way. She would have to tell him no.

Her mouth opened to say the words: I'm sorry but I have to go see if Sally needs me and then I'll probably take a nap before dinner.

"Thanks, Loring. A drink sounds great."

She stopped walking. He took half a step before he noticed and swung around to face her. "Emily?"

"That's not what I meant to say."

"What's not what you meant to say?"

"I meant to say I couldn't go."

He grinned. A triumphant old-Loring grin. "Well, apparently your subconscious wants to spend more time with me than you do."

She snorted, then, as the absurdity of the situation hit her, laughed out loud. "I think I have multiple personality disorder."

He held out his arm again and shrugged. "Go with the flow, Sybil."

She considered his words. She hadn't gone with

the flow for a long time. In fact, she'd scheduled and compartmentalized and organized and squeezed more time out of every hour for the last two years than she ever had in her life.

Going with the flow would feel damn good.

She took his arm again and walked with him to the bar set up poolside, feeling giddy and crazy with possibilities she couldn't possibly be giddy or crazy enough to consider.

Two feet from the bar, her phone rang. She hauled it out of her pocket and peered at the display. Massachusetts area code. Oh my God, she'd bet that was a Borwyn and Company number.

Instinctively she moved to take the call, then realized she wouldn't sound professional with the partying crowd around her. Better let them leave a message, then she'd go to her room and call back in privacy and silence.

Of course the call could be anything. Maybe they were just missing information for her file. Except she'd called before she left to make sure they had all they needed. Maybe they were calling to reject her? No way. Not this soon.

They could be calling to offer her the job.

Excitement flooded her, dousing a strange uneasiness she wasn't interested in examining. She glanced at Loring, who grinned and held up two drinks brimming with ice, each the color of a Caribbean sunset. Ha! Get thee behind her, Satan. The call had come at just the right time. If she hadn't gotten this message, she would have downed one of those drinks, maybe two. And if they talked about old times, managed to find themselves alone… Those things could happen. Loring seemed anxious they reconnect—Sally, too.

Emily needed to get away, to retrieve the message and, apparently, her brain. She had a new road to travel in her life, and she wasn't going to get far if she started in reverse.

She shoved the phone back into her pocket, marched up to Loring, the man she'd once loved more than her own life, and gave him a friendly smile, realizing it was exactly like the ones he'd given her time and time again just before he broke a date.

The words came to her instantly and without thinking she recited them with his exact intonation, exact expression—she knew both painfully by heart.

"Sorry, Loring, I've got to cancel. Something's come up at work."

CHAPTER SIX

LORING FOLLOWED Emily down to the southwestern end of the island, squinting in the late afternoon sun. They'd spent the morning sailing with John and Sally, and after a picnic lunch had returned to treasure hunting.

Emily's theory on the second clue, "Time heals all wounds," was that *time* referred to the sundial carved over the entrance to the island's boathouse, and "heals all wounds" to the first-aid kit stored inside.

He wondered if she realized that these clues could only be solved by someone who knew the island as well as she did. The unsubtle hands of Sally and John were all over this treasure hunt, and he and Emily were favored to win by about a hundred to one. At the wedding rehearsal early this morning, it had been clear that none of the other hunting couples had made even a dent in the first clue. Most had given up entirely.

He stumbled slightly on the uneven path—his own fault, since instead of watching his feet he'd been watching Emily stride ahead of him, by far his favorite part of treasure hunting. In fact, the situation could only be improved if she were wearing a thong bikini instead of tan cotton shorts and a yellow top. Wait a second, this was fantasy. She shouldn't be wearing a thong—she shouldn't be wearing a thing.

His hopes for success this week were rising. Disaster had yawned beneath him yesterday evening when he'd been ready to ply her with rum and soften her up with memories of the better times they'd had together, and the call came in from Borwyn and Company offering her the job.

But far from turning out to be his worst nightmare, the offer had spurred him on to try harder. Emily had come back from retrieving the message with her face frozen into what was probably supposed to be a triumphant smile, but which looked to him more like terror. As of this afternoon, she still hadn't called back. And she'd loosened up toward him more and more today. She'd even brought up a few memories of good times sailing on Long Island Sound shortly before they got engaged. Her eyes had gone soft, her smile had been warm and unguarded.

That had done it. Cemented his already strong determination to keep her off the Borwyn payroll.

If she really, truly had changed so much that a career in cutthroat corporate life was what she wanted, he'd be the last person to stand in her way.

But if she was taking the job to prove something to someone, even just to herself, she'd only end up miserable. Suffocated in that environment, her sensitive, ebullient nature crushed and molded into the corporate pressboard personality.

He'd seen her work with the teens she helped, teens who were pregnant and often rejected both by their child's father and their own families. Some were in stages of denial so strong they refused to acknowledge what was happening to their swelling, too-young bodies.

With those kids, Emily could be herself. Gentle and respectful, with strength the girls could depend on, and firmness to set them straight in a hurry when they strayed. She cheered them, taught them, and while she couldn't magically erase what had happened, she gave them options and helped them along whatever path they chose, up to the birth and beyond.

There were plenty of navy-suited automatons to fill the slots of Corporate America, but those girl-women needed people like Emily. And he was determined they'd get her.

Of course, there was nothing remotely self-serving about that desire…

He grinned and nearly ran into Emily, who'd stopped abruptly in front of the boathouse, a small wooden building painted white and nestled among the palms and flowering shrubs at the edge of the sandy beach.

"Look." She pointed into the bay, where the tiny speck of an island stuck up like a leftover crumb on a giant's plate. "See that?"

"Yes?" He bent closer, sighting along her finger, "steadying himself" by putting his arm around her waist.

"That's Daim Island." Her voice came out a little croaky. "*Daim* as in Sally's grandmother's maiden name, not *dame* as in woman."

"Mmm, woman." He murmured the word into her hair; his lips brushed across a few strands. "So tell me about it."

"About what?" She was whispering, staring glassy-eyed out at the sea. He dared hope that his nearness did to her even half of what hers did to him.

"Tell me about Daim Island."

"Oh…um…yes." She drew in a long, slow breath, the way she did when something surprised her—or aroused her. "Sally and I…used to go there and…stuff."

"Stuff?"

She stepped out of his hold, breathing hard, eyes vulnerable and anxious. "Shouldn't we be looking for clues?"

"Is that really what you want to do?"

"I…" She looked down at the sand. "Yes."

He offered her his hand, satisfied to know what she'd wanted to answer. Okay, they'd find the damn clue. Then he was going to kiss her until she couldn't breathe. "Let's go."

She hesitated, then put her hand in his. They strolled to the boathouse and found the familiar slip of paper in the first-aid kit on the shelf behind the door, exactly as Emily had predicted.

"'No man is an island.'" She read the clue, frowned and muttered something about meddling that made him want to laugh. John and Sally's plan hadn't gone unnoticed. Nothing got by Ms. Wakefield.

He reached for the paper in her hand just as she crumpled it in her fist, so that his hand closed over hers. Instead of letting go, he followed her other arm down until he held that hand as well. "So what do you think? Island…Man…"

She didn't draw back, but stared at him in the dim light of the boathouse, blue eyes lit with a touch of anxiety again—but also with a touch of excitement. "I don't know."

"No thoughts?" He drew her forward until she was an inch from his body.

"No." She smiled, tried to stop, and failed. "Not with you melting my brain like this."

He grinned and pulled her closer, flat against him, wondering how he could possibly be staying cool and in control when he was practically out of his mind with how much he wanted her, loved her. "You don't like having melt for brains?"

"No." Her lips curved wider, then relaxed; her eyes half closed.

"You heard it here." He let go of her hands and drew his down the sides of her face, cupping it gently. "No man is an island."

"But I'm a woman," she whispered.

"Believe me, I noticed."

"So I *can* be an island. A woman island."

"Oh?" He leaned forward until their lips nearly touched. "Okay if I kiss you, woman island?"

Her eyes shot open wide. She gasped and pushed him back. "That's it!"

He gritted his teeth. "What's it?"

"Woman Island! The treasure must be on Daim Island." She pointed. "Out there."

He looked out at the island speck in disgust. She had to be kidding. He was going to kill Sally and John. "We have to go out there?"

"Of course."

"Now?" He frowned at the sky. "The sun will be going down in a few hours."

"Oh, it will be fun. There's a little cabin on the other side. It's so cute, with a skylight. At night, Sally and I used to lie in bed and—"

"Bed?"

She froze and looked at him. Swallowed. Blinked.

Loring strode over to the ancient-looking row-boat and started dragging it out toward the water.

He damn well couldn't *wait* to get to Daim Island.

CHAPTER SEVEN

THE OARS of the little boat Sally and Emily had dubbed *Escape Pod,* or *EP* for short, cut gently through the clear sparkling water toward Daim Island. Maybe the clunky falling-apart rowboat wasn't the easiest choice for travel, but the sleek double kayak was missing from the boathouse and *EP* held a lot of wonderful memories.

Emily sat in the stern, trying very hard to think about those wonderful memories while the familiar dot of land approached, and trying very hard not to watch the muscles in Loring's shoulders and chest strain and contract with the pull of the oars. Or watch the way his dark hair had been attractively ruffled by the wind, or the way his blue eyes landed on hers once in a while and didn't seem to want to leave.

The silence between them was anything but companionable. The tension buzzed, alternately thrilling and awkward, painful and full of promise.

All day she'd felt herself being drawn to him more and more, not just because he was sexy, but because sailing with him this morning and treasure hunting had reminded her of how much fun they'd had together those times when he allowed himself to turn work off. She had to remember how she'd spent most of their relationship starving for those all-too-rare blissful moments.

Right now she was torn between wanting to find the damn treasure so she could get away from Loring and build back her determination to avoid him, and wanting to spend time right now making up for every kiss he hadn't been able to give her in the last two years.

Pushing him away in the boathouse with one of those kisses on its way to fruition had been the act of a desperate woman. She just couldn't decide if she was desperate to keep him away or desperate to have him.

He was like a rich dessert, a hot fudge brownie sundae, with whipped cream and chopped pecans—no maraschino cherries, they tasted like cough syrup. A dessert she'd reasonably expected to be able to have every day for the rest of her life.

Until she realized that brownie sundaes could cause her permanent harm—weight gain, clogged arteries, high blood sugar. So, as much as it pained her, she gave them up. Banished the ingredients from her kitchen so she wouldn't even be tempted. And for two years, she wasn't.

Coming to this wedding was like going to dinner at a friend's house and being served—in a huge

silver bowl with a veritable shovel of a spoon—
Mr. Brownie Sundae.

Maybe she'd have the strength to resist; after all,
she knew how bad that sundae was for her, and
she'd resisted for two years. But now that it was
sitting right in front of her, memories had hacked
their way back into her supposedly well-protected
brain—memories of the smooth rich ice cream on
her tongue, the gooey brownie warming her stomach, the hot fudge and cool cream sating her
senses. The longing for another taste was overtak-
ing her reason.

Which was why at this very moment she was
gazing at Loring, wishing she had a spoon the size
of a shovel to dig right in.

A motor boat sped toward them from the far side
of Daim Island and zoomed past, barely slowing
to avoid rocking them in its wake. The sudden
noise and motion knocked her out of her longing
for high-calorie maleness. What was she thinking?
She needed to hold tight through tonight and the
wedding tomorrow afternoon, and then hightail it
out of here first thing the next morning. The last
thing she needed was to spend any more intimate
time with Loring, especially on Daim Island, which
housed so many good and sentimental memories.
Her resistance was dangerously low as it was.

"Nearly there." Her brownie sundae twisted to
peer at the island over his shoulder.

Emily smiled bravely. "The best landing place is on the other side. There's a little sheltered spot where we can pull the boat up."

He nodded. Five minutes of powerful stroking and he'd brought the boat around the narrow tip of the island and landed on the small strip of beach.

They got out and tied *EP* securely to the same tree Sally and Emily had always used.

"Well! We made it." She smiled, nauseatingly aware that she was speaking in this weird ultra-chipper way to avoid sounding nervous, which made her sound about ten times more nervous. "I guess we should look for treasure."

He gave her an amused glance, nodded and swung around, taking in the tiny cabin and the fraction of an acre of land around it. "Shouldn't take us long...."

The words "and then we can get down to business" hung in the air even though he hadn't said them.

They separated to search on opposite sides, Emily avoiding the cabin until the last possible moment, Loring probably saving the best for last.

What was she going to do? Would she have the strength to resist him? Did she really *want* to have the strength to resist him?

She didn't know, hadn't decided, barely registered her surroundings, shuffling among trees, yellow Ginger Thomas flowers and hibiscus. Gloom sank her mood, dragged her feet. Damn it, this wasn't the way it was supposed to be. She was so determined to enjoy being friends with him. Now, having glimpsed heaven again through that near-kiss, she felt as if she'd been hurled down to the other place.

The worst part was that all this up-and-down, yes-and-no emotion made her realize how long she'd spent in limbo, neither happy nor miserable. It was as if she'd been in a state of suspended animation. Maybe she'd rid herself of the old Emily a little too thoroughly.

If nothing else, Loring made her feel.

She pushed through a stand of palm trees and reached the path to the cabin at the same time Loring approached it from the other side.

"Find anything?"

"Not so much as a doubloon." He watched her intently, as though trying to sense whether she was ripe enough for picking, sweet enough to eat right now...

She stepped back and wrapped her arms around herself, as though she could stay safe from him that way.

As if.

"I guess if there is any treasure here, it's in the cabin." He flicked a glance at the pathway through the middle of the island. "Are you ready?"

No. "Um...sure."

She followed him reluctantly up to the cabin, which sat on the high end of the island. One L-shaped room, with a bed. A big bed. A big beautiful comfortable bed. A big...

Okay, forget that part. A propane stove, chemical toilet, the bare necessities. And, as she remembered, a solid padlock on the door.

The padlock, however, was not in evidence. Loring swung open the door and waited for her to precede him, a hint of a smile in his intense eyes, which totally unnerved her—the last thing she needed.

She pushed past him into the room and stifled a gasp.

The queen-sized bed had been made up, the dazzling white coverlet turned down to reveal light-blue sheets and four plump pillows in shades of blue, ready and waiting for the bed's next occupant. Above the bed a sign: *Enjoy your stay.*

On the other side of the room, an enormous cooler sat on the low counter. Champagne in an ice bucket with fresh ice, two crystal flutes on a silver tray. How could anyone have known someone would solve the clue and be here this afternoon?

She flashed back to the speed boat that had roared past them. Sally's partners in the scheme must have just been here to refresh the supply.

Emily stole a nervous glance at Loring. He

watched for her reaction, his deep-blue eyes vivid under the darkness of his brows. "I guess we're supposed to…enjoy ourselves, Emily."

She opened her mouth to respond to his soft words, but hadn't a clue what to say. A motor sounded quite close to the island. A sudden breeze blew through the cabin, then quieted. If only her brain would make up its mind…

"Well?" Loring stepped closer, brushed her hair back, cupped his hands briefly at the base of her neck, then fanned them to lie on her shoulders.

"Well." She gestured lamely at the room. "This is…nice."

"It is. Very nice. Would you like to stay? I'm guessing the cooler has dinner in it. And I know you love champagne…"

And he knew exactly what it did to her. Automatic Libido Boosting System.

A finger of the soon-to-be setting sun found its way into the cabin and lit the sign over the bed, like a statement from the heavens that they should have sex immediately.

"It's going to get dark soon, Loring."

"Not that soon."

"Soon enough."

His hands glided over her shoulders in a light caress. "Then we can spend the night. It's no secret I want to, Emily. And we have a lot of things to talk about."

She swallowed, suddenly panicked, then immediately became disgusted with herself. Why the hell had she spent all this time wallowing in indecision? She wasn't Doormat Emily anymore. She knew what she had to do. "Loring, I'm sorry, I don't think it's a good idea."

His hands stopped moving. "You don't?"

"I mean, it *is* a good idea, but it's only a good idea for here and now. Then, forever after until the end of time, it would be a horrible one."

"Are you sure?"

"I'm sure, Loring. Our lives have gone separate ways. What's the point of digging all that up again?"

He stood gazing at her. She gazed back, determined to hang tough, show him she wouldn't back down, though every part of her body screamed in outrage at her decision. She knew what was coming now. It was what always came when she made a decision he didn't agree with. He'd press his advantage, use his knowledge of her weaknesses, persuade her gently, seduce her slowly, wind her reasoning around and around until she was so hopelessly tangled in it that she'd lost sight of where the thread originated.

"Okay." He took his hands off her shoulders and went over to the cooler, lifted it and started toward the door. "We should probably take this back to the island. We have the clues. No one else will find it."

"Oh…good idea." A stab of painful disappointment showed exactly how good an idea she thought that was. *So, Emily, you want to stay here, doormatlike, and do something you know is wrong, have a romantic dinner followed by a night of carnal pleasure, followed by pain, then more of the nothingness you've been living the past two years?*

Oh yes. She wanted her brownie sundae. In the worst way.

She pulled the champagne bottle from the bucket, watching water and chunks of ice drip off the smooth glass. Those wistful feelings were normal. She'd loved him deeply for a long time. But it was better this way. She'd only get herself in trouble again. Loring might have changed some, but no one could change completely, not really. And she lived in Boston and he lived in North Carolina now, and they both had jobs to go back to.

Better let the past remain in the past.

She left the cabin after him, stumbling on a protruding root, instinctively protecting the champagne. Damn. She hated this push-pull of emotions. She wanted him, she didn't, she wanted him, she didn't. It was better that they were leaving. She'd go back to her room, take a long, hot bath, meditate herself into positive territory and get a freaking grip.

"Hey, Emily." Loring's shout sped her feet down the path to where they'd left the boat.

"What is it?"

Then she saw. She gasped and came to an abrupt halt in the warm sand, clutching the neck of the Veuve Clicquot, the same champagne she and Loring had been supposed to have at their wedding.

Loring stood at the shoreline, clutching *EP*'s rope, which was still tied tightly to the same tree.

With no boat on the other end.

She gazed in horror, out into the cove and beyond, at the still, smooth water. Not so much as a plank of the *Escape Pod*. "What happened? What could have happened?"

He shrugged and held up the rusty metal screw that used to be attached to the bow, rope still knotted firmly through its loop.

"EP's gone home."

CHAPTER EIGHT

"I DON'T UNDERSTAND how the boat could have gone so far so fast." Emily stared out at the ocean, as if she could will *EP* back in to shore to take her away from this mess. A stiff breeze blew, which might explain why the boat had drifted out of sight so quickly, but that seemed unlikely. It was almost as if someone had come along and taken—

Oh my gosh. She suddenly remembered the noise of the boat motor while she and Loring had been up at the cabin, and she had an entirely new theory of how they'd become stranded.

A theory named Sally.

"Excuse me. I have a call to make." She whipped her cell phone out of her pocket, waved it at Loring and marched over toward the other side of the island for privacy, punching in Sally's number. Her friend picked up on the second ring.

"Sally, exactly why am I stranded on Daim Island with Loring, a bottle of champagne and a big bed?"

"Oh, um, hi, *Emily*." She emphasized Emily's name, no doubt so John or whoever was with her could share the joke. "Wait, did you say you're stranded?"

"*EP* 'floated away,' even though we tied her. You know anything about how that could have happened?"

"Wow. No. No idea."

Emily rolled her eyes. Right. "Can you send someone to pick us up?"

The line went suddenly quiet, then she heard the faint sound of whispering before Sally cleared her throat. "Emily. Are you *sure* you want to be picked up?"

Emily opened her mouth to say *Yes indeedy, I certainly am,* then closed it and bit her lip. *Grrrrr.* Hadn't she had to make this agonizing decision already in the cabin when Loring asked her to stay? What sick twist of fate was handing it back to her to make again? "Yes. I want to be picked up."

"Listen to me." Sally's voice dropped to her most gently persuasive tone. "Loring has changed. You must have sensed it. Think of how miserable you've been without him these past two years."

"Miserable?" Emily bristled. "I've been better than I ever—"

"If you don't give him a chance now, you'll wonder for the rest of your life whether you made a mistake getting rid of him a second time."

Damn. "But I... But I..." She screwed her face

into a tight mask of frustration. But she what? She nothing. She confused.

"We'll send a boat to pick you up tomorrow, in time to get ready for the ceremony."

"Sally, I can't." Emily's voice came out a pathetic whimper. *What* was she so afraid of? Her weakness for him? Hadn't she proved just now she could conquer that? Was it fear she'd go back to being a doormat? No way. She was strong now.

Then what?

"Why can't you stay?"

"Because…my life is in Boston and his is—"

"Oh, please. There's a ton of happily married couples who've dealt with worse problems than that. Give him a chance. We'll send a boat in the morning. Okay?"

Emily swallowed. Lifted her eyes to the blue tropical sky. When she twisted around, she caught a glimpse between the trees of a gorgeously filled-out royal-blue T-shirt. Damn it, she was going to give in. Because even though she detested admitting it, a lot of what Sally said made sense.

"Okay."

"Good. And Emily?"

"Yes?"

"Have some fun for a change."

The line went dead. Emily narrowed her eyes. For a change? She knew how to have fun. There just hadn't been time in the last couple of years.

And before that, fun was whatever Loring felt like doing.

She walked slowly back to the other side of the island; Loring leaned against a tree, arms folded, warily watching her return. He didn't want to be rescued.

And neither did she.

"Sally's sending a boat in the morning. I guess they can't spare one now."

The triumphant smile she expected didn't materialize. One dark brow lifted. "Is that okay with you?"

"Not like we have a choice. I'd try dialing 911, but…" She gestured to the cooler and champagne. "Somehow, I doubt they'd see this as an emergency."

"Do you?" A smile touched the corners of his mouth; he detached himself from the tree behind him.

She shrugged and looked down at the sand. "I think I can handle it."

"Good." He grinned and hoisted the cooler again. "Because I'm damn sure I can."

They walked back to the cabin, Emily's spirits ricocheting upward. Twenty minutes ago she'd been trapped between the need to find strength to leave the island and the desperate desire to stay. In one stroke, she now had the have-cake-and-eat-it-too pleasure of having proven herself strong enough to leave and still getting what she'd wanted all along. A night with Loring on this island, just the two of them, in a cabin. With an enormous freshly made bed.

The titillation alone would be spectacular, even if she couldn't take the final step of enjoying the bed the way she knew he'd want to.

With a start, she realized she wasn't expecting him to try and persuade her to make love if it didn't feel right to her. The old Loring would have stopped at nothing to get his way. The knowledge made her feel safer and surprisingly free and relaxed. Maybe he really had changed enough. Maybe they could make their relationship work. Somehow.

Because even beyond the sexual pull, she still enjoyed just being with Loring. The past few days had underlined that, and showed her things could be better between them. Look how successfully they'd teamed up to find this treasure, taking turns leading, respecting each other's intuition and intellect. Not that life was a treasure hunt, but it boded well.

Or was she being Pollyanna's twin?

She set the champagne back into the bucket, then hauled it right out again. Why wait?

"Champagne?" She untwisted the wire cage, carefully, when she sensed the cork was eager to come out.

"Can't let it go to waste." He opened the cooler and started lifting out cans and containers. "Look at this. Caviar, pâté, a roast chicken, salad, chocolate cake, condoms—"

Pow. The cork exploded before she could stop it; champagne erupted from the bottle. Emily burst out laughing and lunged for a glass to catch the overflowing liquid.

"Wow." Loring grabbed a napkin to help mop up the mess on the floor. "I'd say that bottle has a keen sense of comic timing."

"Caviar and *condoms?*"

He looked up and winked. "I guess she thought of everything."

"I guess."

"Consenting adults only." He tossed the napkin on the counter and grabbed a wet wipe from a nearby container to rinse his hands. "If you don't consent, then it's out. No tricks, no seduction, no—"

"I know, Loring. I…trust you."

His hands stilled; he turned to look at her and smiled. Not a big cheery smile, not a friendly warm smile, not a smile of polite comfort, but a smile of genuine happiness that connected them in a long breathless moment, the way they'd connected from the day they met, before everything started to go wrong. "Thank you. That means a lot. I haven't always made it safe for you to trust me."

Emily tried to swallow and couldn't; her throat jumped convulsively. "The past is in the past."

His smile grew into a grin. He nodded and gestured to the champagne. "Then let's drink to the future."

"Excellent idea." Her giddiness increased. Something had loosened, opened up between them. As if a storm had passed through, the air in the cabin and in her lungs seemed fresher and lighter.

She poured champagne into the second glass, then topped both glasses off once the foam subsided. Her movements slowed, became precise and leisurely. She found herself immersed in the moment, pouring champagne for herself and for Loring as if they were alone in their honeymoon suite, the way she'd imagined it so many times. Dangerous thinking, but somehow she didn't feel threatened. Somehow the night promised to be perfect, no matter what happened.

Sally was right: Emily had been having entirely too little fun.

She nestled the bottle back into the ice and recorked it with a stopper dangling on a silver chain from the bucket handle. The glasses felt cool and heavy in her hands as she crossed the room to where Loring stood watching her, blue eyes alight, as if he'd gotten the same excited pleasure out of watching her pour champagne for the two of them as she had pouring it.

Oh, she had a feeling this was going to be a really fine evening.

"Cheers." She handed him his glass and clinked hers gently against it. "To the wedding tomorrow."

"And to the wedding that never was."

"Yes." She swallowed hard, trying to keep her tone as light as his. "To…that."

They took a sip at the same time; their eyes met over the rims of their glasses and a powerful electric current started humming between them.

"Mmm."

She was pretty sure she was referring to the champagne, but Loring looked so sexy with his dark hair slightly tousled, his body strong and tall and casually powerful in tan shorts and blue T-shirt, that she wasn't entirely sure the champagne was all she found delicious.

"Mmm is right."

And the way his eyes devoured her, she wasn't entirely sure what he was referring to either.

"Let's take this outside." She gestured to the bottle.

He scooped the bucket up and followed her out to the tiny veranda in back, where a narrow bench rested against the house, positioned perfectly for sunset-watching.

They sat nearly shoulder to shoulder, the empty air between them buzzing with promise. The sun had started its descent into the ocean; the blue of the sky had already deepened, and the heat of the day eased into comfortable warmth.

"When I was in Paris, Mme. Rabeaux and I would go out onto her balcony most evenings in the summer. We'd sit and talk, drink wine or brandy. She'd tell me about her youth, the wild times, the men she knew, how she hung out with people who'd known Picasso and Matisse, Sartre and Simone de Beauvoir. She made it sound as if she'd experienced a pumped-up version of life that the rest of us don't have access to, and I think that went a long way toward making me realize the corporate life wasn't where I wanted to be. Maybe that sounds strange."

"No. No, it doesn't." Emotion sat high in Emily's throat. Loring had never opened up like this. The old Loring had everything figured out. Everything. How his life would go, how theirs would, and to a much-too-great degree, how hers would. If she brought up an interesting point, he'd heard it already and also knew why it wasn't valid. If she was fascinated by a sight or a flavor or an idea, either he knew why she should strive to appreciate something better, or he simply wouldn't have time to listen.

Sally was right. He had changed.

"I'd like to show you Paris, Emily. I'd like you to meet Mme. Rabeaux."

She loosened her grip on the flute before she crushed the thin crystal. What was she supposed to say to that? Was he offering? Truly? What did that mean? Would they travel as friends? Sleep in the same hotel room? How did he plan to—

"I think you'd love it."

She sipped more champagne, then more. *Relax.* He wasn't really inviting her. He just thought she'd like it. Which was fine. She'd just forget that for a moment she'd been mentally packed. "I'm sure I would."

Loring drained his glass and reached for the bottle to pour them more. When she held out her glass Emily was surprised to find that she'd nearly emptied hers as well. She could already feel the glow of alcohol, carried by the bubbles too quickly into her bloodstream. She should be careful. Champagne always made her a little reckless, a little wild.

A frown creased her forehead. Why the hell should she be careful? It had been a long time since she'd felt reckless and wild. Of course, for her, reckless and wild used to mean things like not paying parking tickets right away.

She glanced over at Loring, his head resting against the house, the strong column of his throat shifting when he swallowed champagne.

And she suddenly knew exactly what she wanted reckless and wild to encompass tonight.

"The funny thing was…" He turned and grinned at her. "I promise I'm not going to talk about Paris all night."

"It's okay. I want to hear it." She did, with surprising passion. She wanted to know everything that had gone on after she'd left him, find out whether he'd truly changed as much as he seemed to have. Because then…

She couldn't finish that thought right now.

"Sitting listening to Mme. Rabeaux on those warm beautiful evenings, I got the feeling that having known all those incredible people in that incredible city was part of what made her so vibrant and amazing, what made her life so long and so satisfying and full of joy. She felt most alive when she was around greatness." He cleared his throat, examined the bottom of his champagne glass carefully. "And I feel most alive when I'm around you."

CHAPTER NINE

LORING LIFTED his gaze from the bottom of the glass to Emily's face. He'd taken a risk exposing his feelings when she felt so vulnerable here. But at the sight of her face glowing in the sunset, flushed from champagne, eyes sparkling with the light they lit in each other even if she wasn't aware of it, his longing had been so intense he couldn't help putting some of it into words.

She stared at him, at first with some fear, but then the fear rapidly receded into the dreamy-eyed reality of her feelings. She still loved him. She had to.

"I...I don't know what to say to that, Loring."

"I just wanted you to know."

"Yes. Okay. Thanks." Her head bobbed up and down, the flush deepening on her cheeks, pleasure visible in her eyes even though she avoided looking directly at him.

His internal cheering section began whooping it up. She was embarrassed, but she hadn't freaked. Yes, he'd been bad for her, yes, she'd been right to turn her back on their engagement. But what was between them was still strong and could be fanned back to life, built into something that would be good for both of them.

Unless she took the job at Borwyn and Company. That environment would crush the life out of her, and accepting the offer would make her stay in Boston permanently, at least for the short-term. He wanted her in North Carolina with him. She'd love it there as much as he did: the beauty, the charm, the slower pace of life. And there were girls at his school who needed her expertise. Asheville Prep's counselor would soon be leaving to have a baby herself. If ever there was a sign…

"So you're taking this job at Borwyn?"

She sipped champagne, the pleasure fading from her eyes. "Yes."

The cheering inside him grew louder. An entirely unenthusiastic response. He was on the right track. He leaned over, nudged her with his shoulder. "Is it really what you want?"

She turned miserable eyes to him, eyes that made him want to sweep her into his arms, make love to her until she felt utterly safe, then carry her off to his castle and protect her from any and every negative thing that could possibly happen. Two years ago, he would have. But that kind of domination was exactly why she'd left him.

"I don't know if it's what I want." She put her glass on the bench next to her. "This is a really confusing time for me. I was so clear for so long on what I wanted, and now that I have it..."

She made a helpless gesture, her expression anxious, troubled, vulnerable. He couldn't help himself. He leaned over before he could change his mind and before she could see it coming, and kissed her. Once gently, then deeply and more deeply—he'd been starving for this, for her, for the past two years.

To his wild relief, she responded, opened her mouth to him with unexpected passion, and his own exploded. He put his glass aside, stood, drew her tight against him, then lifted her up, half expecting her to resist.

She circled his neck with her arms, his waist with her legs, and clung tightly, feverishly pressing her lips to his neck as if she wanted to taste every inch of him.

He had no problem giving her that chance. A dozen long strides and he was back at the cabin's door.

No, he shouldn't jump in and fix her world the way he thought it should be fixed. But he wanted Emily back in his life—hell, he wanted her in his house as his wife, where she damn well belonged and had since he met her. He'd just had some growing up to do before he was ready and worthy of her. Now that he was, he could help steer her away from the same mistakes he'd made.

He pushed into the cabin and laid Emily reverently in the center of the bed; she looked up into his eyes, her arms still clinging to his neck, and his heart swelled until it hurt.

"Emily." He undressed her slowly, glorying in the sound of her name, the taste and feel of her body, doing everything he'd wanted to do to her since she'd walked out of the Lemon Drop bathroom naked—hell, everything he'd wanted to do to her since the day she'd left him.

When he couldn't wait any longer, he protected himself with one of the condoms he'd thank Sally for the rest of his life and slid into her.

The contact was electrifying. Emily gasped and he lifted slightly to see her face. She gazed at him while he moved, her eyes wide, lips barely curved into a smile, as if he was the most wonderful sight she'd ever seen. Nothing in the world could possibly have felt more right.

"I love you." He whispered the words he couldn't help saying, moving slowly inside her, waiting for her response. Her initial stiffness relaxed into his rhythm; she wrapped her arms around him and responded with her body as she couldn't yet with her words.

That was enough. She loved him. He loved her. He needed to show her how much, what he wanted for both of them, and soon, tomorrow, while she was at this crossroads, before she went home, away from the spell cast by this island, and started thinking again that she could be happy without him.

He needed to do what he'd dreamed of doing since she'd walked out of his office two years ago, leaving him clutching his desk, arrogant and foolish, his heart ripped to shreds.

He'd return his ring to where it belonged: Emily's hand.

THE AFTERNOON couldn't have been more perfect for a wedding. A nearly cloudless sky, comfortable temperature, cool sea breeze—the fates had smiled on John and Sally as brightly as their gathered friends and family were smiling now.

To the strains of a Mozart string quartet, Emily did the step-together, step-together bridal walk down the aisle between rows of folding chairs set out on Gloryside's beautiful grassy front lawn. She kept a smile on without trying, clutching her bouquet, leading the stunning bride toward the makeshift altar, where the minister stood with John... and Loring.

Emily was sure the minister looked very regal and that John made a tremendously dashing groom, but in her utterly unbiased opinion, the best man was so handsome in his charcoal morning suit that she practically forgot to breathe.

They'd had such a wonderful night together in the cabin. Sex, food, more sex, champagne, more food, sex, then sex and for a change of pace, more sex. Their lovemaking had always been good, but last night had left "good" in the dust and proceeded to "extraordinary" at top speed.

She loved him. Who was she kidding? When he'd whispered those words to her, she'd panicked almost instinctively, then realized she couldn't live in denial anymore about how she felt, and would probably always feel.

But what could she do? Tomorrow she'd go home and accept the job at Borwyn and Company, start her new life of strength and independence as she'd dreamed of doing for so long.

Loring gave her an appreciative once-over, raised an eyebrow, puckering slightly as if he were whistling—or wanting to kiss her—and winked.

Mmmm.

She *thought* she was going to accept her dream job.

She was pretty sure.

She reached the altar, she stood aside and watched while John and Sally took hands and faced the minister. They were so much in love;

things had gone so smoothly for them. She couldn't help feeling a little envy mixed in with her happiness.

The minister welcomed the guests, the bride and groom and their families, the sun shone, the breeze blew. Emily drank in every moment. An exquisite soprano friend of Sally's performed an equally exquisite Schumann song. Members of the bride's and groom's families gave selected readings. The minister spoke about being true to themselves and to each other.

Beautiful words. But how could she be true to herself and to Loring when the two were at cross-purposes?

Then, finally, the vows, recited in a loud clear voice by John, a husky softer one by Sally.

Emily's eyes found Loring's at the same moment his found hers, as if they'd been programmed to look at each other at this point in the ceremony. No, this wasn't their wedding, the vows being exchanged weren't theirs, but by the adoring way Loring gazed at her, anyone might think it was.

Worse, she knew she was gazing back at him exactly the same way. In that powerful moment under the flawless Caribbean sky, she wanted to give up her hard-won shot at a high-powered career, toss aside the last two years—all her work, her pain, her determination, her dreams—marry him and be carried off to North Carolina to have his babies.

No way.

The island had cast a spell over her. Okay, be real. Loring had cast a spell over her. More than ever she needed to try on her new life for size. Prove to herself that she could be utterly and completely self-sufficient.

Then, away from this fantasy existence, if she and Loring still wanted to, if they could find common ground, if she could find a job in North Carolina or he could find one in Boston, if, if, if... It was so damn complicated. She didn't want to lose him again. But more important, she didn't want to lose herself again. Ever.

"I now pronounce you husband and wife."

The crowd erupted into cheers, Emily dragged her eyes away from Loring's and joined in, heart swelling with joy. John and Sally would be happy forever; she knew it in her heart of hearts.

A good two minutes later, when the cheers of the crowd grew good-naturedly raucous, John finally released his new wife from their first married kiss. Emily laughingly took Loring's arm and followed the beaming bride and groom down the aisle and to the back of the house where the reception was to be held.

Sally separated herself from John, then turned and launched herself at Emily, hugging her tightly.

"I'm so happy about you two," she whispered.

Emily gave a faint start. Huh? What had Loring said to her? And since when did he kiss and tell?

"I think the happiness is supposed to go the other way, Sally." She smiled at her friend's radiant face. "You guys deserve a really special life together."

"Thanks. I'm so happy I could explode." Sally took a deep breath; her eyes misted and she moved toward her husband as if his body contained a magnet set especially to attract only her.

Emily followed, grinning, in time to hear the last of Loring's words to John: "And thanks for your help bringing Emily around."

She stopped, her grin drooping. Frowned. Cocked her head and consulted the potted topiary to her left. Had she heard that? No. She couldn't have. Sally had been acting on her own, right? She and John weren't playing matchmaker on Loring's instructions. Were they?

That wouldn't feel terrific. That would feel a lot like the old Loring.

The breeze gusted, threatening the circlet of baby's breath in her hair. But he wasn't the same old Loring. No, he hadn't exactly jumped with excitement at the idea of her taking the job, but he seemed to have her best interests at heart for once. Not his.

Right?

Loring approached her, his eyes lit in a curious purposeful way that made her very nervous. She knew that look, that walk, that manner. He was on a mission, out to make something happen. *Thanks for your help bringing Emily around.*

"You look gorgeous." He leaned down and kissed her. "Any chance I can sneak you away for a private glass of champagne? I don't think we'll be missed."

"Leave the wedding?" She blinked stupidly at him. "Now?"

He jerked his head toward the guests lining up to speak to the bride and groom and their parents. "We'll be back by the time the party starts in earnest. Please, Emily."

Instinctively she wanted to say no. He seemed so intense, so insistent. She had too many bad memories of him this way and it made her want to retreat for all she was worth.

Calm down. She shook off her paranoia. He probably just wanted to make out, which would suit her fine. And a glass of champagne would help her relax. Maybe she was dehydrated. Maybe she was tired from lack of sleep.

Maybe she was completely freaked out by his comment to his brother.

No, she was overreacting. He'd changed, learned to give her the space she needed, not manipulate her to get what he wanted. He'd proved it over and over again, just in the last few days.

"Okay. I guess no one will miss us."

"Atta girl." He left to ambush a caterer holding a tray of drinks.

Atta girl? Who was this person? Where had her new and improved lover gone?

He returned, holding two glasses, and started down to the beach, looking over his shoulder occasionally to make sure she was able to negotiate the path in her high-heeled sandals.

She glanced back at the party. "Loring, are you *sure* it's okay to—"

"Yes."

She gritted her teeth. Interrupting? Not hearing her out? Insisting his views were correct? This was entirely too familiar.

"It won't take long."

"What won't take long?"

"You'll see."

By the time she reached the cove, she had to confess her warm fuzzy feelings of a few minutes earlier were threatening to become cold and bald.

He walked ahead out onto the beach and stood

there for a moment with his back to her. Then, as she struggled on the sand toward him, he turned abruptly and held her glass out, cupping the bottom strangely in his hand instead of holding it by the stem.

What was this?

"To us." He lifted his glass, then took his hand away from hers when she had a firm grasp.

She stared down at the bubbly liquid and froze.

For a second, she didn't even know what it was. Something in the bottom of her glass, covered with bubbles, as if a swarm of tiny bugs were trying to devour it.

Then the shock hit and her whole body seemed to shut down.

The ring. *Their* ring.

"I've kept it for the past two years. I always dreamed of giving it back to you. I never gave up hoping this day would come." His voice was passionate, eager; he moved forward and took her hand, gazing earnestly into her face. "You've never left my head, Emily, even for a second. And God knows you've never left my heart."

She gaped at him, utterly unable to take this in. "You're asking me to marry you again?"

"Yes." He smiled, confident, totally in control, as if he were Ed McMahon telling her she'd won Publisher's Clearing House.

"After four days?"

"After two years. We belong together, Emily. I want you to move to Asheville. I can get you a job doing what you love, what you were born to do. There's a counseling position open at Asheville Prep."

She couldn't believe what she was hearing. She couldn't believe. *I* want to marry you. *I* want you to move. *I* can get you a job. It was still all about him. He was so sure of her answer, he wasn't even asking if she'd like to. So sure she'd chuck everything she'd worked for over the last two years, so sure she'd change her entire life for him in one stroke...

"Is this why you told me not to take the job?"

The confidence started to slide off his face. "Of course not. That had nothing to do with this. You'd be miserable at Borwyn, Emily. On some level you already know that. I can see the reluctance in your face when you talk about it. I lived that life and I came out the other side only after an incredibly painful trip. I don't want to see you have to do that."

I, I, I, me, me, me. "Don't you think I should find that out for—"

"Emily, I—"

"Yes, Loring?" She interrupted as rudely as he

had. She couldn't stand that impatient way he said her name.

"Emily." To his credit, he forced softness into his voice. "Can you blame me for wanting to spare you misery?"

"What makes you so sure I won't love it?"

"I know you. You'll—"

"You don't know *squat*."

Her temper spiked, anger getting the better of her, but she was beyond caring, preparing to ride the wave of glorious outrage in a way she'd never had the courage to do before. The fact that she hadn't been one-hundred-percent sure about Borwyn herself was not going to stop her now.

The choice between taking the job and knuckling under to Mr. Thanks-for-your-help-bringing-Emily-around, Come-be-my-slave-again, was a freaking no-brainer. Did he really expect her to ditch her life plans and dreams after four days playing treasure hunt?

"This has been your goal from the beginning, hasn't it. Your usual operating mode. Another manipulation, to get Emily to do what you want. The hunt, the boat, the condoms in the cabin."

He looked genuinely surprised, she had to give him that. "That wasn't me."

"'Thanks for your help bringing Emily around.'"

His expression froze. *Gotcha.* "That wasn't how it sound—"

"Oh, please." She held out the champagne glass with the ring for him to take back.

He made no move, just stared at her, shock and pain finally registering on his handsome face.

If she stayed another second, she'd start feeling sorry for him. And for once, this was going to be about *her*.

"At the risk of repeating history, Loring, I'm afraid this isn't going to work out."

When he still didn't move, she tossed the entire glass of champagne, ring and all, onto the sand at his feet. And for the second time in her life, she turned and walked away.

CHAPTER TEN

EMILY STARED at herself in the mirror over her bathroom sink.

God, she looked horrible. Any tan she'd gotten in the Virgin Islands had faded a few weeks after she got back, and the intervening two months hadn't done much to put the sparkle in her eyes or any color in her cheeks.

Far from it.

Worse, her navy suit drained whatever color she did have. By now she hated navy. She hated black. She hated beige. She wanted to show up for work in a red miniskirt and black tube top. Wear her hair down and dance a chorus-line number on top of the desks in her area.

One of her colleagues had been busted last week for inappropriate socks.

Inappropriate socks!

She splashed more water on her face, rubbed it dry and went into her bedroom. Took down her hair, shrugged out of the damn navy jacket and glanced at the clock. Seven-thirty. She was home early tonight. Maybe she'd celebrate by finding something to eat besides cereal. She was losing weight and she didn't have a whole lot extra to lose.

Yes. She hated her job. Her colleagues were nice enough, but they were so lacking in humanity, lacking in creativity. They threw lavish parties, consumed alcohol, ate fabulous food, but didn't seem to be able to relax enough to enjoy any of it.

Neither could she.

She remembered those cozy afternoons with the teen mothers, sitting at their kitchen tables going over their history homework, making it come alive for them, while their babies slept.

Compare that with sitting in meetings with prematurely wealthy twenty-somethings endlessly discussing when they should meet next and with whom.

Ugh.

Worse, even though the work was challenging, at times fascinating, she never felt like she got anything done. Bits. She worked on bits. Her bit got passed along and joined to someone else's bit. She missed the personal satisfaction of seeing something she'd created or nurtured on her own grow, blossom, come to fruition.

Meetings, meetings, more meetings.

Borwyn and Company did good work, of course they did, helping at-risk companies that might otherwise not survive. But every time they recommended layoffs, she found herself wanting to make soup to deliver to those her input helped put out of a job.

Time to face reality. She was not cut out for this and had reached her limit on trying. She'd been stubbornly sticking it out, partly because she wanted to be absolutely certain and partly because she hated to admit she could have chosen so badly. But it was time to own up to the childish part of her that had also been reluctant to concede to Loring. Time to acknowledge that he'd been right. That he *had* been thinking at least partly of her when he urged her not to take the job. Which meant she'd mistrusted him unfairly and hurt him unnecessarily.

Ouch.

She pulled on sweats and a sweatshirt—would spring ever come?—and went back into her kitchen to find something to eat.

At the same time, she was glad she'd done it this way. Quitting now—she smiled, even the *thought* she could quit made her happy—was an entirely different animal from not having tried. Far different from accepting Loring's second proposal and running away from opportunity to the safety of life with him.

This way she would never worry that she'd missed something important or that she'd be knuckling under to him once again. This way she could admit failure proudly and leave from a position of strength. This way it was *her* choice. To go back to Loring, go back to doing what she loved, admit her mistake, and live happily ever after.

If he'd take her.

She shook off the fear—one major life decision at a time—and put a frozen lasagna into the microwave, then poked through her mail. A letter from Sally's address in Manhattan, heavy, as if it contained photographs.

Yes. Pictures of her, pictures of St. Thomas, pictures of Loring.

A picture of her and Loring.

Her heart gave a huge leap; she sank down on her kitchen chair, clutching the photograph. God, she looked so happy. Sally had caught her grinning for all she was worth at the camera. Loring was staring at her as if she was the most precious thing he'd ever come across.

An unexpected sob tore out of her throat, sounding like a mutant hiccup. She laughed then started to cry, looking at the expression on his face, missing him like crazy.

She loved him. She would always love him.

Her phone rang. Her boss, Rick Handel's harsh nasal tone came on the line. "Emily, I needed the report on the CEO of Beta-X Systems tonight."

"I left it on your desk."

"This isn't what I wanted. I sent you an e-mail this morning. Didn't you get it?"

Her back tensed; her jaw tensed. "I didn't get an e-mail from you this morning."

"This whole thing needs redoing. We're going at the research with the wrong angle. I need it done tonight."

Weariness. Unutterable weariness. Worse, indifference. She stared at the picture of Loring, at her glowing face so close to his.

And in no uncertain terms, told Rick Handel exactly what he could do with his report.

LORING TOOK a sip of his beer, staring at the view of the Blue Ridge mountains from his back deck, breathed in the fresh pure air and felt his body starting to relax. Exhausting day. Amy Campole, their pride and joy valedictorian, had come into his office in tears. She and her boyfriend had used protection, but something had gone wrong. Her parents would kill her. What should she do?

He let out a sigh. He'd helped her as best he could, touched that she'd confide in him above one of her female teachers. But she'd called three times since, and he knew she required a lot more than the reassurances he'd given her. Her life would never be the same, and if her parents did come down hard on her, she'd have to have somewhere to go, someone to turn to. He was willing to help, but wasn't equipped to give her what she'd need.

The school's counselor had developed complications with her pregnancy and her doctor had ordered bedrest. Her absence left a hole Loring had hoped the school wouldn't need to fill this soon. And she'd decided to stay home full-time, so she wouldn't be back in the fall.

All he could think about was Emily.

But that wasn't unusual; she was all he thought about anyway.

He worried about her, worried she'd be miserable in her job—and okay, worried she wouldn't be. He'd resisted calling her, not wanting to compound the colossal miscalculation he'd made on the island. Just because he knew what he wanted from life and from her didn't mean she was at the same place. And it certainly didn't mean he was entitled to shove his experience down her throat and insist she feel the same way. He'd been so damn hyped up when he proposed on the island, so anxious to have the deal sewn up—no different from the man she'd left the first time.

The worst of it was that he did know better now. And was paying because of it. Since he'd met her, he'd been so thoroughly convinced that they belonged together that until this past month, he hadn't allowed himself to believe their relationship could really be over.

But during the last few weeks, he'd gradually and painfully stopped expecting her to call. Not that he'd hoped she would capitulate—half of him did want her to love her job so she could become the person she so desperately seemed to want to become. But he'd hoped she would call just to hear his voice, to share what was happening in her life.

And yes, because she missed him and couldn't live without him.

Maybe it was better this way. All or nothing. But if this was how better felt, he wanted worse.

Impulsively, he got up from his chair, went into his bedroom and retrieved the box of cuff links from his closet. He held up the ring—her ring— and watched it glitter in the light, as cold now as it was warm on Emily's finger. He couldn't ever see getting to the point where he could sell it.

His doorbell rang; he sighed and stuffed the ring in his pocket. Amy? He didn't begrudge her the time he spent calming her, but he didn't feel like talking to anyone tonight.

He opened the door. The bottom dropped out of his stomach.

"Emily."

"Hi, Loring." She whispered the words, gave a little nervous wave.

"Hi…"

He meant to invite her in, act hearty and friendly and glad to see her. But she was so damn beautiful, even thin and pale and anxious looking, that his heart nearly tore in half. Heartiness was beyond him.

So instead, he held out his arms. To his profound joy and relief, she came into them and pressed herself against him.

"I…I'm…" She laughed, though he heard tears in the sound. "I had this whole, 'I'm sorry, you were right, I did hate the job but I had to find that out for myself' speech worked out, and now I can't remember it."

He chuckled, burying his face in her hair, inhaling her scent in greedy lungfuls, holding her probably too tightly but not able to stop himself. "I have an 'I'm sorry I was once again overbearing and insensitive' speech worked out. Would you like to hear it?"

She drew back, looked into his eyes and he saw everything he needed to see, hoped she saw everything she needed to in his.

"Let's skip the speeches."

He grinned, then lowered his face to her eagerly upturned one, gathering her again as close as was humanly possible.

She kissed him in that way that was at once eager and sweet and sexual, the combination that turned him on as nothing and no one else could.

Before he'd had enough—would he ever have enough?—she turned her face into his shoulder.

They stood, rocking slightly, arms tight around each other, and it was somehow more satisfyingly intimate than the kissing had been.

"Oh, Loring. I was so nervous coming here. Afraid you wouldn't want me back, wouldn't take a chance with me again. And worse, afraid that after I'd come all this way and gotten myself so worked up, you wouldn't even be home."

"I'm home." He kissed her again, his lips lingering over hers. "And if you want to be, you are, too."

She slid her arms around his neck and drew back to look into his eyes. "I quit my job. That, I did for me, whether you still wanted me or not. I'm willing to move here if that's what will work best for us to be together now."

He couldn't speak right away, and had to take a breath before his throat relaxed enough for words.

"There's a job at school." His voice broke anyway. "You're desperately needed there and here."

She smiled, eyes shining blue, a flush coloring her pale face rosy. "Do you still have the ring?"

"You mean this one?" He chuckled and pulled it out of his pocket.

Emily gasped. "You carry it around all the time?"

He shook his head. "I must have known subconsciously that I'd need it tonight."

"I guess you did." Her gaze turned shy and

uncertain; the protective side of him kicked in as it always did around her. This time he waited to hear what she'd say, even though he had a pretty good idea, and the thought made him feel giddy, like a kid who has finally earned a coveted privilege.

"Sally told me you had nothing to do with the matchmaking schemes she and John cooked up."

"No, but I was damn grateful to them for their help in trying."

"I'm...sorry I didn't have more faith in you."

"Oh, Emily." He leaned forward and kissed her worried forehead. "Based on our history and the fact that you overheard me thanking John for the chance to spend more time with you as if I was part of the scheming, I don't blame you at all."

"I love you, Loring." She brought her arms down and put one hand to his chest, looked him full in the eye, calm, strong and sure—the new Emily. "I want to wear this ring for the rest of my life. And any changing we do from now until death do us part, I want us to do it together."

He nodded, slid the ring on her finger, too choked up to speak.

"It's so beautiful." She held the diamond up to the light, then lowered her hand to clasp his. "I think we found something much better than treasure."

He kissed her, let his tongue taste her lips; she

responded with a soft moan that made him start to get hard. "Each other?"

"Mmm." She pressed against the rapidly expanding front of his pants. "To love, honor, cherish and sexually exhaust."

He scooped her up in his arms and headed for his bedroom, where he intended to install her for the rest of her natural life. "This time, Emily, it's going to work out."

FAIR GAME?

Julie Kistler

CHAPTER ONE

Five weeks before the wedding

"ANDIE? Don't tell me you're still in bed?" As her mother threw open the curtains, letting sun flood into the bedroom, Andie Summerhill pushed her hair out of her face and lifted her head off the pillow.

"G'morning." She found a sleepy smile. "I was enjoying sleeping in."

"Andie, it's almost ten."

"Really?" Twisting her hair into a topknot with one hand, Andie squashed down the stack of pillows with the other to get a view of the alarm clock. "It was a late night," she yawned.

"You ended up pitching in and helping with that cocktail party last night, didn't you?" Margaret Summerhill asked shrewdly.

"Well, as a matter of fact..."

"Oh, Andie." Her mother shook her head. "Sweetheart, they're never going to take you seriously as management material if you keep acting like the hired help."

Andie kept her smile in place as she tried to change the subject. "It was for the Rosencrantz catalog pre-show. Some gorgeous stuff coming up in that auction, Mum. I'll bring you a catalog."

But her mother refused to be put off course. "I still think they use you shamelessly at that place," she noted with a sort of tsk-tsk sound. "You're supposed to be moving up the ladder into management at the auction house, not filling in as a caterer. You really should come work at S and S."

It was a familiar theme, and Andie was very good at avoiding it. Although she loved her family dearly, she had no intention of working at the brokerage house with the rest of them. Oh, sure, they all adored the place and she understood that they wanted to share their enthusiasm. But they were numbers people. They liked high finance. And Andie did not.

"I didn't mind helping with the party," she said quickly. "In fact, I had a lot of fun last night."

"Andie, we've talked about this," her mother reminded her. "Fooling around with parties just isn't the kind of work you should be doing. You're too smart to waste your time on that kind of..."

The next word coming would be *silliness*. It was always *silliness*. But this time her mother broke off and started again.

"It just isn't serious work. You know that, right?" she asked awkwardly.

Andie kept her mouth shut. Her career plans—or lack thereof—were something of a sore spot in the family, and she really didn't want to discuss it further. How many times had she and her mother sat down and made lists and plans and tried to figure out what exactly the right career for Andie might be? Too many. Her impromptu work on last night's cocktail party was the most fun thing she'd done at the auction house. But she didn't share that information. Any sign of discontent with her new job at Peacock and Sons—her fifth job in the last two years—and her mother never would give up trying to get her to move into the financial world and join the family firm.

Andie stood up, stretching and yawning again. "And why do I need to be up on a Saturday morning, anyway?"

Margaret Summerhill's smile broadened, and there was a mischievous gleam in her eye. How very unlike her mother, Andie thought. As steady, calm and reliable as the venerable Summerhill and Summerhill brokerage house, Mrs. Summerhill was not given to mischief. And yet that sparkle was definitely there.

"What gives, Mum?"

"Your brother is bringing Kate to lunch," she confided. "I think they may be making an announcement. You know, that kind of announcement."

Andie tried not to groan. When it came to the prospect of marrying off her children, her mother was incorrigible. "But they've only been dating for a few months. That's pretty quick for Rob to be popping the question.''

Rob, the eldest of the three Summerhill children, was as thoughtful and careful as the rest of the family. Well, except for herself, Andie acknowledged. The youngest, she'd always been the round peg in this neatly squared-off household. But Rob did seem to be quite happy with Kate, a fellow investment broker who fit in with the Summerhills far better than Andie. Still...

"Six months is plenty of time," her mother said with conviction. "And speaking of time..." She tapped her watch. "Lunch is at twelve-thirty, which is why you need to be up and getting ready. I was hoping you could lay the table and arrange the flowers. Can you, sweetie? You always do such a nice job."

"Love to."

"Excellent." Mrs. Summerhill had her hand on the doorknob, but she turned back. "And wear something extra pretty, all right? The pink dress is nice. I've got Cook making the mandarin chicken salad that Kate likes, and I want everything to be just right for Rob's announcement."

"All right, but he may not be announcing anything," Andie warned.

Her mother wasn't listening. Halfway through the door, she mused, "Now, if I could just get Celia settled."

A smile curved Andie's lips as the door closed behind her matchmaking mother. "Better Cee than me," she said out loud. She wasn't sure if her status as youngest child was keeping her safe from her mother's machinations or if she had simply given up on trying to push Andie into settling down. Sometimes it was kind of nice being the round peg.

Whatever the reason, Andie was very glad her mother wasn't on *her* case all the time about dates and prospective partners. Poor Rob. And poor sensible, dutiful Celia. With their mother on the marriage warpath, the two of them didn't stand a chance.

Of course, Mum spent just as much energy trying to keep Andie on the straight and narrow when it came to work, so she supposed it evened out. Celia had a great job as a financial analyst that their mother approved of, but she got pushed to find a stable, responsible boyfriend. Andie dated a lot, but she got pushed to find a stable, responsible job. Six of one, half a dozen of the other.

Padding off to the shower, Andie shifted her thoughts to more pleasant things. What table linens should she use for lunch? And what about china? Grandmother Summerhill's Minton with the rosebuds or Great Aunt Ruth's Wedgwood? Which would look better with mandarin chicken salad? Decisions, decisions...

DUTIFULLY ATTIRED in the pink dress her mother liked, Andie decided the table was perfect. The roses and lilies from the garden, prettily arranged in the center, set off the Minton luncheon plates to a T. Cook's yummy chicken salad had come and gone, and a luscious warm chocolate pudding was waiting in the wings, but food and table settings were the last things on anyone's mind.

Even Andie's father, who was usually oblivious to emotional undercurrents, seemed to have noticed that something was up with Rob and Kate, who had been sending wordless messages to each other throughout the entire meal. It was incredibly romantic. Andie had to admit that her mother was right. They were definitely making an announcement, even if there was no ring on Kate's finger.

But when?

Everyone was on pins and needles waiting, since they all knew something was coming. And poor Mum, usually so calm and collected, looked about ready to collapse with the strain of waiting.

"Kate and I..." Rob began, and the other members of the family all leaned forward, literally on the edge of their seats. Rob took Kate's hand, and she blushed prettily. "We have an announcement to make."

Andie couldn't stop herself. "We know, Rob. Get on with it, will you?"

"Oh." Rob looked nonplussed. "Is it that obvious?"

"Yes," Andie returned with a laugh, ignoring the frown she was getting from her mother. *I couldn't help it,* she mouthed.

"Well..." He took a deep breath and squeezed

Kate's hand harder. "Kate and I have decided to get married."

For a moment, everyone just sat there and beamed at each other, pleased as punch, and Andie signaled that the maid could bring in the dessert. She'd thought it would be the perfect follow up to Rob's happy news.

"Excellent," their father said, almost trailing his cuff in the chocolate pudding as he leaned over the table to thump his son on the shoulder. "Excellent. Kate is terrific, and she will fit into this family beautifully." His smile widened. "She already does."

Kate's blush intensified, and Andie felt as warm and soft inside as the melted chocolate. She adored romance and weddings and all that went with them. And this was the first wedding in her immediate family. It was so exciting. She grinned at her sister Celia, who was sitting next to her, and they both offered their congratulations.

"Lucky you, Rob!" Andie said, while Celia chorused with, "This is wonderful news for both of you."

"Oh, yes, it *is* wonderful," Margaret Summerhill rushed to add. Dropping her napkin, she came around the outside of the table and gave Rob and Kate each a kiss. "We couldn't be happier for both of you." She paused, and Andie could see the questions forming on her lips. "When will you pick out the ring? Have you set a date? Where were you thinking of having the ceremony?"

"Mum, they have plenty of time for all of that," Andie put in, noting the rather panicked look on Kate's face. She hoped they weren't scaring off the poor girl before she even got to the altar. As far as she remembered, Kate had been raised by an elderly aunt who had died some time ago, and she was used to doing things on her own. All this family interference and enthusiasm might be a bit much for her.

"Well, you have to plan ahead, you know," Mrs. Summerhill declared. She stood back from the table, smiling happily at her family.

Whatever else she was, Margaret Summerhill was a planner. Whether it was a client's portfolio or her son's wedding, the arrangements would be made in a rational, logical, linear fashion if she had anything to say about it.

"There's oodles of time," Andie reminded again. "With all due respect, Mum, I have way more experience at throwing parties than you do. So you'll have to trust me when I say that it can be done, especially if they haven't set a date yet. Maybe next summer would be nice. Or even fall."

She knew very well that putting together a big event like a wedding could freak out anybody, especially someone as work-oriented as Kate, who had probably never even held a dinner party. Andie sent her sister-in-law-to-be an encouraging smile.

"Yes," her mother argued in her best no-nonsense tone, "but Kate has decisions to make, and the sooner the better. She'll have to decide whether she wants a wedding planner or not. The church, the caterer, the cake designer, the dress… And, of course, she has to pick a place for the reception. Shelby Farnsworth had hers at the Art Institute and it was lovely, just lovely, but I still think your second cousin Laura's reception at the Arboretum was even nicer. But an outdoor wedding in Chicago is so risky. Better not to chance it, if you ask me.''

"But—'' Kate began.

"Lots of choices to make,'' Margaret went on. "Not to mention attendants and parties and your registry. You only get married once, and both of you will want things just right.''

"Oh, dear,'' Kate murmured. She looked quite apprehensive. "Of course we want things to be done right. But…''

"What's the matter?'' Dad asked. "I hope it's not financial considerations, because we can certainly help out.''

"No, Dad, nothing like that.'' Rob glanced at his fiancée. "It's just that… We need to get this wedding taken care of as quickly as possible. We have to get married next month.''

"Next month?'' his mother echoed. "As in four weeks? I was thinking more of next year. Why next month?''

"Well, five weeks,'' Rob said awkwardly. "But that's the max.''

Andie's brain flashed through possible reasons for her responsible older brother to be in such a hurry to get married. Rob was never in a hurry for anything. The obvious reason to get married in haste was pregnancy, of course, but Rob with a pregnant bride? So unlikely as to seem impossible. Of course, if that was it, she would have to look at her brother in a whole new light. How very entertaining. Andie sat back, waiting for an explanation.

"It's my fault," Kate began. "You see, I have this terrific job offer."

Now *that* made sense, Andie thought. It wouldn't be her style to choose a wedding date based on business opportunities, but she had no doubt it seemed perfectly logical to everyone else at the table.

Rob smiled. "I wouldn't say it was your *fault*, sweetheart." To the table at large, he announced, "I'm so proud of Kate. She's been asked to help set up a commodities exchange in Luxembourg, and—"

"It's an amazing opportunity," Kate said. "Very lucrative, as well. And—"

"—of course we want to do it," Rob continued.

They were finishing each other's sentences. Andie smiled. It was adorable.

"And they'll hire Rob, too. Kind of a—"

"—spousal hire. But only if she has a spouse," he said ruefully. "We knew we wanted to get married, anyway. It's just that this speeds up the timetable a bit. I can't let Kate go off to Luxembourg next month—"

"—without you? Oh, heavens, no," Kate concurred, shaking her head. "We're totally a team. Rob is coming with me, and we're getting married before we leave."

"Married, I expected. But Luxembourg?" Mrs. Summerhill asked. "Oh, my."

"This is happening awfully quickly, Rob," their father noted with just a hint of disapproval.

"Yes, I know," Rob put in ruefully. "We're awfully sorry about that, but it's an amazing opportunity for Kate."

"And for Rob," Kate added. "And it's not a permanent move. Two years. Three tops. Luxembourg City is really lovely. We're hoping you'll all be able to visit."

"Well," Mr. Summerhill began, and they could all tell he had now made up his mind that he liked this idea. "It sounds wonderful for the two of you. Really start you off with a firm foundation. I have an old friend, George Mittermeier, with the embassy there. You remember George, don't you, Rob? He could be a world of help. Great guy. He'll set you up right."

Margaret Summerhill set her hand on her husband's arm. "That's an excellent idea, Warren. And we will visit, Rob. Well, this will certainly be exciting, won't it? A major move and a wedding, all at once."

"Yes, I know. Sorry about the timing." Rob looked properly apologetic, but there was an underlying current of anticipation and animation Andie hadn't seen in her brother in a long time when he turned and smiled at his new fiancée.

Their mother leaned forward, and Andie wondered if that was a tear in the corner of her eye. "Don't worry, sweetheart," she said quickly. "We'll just have to make it work. We can do that."

"We want to keep it simple."

"Yes, exactly." Looking very serious, Kate said, "We've discussed it, and a simple, understated wedding seems right for both of us. We thought..." She bit her lip, gazing hopefully at her future mother-in-law. "We thought perhaps we could accomplish that in a month."

"We can certainly try." Mrs. Summerhill put on a brave smile.

"You'll have to be flexible," Andie said helpfully. "For instance, you'll pretty much have to choose dresses off the rack. And keep the numbers down. But I think small, simple and elegant can be done beautifully in a month, even at the most popular places. I have some connections, and I could make some calls. Definitely doable."

"Oh, Andie, I'm so glad to hear you say that." Kate glanced quickly at her fiancé and then back to Andie. "But first, I would love to ask both you and Celia to be bridesmaids, if you will."

"Of course," Andie responded.

It took Celia an extra second or two, but then she hastened to add, "Yes, of course. Certainly. Love to."

Andie could see that her sister looked a little uneasy about it. Anyone who knew Celia knew that she hated parading around in front of a bunch of people, especially in a fancy dress. Especially if it was skimpy. She had always been a bit shy about things like that, whereas Andie had stood up in about twenty weddings and never got tired of it, no matter what she was asked to wear. Once she had a few more bridesmaid dresses in her closet, she could start her own store. Or throw a really dynamite party with old bridesmaid dresses as the theme.

"Don't worry," Andie whispered, patting her older sister on the leg. "I'm sure Kate will pick out really nice dresses, and it will be a breeze."

"You see, that's the thing, Andie." Kate looked stressed again. "I don't know a thing about choosing dresses or where you go or what you do. And we have so little time. I was hoping..." She paused. "I know it's a lot to ask if you're a bridesmaid, too, but, well, I don't know. Do bridesmaids do a lot?"

"I think it depends," Andie said kindly.

"That's exactly what I mean. I'm so bad at this sort of thing." Kate sighed. "I was hoping you might be willing to be my unofficial wedding planner. I can't hire an official one since I wouldn't even know what to ask. You're the only person I know who can throw together a wedding in five weeks."

Andie blinked. "Really? You would want me to do that?" She was truly touched. "I'd love to."

"Andie," her mother began, a worried look on her face.

"Don't worry, Mum," she said quickly. "It's just a favor for Kate. Not a lifestyle choice."

"Okay. If you're sure." But her mother still looked a little worried. Andie's smile widened. To hear Mom talk, you'd think throwing a few parties was an addiction and Andie needed a twelve-step program to keep her away from hors d'oeuvres and martinis. "I just don't want anything to interfere with your real job at Peacock and Sons. I know that has to come first."

Meaning, *You've had five jobs in two years, and if you lose one more, chances are iffy we'll be able to find you another position we approve of...*

"I'm sure I can handle it," Andie told them.

"That is such a relief." Kate sat back in her seat. "Whew."

"Thanks so much, Andie—you're amazing," her brother murmured. She could tell by the heart-felt look in his eye that he was really happy she'd said yes, and that he, too, was relieved to put the details in her hands.

"Well, I'm sure Andie will do a wonderful job," her mother interjected, clearly trying to sound supportive. "She always does."

"Andie, you and Kate can pick dresses without me, right?" Celia asked. "I hate trying on and modeling." She shuddered. "Besides, I have this important client I'm handling right now. He's kind of difficult and, well, I need every minute. You understand. And I trust you implicitly.''

While she appreciated their confidence, Andie realized she had to get cracking if she was going to pull this wedding off. "Kate, you and I are going to need to put our heads together and look at some magazines and things so I get an idea of what you want.''

"Oh, you go right ahead," Kate said sweetly. "I trust you, too, Andie. You know best.''

Andie looked at the faces around the table. Everyone was smiling, content to know she was taking care of things. How very odd. She was used to being the flake, the non-conformist, the round peg. Being the go-to girl was something new. But when it came to parties and weddings, she was the one in the family with the most experience. The others' brains just didn't work that way. She didn't mind, really. It was just…odd. She wasn't sure exactly when she'd acquired this expert status. She just hoped she didn't screw up.

"You should definitely use that friend of yours who makes those wonderful cakes," her mother told her. "You know, the one who did the cake for my birthday party?"

"What about a bridal shower?" Celia asked. "You and I can be the hosts, as the bridesmaids. That would be nice, wouldn't it?"

"Oh, and a small engagement party here at the house," Mrs. Summerhill chimed in. "Nothing fancy. But we could use the ballroom. Haven't used it in years.''

"Okay. Yeah, I think I can do all that." Andie wasn't a list-maker by nature, preferring a more seat-of-the-pants approach, but she was mentally taking notes, anyway. Ideas, ideas. Maybe a pretty little afternoon tea for the bridal shower. She could get tea cakes for that, as well as the wedding cake, from her friend Mariette, who did amazing things with butter cream and flowers. And she could check out dresses from Armand's—different skirts and tops in the same fabric. This was going to be such fun.

Andie rose from the table. "I guess I'd better get started," she said with a certain spark of enthusiasm. "I think I have a pretty good idea of your taste, Kate, but I'll be in touch to run things by you, okay? And congratulations again, you two. The wedding, Luxembourg and wedded bliss... It's all going to be awesome."

As she hit the door, however, her mother called out, "One more thing, Andie. Could you find a date for Celia for the wedding?"

"Mother!" Celia protested. "I can find my own date."

"But you won't," her mother returned patiently.

"Yes, I will."

"Celia, we always go through this, and you always end up going solo." Affectionate yet firm, her mother added, "I think this is one time when an escort would be very useful. You're a beautiful, eligible young woman, and you should be taking steps, just as Rob did. You'll never find the right man unless you start trying out a few here and there.''

Oh, dear. Poor Cee. Mum really did have a bee in her bonnet this time. With Rob off the market, she was moving down the line to her number-two child, Celia.

"Mother, I promise you," Celia said with determination, "I will find a date for the wedding."

"Andie," their mother said, "put it on your list."

Andie shook her head. There wouldn't be a spare minute to get a date for herself, let alone Celia. If she decided between now and then that it was important, well, she had a handy list of suitable escorts—male friends who always filled in when she needed them—but Celia was a trickier issue. The combination of shy, stubborn and picky made it tough for her to find dates.

But if Mum had her heart set on it, maybe Andie could scrounge up a nice guy to escort Celia, just to get her poor sister out from under their mother's microscope. It was the sisterly thing to do, right?

CHAPTER TWO

Two weeks later

RECLINING CROSSWAYS on a wicker love seat in the sunroom of the carriage house, Andie chewed on the end of her pen, frowning at the unimpressive scene before her. After clearing out all the furniture, she'd had five small tea tables, the love seat and some serving tables set up here. She'd borrowed enough wicker chairs to cluster around the tables in cozy little groupings, and that worked fine. The lace tablecloths looked lovely, but the overall effect was flat, boring. Would the eclectic assortment of mismatched plates and teapots, plus tiered silver trays spilling over with sweet little sandwiches, pastries and Mariette's gorgeous cakes be enough to bring the room to life?

"I don't think so," she mused out loud. "Something is missing. And speaking of which, where's the florist?"

She'd had the idea of sticking potted palms and Boston ferns around the outside of the room, and dropping tiny posies of violets next to each place.

That would certainly perk things up, but something was still missing...

"Hey, Andie, is that you?" Celia poked her head in through the archway into the hall.

"Cee, I'm so glad to see you. What's wrong in here? Why does it look so dull?" The setting for Kate's bridal shower/afternoon tea looked like, well, a bunch of tables tossed into an empty sunroom that no one ever used.

Maybe she shouldn't have planned this tea party for the carriage house. But she'd wanted to separate it from tonight's engagement party, which would be a grander affair, in the ballroom at the main house. Almost everything for tonight's event was set up, whereas the shower was still disorganized. Of course, the engagement party was totally catered from stem to stern, while the shower was truly Andie's party. She had wanted to do every detail herself, with no servants, and no caterers. Grand and elegant for her mother's black-tie engagement party, but off-beat, off-balance and eccentric for Andie's bridal shower down at the carriage house.

Tossing Celia a stern look, Andie added, "I need help. You're supposed to be my co-host, remember?"

"Yes, I know." Celia had the decency to look guilty. They'd both known from the moment Celia proposed a shower that Andie would do all the work, especially when Andie had insisted on the no-caterers policy, but still...

She looked up, wondering why her sister was lingering in the doorway. "Come on in and get started. There are cups and plates to lay out, place cards to write, and I have to paint the butterflies and flowers on top of the teacakes myself, because Mariette said it has to be done at the last minute. There's a ton of stuff left to do."

"Oh, dear," Celia stalled. "I'm sorry, Andie. I'm kind of tied up with something, and I don't know if I can help."

Andie laid her head back, letting her ponytail hang over the arm of the wicker love seat. "Aw, come on, Cee, don't tell me that."

"But I brought someone with me. Maybe he can pitch in." Toting a large briefcase, Celia finally entered the room all the way, but her gaze was directed behind her. "Jason? I'd like you to meet my sister."

Celia had a man with her? That made Andie sit up and pay attention. Who was this? And where did Celia find him?

Whoever he was, he was drop-dead gorgeous. Very George Clooney. Yikes. He had dark hair, cut short, and dark eyes that looked shrewd and perceptive, as if he didn't miss a whole lot. He was tall, a good seven or eight inches taller than Celia's five-foot-five, and he carried himself with a certain self-assurance that made his casual black knit shirt and charcoal-gray pants look very good.

Her first impression was that he strode in as though he owned the place. And her second was that he didn't match up with her sister Celia under any stretch of the imagination. Andie's gaze swept over him, looking for more clues. Expensive clothes, worn well. Arrogance. Deep, dark eyes. A cleft in his chin that was very intriguing. A small, amused smile, as if he already knew she was taking his measure and he didn't mind a bit. Major sex appeal.

Well, she'd learned a long time ago never to second-guess the mysteries of other people's relationships. Maybe he was just what the doctor ordered for Celia. Maybe he'd knocked her socks off at first sight and she'd done the same for him. He was undeniably...interesting.

"Andie," Celia offered, "this is my, er, *date*. For the weekend. I brought Jason to meet the family. Jason McKinley, my sister Andrea—well, Andie."

Celia just stood there, looking nervous, as Andie crossed to stand next to her. Andie's voice sounded squeaky to her own ears when she finally said, "Well, Mr. McKinley." *You sound like an idiot, Andie. Get a grip.* Hastily, she added, "It's so, um, nice you could join us for the weekend."

"Call me Jace," he said. His voice was husky and deep, and it made tiny shivers slide down her spine.

"Well," Andie murmured again. "Nice to meet you."

That was two *nices* in the last two minutes, and *nice* didn't exactly cover it. Devastating, intimi-

dating and downright scary were more like it. What
was it about Jason McKinley that made her feel
dizzy and clumsy? She'd met all sorts of people in
her life, from power brokers to the man on the
street, and she never got shy and girly around
them. But suddenly, with this man, she was
tongue-tied.

"Good to be here, Andie. Your parents have a
gorgeous home."

"Thank you. We like it."

He extended a hand, and Andie had no choice
but to stick hers out, too. But when Jason McKinley took her hand in his, some sort of bizarre electrical current seemed to leap between their fingers.
Yow. She yanked her hand back as if she'd been
stung. Now *that* was weird. Maybe the room was
too dry. Maybe she should get a humidifier in here
before the party.

Celia didn't notice the static electricity issue.
She was pulling out her small handheld computer
and fiddling with it. "Sorry to beg off, Andie. You
will forgive me, won't you?" She smiled weakly.
"I'll be back for the tea, of course. It's just that
I've got all this research to do and a huge report
to write up before tonight. I'm *so* sorry, Andie.
Really."

"Oh, it's okay, Cee." Truth be told, Andie had
never really expected her sister to help with the
shower. Celia was terrible at that kind of thing.
Besides, if there was a ton of small details left,
Andie knew it was her own fault for insisting she

had to do everything herself and leaving the household staff and the catering people up at the main house to fool with the party tonight. Yep. It was her own fault. And if Celia was busy, there was nothing they could do about it.

"Thanks so much for understanding, Andie," Celia said. "But I'm sure Jason will help."

Andie cast an uneasy glance at Jason McKinley, who stood there, narrowing his eyes at her, still giving her the once-over in a way she did not appreciate. She was suddenly painfully aware that she was wearing skuzzy short shorts and an old T-shirt, with her hair shoved hastily into a ponytail. Not exactly her best look. Not that it mattered. Of course it didn't matter.

Leaning in closer to her sister, she whispered, "Are you sure you can spare your, uh, date? Are you sure he wouldn't rather stay with you?"

"Oh." Celia turned to Jason and patted him awkwardly on the arm. "You'll be fine with Andie while I'm tied up, won't you, Jason? I'd really appreciate it if you could help her out."

"I'll be fine," he assured her. "I'm pretty resourceful."

Yeah, I'll just bet. Andie was admittedly curious about all of this. For one thing, Celia had a hard time finding dates. She was lovely and sweet, but also shy and very smart. Celia tended to be extremely impatient with stupidity, so it wasn't surprising she couldn't find men who suited her. Now, Jason McKinley seemed intelligent enough, and he treated Celia with kindness and respect. But there was no heat between them. And as for Celia... She seemed self-conscious and ill at ease, as well as a bit cranky.

But then, Andie was feeling a little weird herself at the moment. She didn't blame her sister for being tense. It was probably just work. Celia took her job very seriously, and it sounded as if she had a lot on her plate right now. But where had she found Jason McKinley? So far, he didn't seem like the man of her dreams. But Celia wouldn't have brought him home for the weekend unless she really, *really* liked him, would she? Parading him in front of their mom without being fairly sure about him was a foolish move, and Celia was never foolish.

So was Jason someone important? Or just a fillin? Hard to tell, Andie mused. At least Celia had a date for the party. At least she was in there swinging. Their mother ought to be thrilled, especially since the date in question was a real hottie.

Jason McKinley. His name sounded vaguely familiar. But why? Who the heck was he?

Andie's curious gaze flitted back and forth between them. She wished she had a moment to get Celia alone and find out the real scoop here. But with one last wave, her sister hoisted her laptop bag over her shoulder and took off.

Leaving Andie alone with the mysterious and unsettling Mr. McKinley.

"So, Jason." Andie pasted on a brave smile, trying to decide what she could do with him.

"Call me Jace," he repeated.

But Celia had called him Jason. Oh well. If that was what he wanted... "Right. Jace. Well, if you're really up for helping..."

"Oh, sure—I'm good at lending a hand," he said quickly, sending her a rakish smile.

Why did she get the idea he meant something other than helping set up a tea party?

"Okay then." She preferred to ignore the undercurrents rippling between them. There wasn't anything she could do about them, anyway. Not if he was Celia's date for the weekend. A Summerhill woman would never, ever poach her sister's boyfriend. Or even her I-just-met-him-and-asked-him-home-for-the-weekend fill-in guy. Whichever he was, he was Celia's. *So don't be having any covetous thoughts,* she told herself sternly.

I wasn't!

Yes, you were, she argued right back.

"Is something wrong?" he asked.

"No, no, nothing." They just stood looking at each other for a long moment. Without even thinking about it, she asked, "How do you know Celia? How did you two meet?"

"Business," he returned. "She was doing the financials on a project I'm working on, crunching the numbers to help versus move into the area, and she's obviously very good at what she does. I'm the McKinley in the McKinley Group. Hotels, resorts, that kind of thing. Maybe you've heard of us. We've got three hotels in the Chicago area so far, and we're moving more aggressively into this market."

"Oh." Andie blinked. *"Oh."*

Of course she'd heard of the McKinley Group. And of Jason McKinley. The pieces began to fall into place. Although she had to admit she didn't read the business pages carefully, she was pretty sure he'd been all over them recently because of some huge development deal he had going.

The picture was becoming clearer. "You're the one who's buying up old buildings, right? Historically and architecturally important buildings? And you're rehabbing them and turning them into boutique hotels. I think I had a luncheon in one of them."

"That's me."

"Wow." The project was somewhat controversial, but also kind of cool to her way of thinking. *That* Jason McKinley. Wow.

What had Celia been thinking, dragging the man out here to the suburbs and then abandoning him? Jason McKinley, jet-setting, cosmopolitan ubermagnate, helping set up a tea party? Heavens.

"So you haven't known each other long, then?" she asked, fascinated by this whole thing. "Because, I mean, you're new to Chicago, right?"

"Right. Celia was kind enough to invite me for the weekend as a sort of introduction to the area." He gestured out the window at the view of her parents' rambling estate. "She knew I'd only seen the city itself, and not much of that. It was actually very sweet of her. So much nicer to stay with someone than in a hotel."

He wasn't giving the impression that he and Celia were madly in love, what with the *kind* and the *sweet* and all that. "And yet you own hotels."

"Yes, I do." He smiled again. "Coming here was a good decision, though. I'm enjoying the scenery."

Once again, it seemed there were hidden messages in his words, messages she wasn't quite getting. "Oh? What scenery would that be?"

"Your parents' estate is lovely. And you..."

Was he going to say she was lovely, too? There was a light in his eyes that seemed to suggest that was where he was going. And the soft, seductive voice... If she didn't know better, she might have thought he was flirting with her. The snake.

"Yes?" she asked crisply, deciding she was going to skewer him if he got any more obvious with the flirting. "What about me?"

"Well, you're not what I expected." He tipped his head to the side, as if he were getting a bead on her. "You and your sister..."

"Oh, we're really different. Everyone says that." Now she was on familiar turf. Okay, so he wasn't flirting, just trying to figure out how serene, careful Celia was related to the woman with the tousled ponytail and scruffy shorts. Andie backed up, adjusting a lace tablecloth that was off-center.

"Don't worry. The rest of the family is like Celia. I'm the odd one."

"I didn't say you were odd, just different."

"It's not a big deal. I hear it all the time." She sent him a reckless grin. "But Celia is terrific. Centered, stable, so smart. A terrific person."

"Yes, I know."

Okay, so maybe she shouldn't sell her sister like that. He already knew about Celia's good qualities. She changed the subject. "So will you be staying in Chicago long?"

"I'm not sure. But I'm from San Francisco and that's where the company headquarters are. I'm thinking about making Chicago my base of operations for the McKinley Group." He shrugged. "The state has offered me some tempting tax incentives to bring my HQ here."

"I see." So there might be long-term prospects. For Celia.

"Was there something you wanted help with?" he asked. "For your party?"

"Oh, right." In her curiosity about who he was and what he was doing here, she'd almost forgotten the party.

She gazed around the room and then back at him. Somehow folding napkins into butterflies and frosting flowers on tea cakes didn't seem up his alley. If only there were skyscrapers to buy or million-dollar deals to hammer out. "I don't suppose you would be interested in setting the tables?"

"It's not something I've ever done before, but if that's what you want," he said dubiously.

"Right."

She'd had her brother bring over a bunch of boxes containing napkins, sugars and creamers, silverware and other things she would need from the main house, and he had stacked them all against the wall. Andie stretched up on tip-toe to reach the top box. It had never occurred to her before that if she stretched like that, her shorts would stretch with her, exposing more of her backside than she'd intended. But there was a definite breeze going on down there. Maybe Jace hadn't noticed. Surreptitiously, she peeked over her shoulder. Oh, he'd noticed.

Andie felt hot color flood her cheeks as she tugged down on her shorts. As if by magic, Jace appeared at her side to get the box for her.

Recovering quickly, she pretended to be occupied with the teapots set out on the sideboard, and instructed him on the fine art of teapot selection. "I'm putting four people at each table, so I think two teapots per table ought to do it. There are silver trivets in one of the boxes, and you'll need to stick them on opposite corners of the tables."

"The tables are round," he put in.

"And?" she asked, confused.

"They don't have corners."

"Right."

Men could be so literal. Andie stood, hands on her hips, giving him a rather perturbed expression.

She wished she had her mother's patented don't-mess-with-me look in her repertoire, but she already knew she just looked silly when she tried it. Slightly put out was the best Andie could muster.

"Okay, you see where the chairs are? Take plates out of the stack over there on the sideboard and set one in front of each chair." She demonstrated by grabbing four mismatched luncheon plates and laying them out on the nearest table. "Violas."

She went on to stick teacups and saucers to the right of the plates, laid out the silver, added trivets and teapots, replaced two of the plates to coordinate colors better, exchanged one of the teapots, and then rearranged everything to suit her. Twice.

"Is there a reason you're putting empty teapots out now?" he asked. "Don't you need to put tea in them first?"

"Well, yes, but…" Andie tucked a piece of hair behind her ear. "I wanted to pick which ones went best with the tables. You know, visually. Then I'll take them away when I brew the tea, fill them up and bring them back. Besides, I'm giving them a choice of teas. So I can bring back the kind they want."

"Okay, I'm sure that makes sense to you, if not to me," Jace told her, a hint of amusement in his voice. "I think you'd better set the tables, though, considering you did that one yourself and still rearranged it six times."

"I rearranged it twice," she corrected him. Darn him for having a point.

Idly, he picked up an antique teacup from the sideboard and dangled it from one finger, regarding it with a great deal of suspicion and distrust. "It's awfully small, isn't it?"

"That is Sevres. You break it and I'll have to kill you." Andie snatched it away from him. "I don't suppose you can fold napkins into butterflies? It's sort of…geometric."

After several minutes, with Andie hovering over him and directing every move, all he had was a few mangled pieces of bright-colored linen that did not resemble butterflies in the least. Even though he was being an awfully good sport, he wasn't taking this very seriously. And it was more of an effort to try to teach him things than just to do it herself.

"You're hopeless. There must be something else we can find for you to do." She glanced at his fit, lean body, at the easy way he carried himself. "Hmmm… Too bad I don't need anything in the area of slam-dunking or scoring or something."

"Dunking?"

"I'm thinking you're probably very good at basketball," she said. "You know, sports. Guy things. But I'm afraid those skills won't help us put on a tea."

"Actually, I'm better at baseball." He grinned. "In baseball, I can score with the best of 'em.

Home runs. Touch all the bases. Yeah, that's my game.''

Score with the best of them, huh? "I'll keep that in mind," she said dryly. "But for right now... Wait. I just thought of something I know you can do." She gave him a determined smile. "I'm going to guess you're good at being assertive. So how about calling the florist's and finding out why they're not here with my flowers yet?"

"That I can do," he assured her. He pulled a cell phone out of his pocket. "Name of the place?"

"Garden Gate Florist." She quickly recited the number. "If they give you any grief, twist arms. They owe me posies, palms and ferns."

"What's a posy?"

"They'll know. Just call, okay?"

As he wandered out into the hallway to track down the florist on his phone, Andie breathed a sigh of relief. Odd how much larger the room felt when he wasn't in it. *You just bossed around a business tycoon who could eat you for breakfast with one hand tied behind his back.* "He'll get over it," she said out loud. *Yes, but will you?*

While Jace was gone, she set her mind firmly on other things. Her guests would be arriving in two hours; the caterers weren't here, the flowers weren't here, and she still needed to get herself ready. Quickly, she folded the napkins and finished the table settings. Well, that did look a bit better.

The bright-colored butterfly napkins livened up the tables, even though the room still looked too plain.

"I need place cards," she muttered to herself, shoving the love seat against the window and fluffing the pillows. "We can set the gifts on the loveseat. I hope I remembered to wrap my gift. Oh, and I have a whole lot of miniature cakes in the fridge that need flowers. And what am I going to wear?"

As she polished fingerprints off a knife, she couldn't help thinking about something else she needed to do. "Sometime today," she said slowly, "I am going to corner Celia and find out what the heck is up with her and Jace McKinley."

Behind her, Jace announced, "Okay, that's taken care of," making her jump about a foot in the air. She dropped the knife on the table, and it clattered against a plate.

"What's taken care of?"

"The florist. He's on his way. I got him to throw in some extra ferns and posies, whatever they are, for being late." He smiled, looking quite pleased with himself, and it was as if there was suddenly a lot more sun in the room.

Andie couldn't help grinning back. The man had charm to spare, that was for sure.

"Looks great in here," he commented, picking up a teaspoon. Without thinking, she immediately edged over next to him, took it away from him, and repolished it to remove his fingerprints. "Can

I ask you a question?'' he inquired. ''Why isn't there any food here? This is a lunch, right?''

''Actually, it's afternoon tea, not lunch. And the food is all in the kitchen, ready to be served when we need it.'' She stood there, holding the teaspoon a little too close to him, close enough that she could stick it in that indentation in his chin if she'd had a mind to. She couldn't help noticing that his eyes were the same delicious color as the chocolate frosting on some of the tea cakes. Warm. Inviting. Hard to resist.

''What's on the menu?''

''Chocolate,'' she murmured.

''Chocolate? For lunch?'' he asked, looking mildly surprised.

Snap out of it, Andie. ''Not chocolate all by itself,'' she explained quickly. ''I ordered these special little cakes from my friend who is an incredible baker, and they're already here. In the fridge. In the kitchen. Some of those are chocolate, but the rest of the food, which I made ahead—not the cakes, because my friend did those, but the rest of it—is the usual afternoon tea stuff.'' She was aware she was babbling, but she couldn't seem to stop. ''You know, tiny sandwiches with the crusts cut off, salmon, chicken, cucumber, that kind of thing. Scones with Devonshire cream and lemon curd. Strawberry tarts. Oh, and the cutest sugar cookies cut into boy and girl shapes. They're decorated to look like little brides and grooms. So cute.''

"And you made it all yourself?" he asked, still standing too close to her. "I'm impressed."

"I like that kind of thing," she went on, the words just spilling out. "And I wanted this to be special, kind of like my gift to Kate. As her bridesmaid, you know, more than her wedding planner. I wanted to do everything myself. No servants. No hired staff. Just me."

He didn't back away, just stood there, breathing on her. Andie had to be the one to step back.

"I need to go put some final decorations on the tea cakes," she said suddenly. "So, why don't you stay here, and then you can, um..." *Think of something, Andie.* "You can help the florist. I want the palms scattered around the outside of the room, and they'll have to hang the ferns." She frowned. "If they have time. If not, punt. As for the posies, they'll go on the tables."

"On the tables?" He arched a dark eyebrow. "I'm not messing with your tables. The posies will wait for you."

"Fine, fine. I'll handle posy placement." She threw up her hands. "And if the florist isn't here in five minutes, call him back."

"Gotcha."

She had the idea that he knew exactly what she was thinking—that she had to retreat to the safety of the kitchen and the cucumber sandwiches for her own sanity.

It didn't matter. She *was* fleeing. Jace McKinley and his warm chocolate eyes and his cleft chin, so perfect for sticking your pinky finger into, were off-limits. Celia didn't get many dates. Now that she had one, her very own sister was not about to move in on him.

"Celia brought him—Celia gets first dibs," she told herself fiercely as she marched back to the kitchen. "The *only* dibs."

CHAPTER THREE

Later that afternoon

HE WAS SUPPOSED to be paying attention to playing tennis, but all Jace could think of was the sister Andie. Who knew he was going to arrive at the Summerhill family estate and meet such a fascinating woman?

"Surprise, surprise," he murmured as Rob served up an easy lob. He returned it with little effort. If he'd wanted to, he could have polished off Celia's brother on the court in about three seconds. Nice guy, but no tennis player. Jace had enough competitive instincts for both of them, apparently, but he dialed it back out of courtesy for his hosts. Wouldn't be polite to wipe the court with the son of the family.

Rob missed the shot, anyway, slamming the ball into the net, and Jace stood back, waiting for the next serve.

Automatically, he returned it, but his thoughts kept returning to the redhead. Andie Summerhill. Andie with her little shorts and her snippy instructions about teapots and napkins. He liked her. He liked the way she ordered him around, oddly enough.

Jace wasn't a guy who enjoyed being ordered around, but somehow, the way she did it, it was kind of fun. And then there was the way she pranced around, the way energy seemed to seep out of her, no matter what she was doing. And the enticing way that streak of dust had curved around her adorable bottom in those frisky little shorts…

He shook his head just as the fuzzy yellow ball streaked past him down the line. "Good one," he called out to his opponent as he went to retrieve it.

He wasn't sure what he had expected to accomplish by accepting Celia Summerhill's invitation to join her family out in Lake Forest for the weekend, but running into a lively redhead he was actually attracted to wasn't it. "Uh-oh," he said out loud as another hard-hit ball sailed past him. Had he just admitted to himself that he was attracted to Andie Summerhill? "Bad move."

"That was the game," Rob yelled. "I got a game off you."

The guy sounded so thrilled. "Yeah, great job," Jace responded. He bounced the ball, getting ready to serve. Okay, so he'd been bored in the city, and decided it might be entertaining to get out of downtown Chicago for the weekend. And then he'd heard Celia tell her sister he was her date for the weekend. Which was not exactly how he had understood the arrangements, but it wasn't that big a deal. So he'd misunderstood. He could let Celia know he wasn't interested some other time, when it was convenient, when he didn't have to sort it out in front of her family.

But then he'd seen the sister. The redhead with the bouncy ponytail and the sparkling green eyes. And suddenly it was a whole new weekend.

"Are you ever going to serve?" Rob called from the other side of the net.

"Oh." He'd been standing bouncing the ball for about five minutes. "Sorry."

How bizarre. Jason McKinley, top dog, top shark, the man known for his amazing ability to focus on his objective even in a blizzard of distractions, had lost sight of a game because he couldn't stop thinking about a woman. Weird.

What was it about her, anyway? He tossed the ball in the air, bringing his racquet around hard into the serve. Oops. There it went, well over Rob's head, smashing straight into the fence behind him.

Rob looked at him in surprise. "What was that?"

"Just a little distracted," Jace mumbled.

"I guess."

But Jace barely heard him. Frowning, he wondered when he would get to see Andie Summerhill again. And how quickly he could finish off this tennis match.

ALL THROUGH the tea, Andie kept hoping to get her sister alone so she could talk to her, but there was no opportunity. Bridal showers were supposed to be about the bride, after all, not about who was dating whom and what they meant to each other.

Besides, since she had wanted to keep the party small and private and casual, Andie had shooed away the servants and left herself with most of the serving duties, like brewing the tea and refilling the tiered trays of cakes and sandwiches. She hadn't planned any racy games—Kate was *so* not the type—but the food and the conversation and unwrapping gifts kept the guests well occupied.

She had to say, it was a lovely party, and best of all, Kate seemed pleased. Andie smiled. A good party was one of her most favorite things.

After the last guest left, Kate thanked Andie and Celia profusely and went back to the main house to take a nap before dinner and the engagement party. Finally Andie was able to get to her sister.

"Cee, I can't believe you left your boyfriend with me all afternoon," she complained. "Poor guy. He's Jason McKinley of the McKinley Group! Good grief! And I had him folding napkins and harassing the florist." She scanned the room, taking in the abundant greenery spilling from every corner. "He did a bang-up job making the florist behave, I have to say."

"I wouldn't call him my boyfriend exactly," Celia hedged. She piled the last load of dirty cups and saucers onto a silver tray to take back to the kitchen. "I'm sorry, Andie. I was frazzled today. Too busy to think. But I did get my report done."

"I realize that, but I still don't think it was very nice to just ignore him all afternoon." She also thought that if he were *her* date, she would want to spend time with him. Like, every single minute. Why didn't Celia?

"That's the second time you've said *all afternoon*," Celia protested. "I only left him with you for about an hour or so. Then he and Rob went to play tennis during the shower. He was hardly ignored. I'll see him again at dinner." She picked up the tray, headed for the kitchen, and Andie trailed behind her. "Besides, I told him up-front that it was a busy weekend. We thought that might be the best way to introduce him to everyone, while there were other things going on. So he wouldn't get the third degree, you know."

Interesting logic. Very crafty, especially for Celia, who had never shown a propensity for that sort of strategy. And it also made their relationship sound more real. "So Jace is more than just a fill-in, then?" Andie inquired.

"I don't know what you mean by fill-in."

"I mean," Andie explained patiently, "did you bring him home to meet Mum and Dad because he might be the one and you want to know if they approve? Or because he looks good on your arm and it will get Mum off your back?"

"Neither."

"Then what?"

"Well, somewhere in between, I guess." Celia stacked the cups next to the rest of the dirty dishes on the sink. "Jeez, Andie, you sound like Mum. Where did you meet and how long have you known each other and what does he have in the bank…"

"I already know most of that," Andie admitted with a smile. "I asked him."

"You did?" Celia groaned. "What did he say?"

"He said he thinks you're sweet and kind and smart, that you met when you were working on his financial deal in Chicago, and that you brought him out for a weekend in the country because he doesn't know the area." Andie began to fill the sink with soapy water, intent on the careful process of hand-washing the fine porcelain. She considered for a moment. "I think that was it."

"Okay, well, that sounds good." After scrounging around in the drawers for the towels, Celia began to rinse and dry the teacups as Andie passed them to her. "The party went well, don't you think? Kate seemed to enjoy herself."

"Why, Celia, are you trying to distract me?"

"Yes." Celia set the clean china on the kitchen table. "Is it working?"

"No." Andie frowned. "The thing is, Cee, he's so different from what I would expect of you. I mean, sheesh—Jason McKinley of the McKinley Group." She leaned back against the sink. "And you haven't mentioned him before. So… Do you really like him? I mean, *really* like him?"

"Why?" Celia asked, color rising in her face. "Are you saying that you don't like him?"

"Me?" Andie began to feel a little defensive herself. "It's not that I don't like him. Actually, I thought he was handsome." *Very* handsome. "And, you know...powerful. Like he has all this magnetism happening or something. I'm just surprised because he's so different from the other accountants and bankers you've dated." *And because he was kind of flirting with me. Which would be very wrong if he was, but I'm not exactly sure...*

"So maybe it was time for a change," Celia declared, lifting her chin.

Slowly, Andie said, "I can't argue with that. I just get the feeling there's more here than you're telling me."

"Nope. Nothing more." Celia finished stacking the collection of washed and dried saucers and tea-cups. "Listen, Andie, this is the last of the dishes, isn't it? I would love to have a chance to relax and maybe take a bath before dinner tonight, so if we're done..."

The words were out before she could stop herself. "So you're not running right back to see Jace?"

"No." Celia shook her head. "Why are you so pushy about this, Andie? It's not like you. You're usually so laid back—live and let live."

Oops. That was all true. In fact, Andie prided herself on being the easygoing one who never judged other people's choices. And here she was, all Judgy McJudge.

"I'm not engaged to the guy," Celia continued. "I do like him. He's my date for the weekend, and I wouldn't have asked him if I didn't like him, if I didn't think he had, you know, possibilities. Okay?"

"Sorry."

"I'm sorry, too, Andie. I don't mean to get on your case." Celia sighed. "But I don't want you on mine, either."

Andie gave her sister a quick hug, apologizing again. She really was sorry. Celia did look a bit strung out. Maybe it was the pressure of having a new boyfriend around. Or having any boyfriend around. "You go ahead and have a good soak. I'll see you tonight."

And I will not ask you any more questions about Jason. Not even one. As soon as her sister was gone, Andie did a quick look around to make sure they hadn't missed anything. Idly, she picked up one of her favorite teapots, a Cardew shaped like Alice's White Rabbit. She stared into the little black eyes, as if somehow the porcelain bunny might provide answers. But she was no further along in understanding the mysterious Mr. McKinley than she had been when she started. Except, of course, that she had interrogated and annoyed her sister, which actually knocked her several steps back.

ANDIE was feeling a little stressed out herself by the time she got to the dinner table. This early dinner was just for the family, plus Celia's disconcerting date, of course. It was her mother's way of getting them all together and touching base before the engagement party.

So there they were, around the dinner table, chatting away. The family had disposed of the "How did you two meet?" and "What do you do for a living?" questions for Jace and Celia right off the bat, which was a relief to everyone, and meant they could get back to stocks and bonds and interest rates and the proposed commodities exchange in Luxembourg. Now they'd turned to arguing about the fundamental fairness of the latest securities regulations. Andie carefully chewed her beef Wellington and did her best to stay out of it. She noticed that Jace McKinley wasn't really into the discussion, either. He lifted an eyebrow at her as he raised his glass of merlot.

What did *that* mean?

When there was a lull in the conversation, Andie's father apparently decided he ought to do a better job of including their guest. "So, Mr. McKinley," he said gruffly. "How are you enjoying your stay in Chicago?"

"Very much. I didn't know much about the city, so this has been an education for me." Jace smiled at Celia, who was seated next to him, of course. "Celia has been very gracious about filling in some of the blanks."

"How nice," Mrs. Summerhill remarked. "Do you plan to be in Chicago long?"

In other words, *do you have any long-term intentions toward my daughter?* Andie would have been annoyed with her mother if she herself hadn't asked the same question a few hours ago.

"I'm not sure about that," Jace answered. Which was, as she recalled, what he had said to her, too. "I'm thinking about moving my company's headquarters here from San Francisco. In fact, I'm pretty sure I'm going to do that."

He hadn't sounded so positive before. Andie's interest perked up. Did his decision have anything to do with Celia?

"Oh, really?" her mother probed. "So you'd be moving to the area permanently?"

"Well, I don't know." He shrugged, lifting his shoulders inside his expensive Italian suit. Andie's eyes lingered there, sliding to where his tanned skin met the bright white collar of his shirt. The man knew how to wear clothes, that was for sure. "I may be retiring before long, in which case it would just be the company, not me."

Pulling herself from the shirt-collar reverie, Andie leaned forward. What had he just said?

"What? Retiring?" her father demanded. "At your age?"

"I've done most of what I set out to do with the McKinley Group," Jace said casually. "The company is in great shape. Very sound. I have great people at the helm. I always wanted to retire and have some fun when I hit certain financial goals. I'm closing in on my goals, so the time may be right within the next year.''

That raised a few eyebrows around the table. Andie's grandfather had never retired, had died at his desk at Summerhill and Summerhill at the age of ninety-four. That nose-to-the-grindstone ethic was pretty much carved onto the family crest. Work was encouraged for its own sake, as well as for the financial security that went along with it. Fun wasn't anywhere on the list of priorities.

"I don't like getting too safe," Jace continued. "Taking risks, taking chances, never sitting still…" He grinned, so confident about his choices that he didn't notice the gasp that came from Andie's mother. "That's what it's all about in my book. What good is the money you pile up if you can't risk it all on one roll of the dice or spend it on a yacht and sail around the world? The McKinley Group has been a great adventure, but it's time for some other kinds of fun.''

"Fun?" Margaret Summerhill's eyes widened. "Celia," she asked in a choked sort of voice, "did you know this?"

"Um, not exactly. Not in so many words, I mean." Celia's eyelids fluttered. "We hadn't really discussed it."

"I'm sure that Jace wouldn't expect Celia to share his philosophy," Andie interjected. Trying to lighten the mood, she added, "Or maybe our sensible Cee will talk him out of it."

What she was really thinking was that Jace Mc-Kinley was a breath of fresh air around this dinner table, and maybe Celia had latched onto something wonderful here. Lucky Celia. For the first time in her life, Andie envied her sister.

But she quickly squelched that feeling. *Go for it, Celia!* She cheered inside. *Rock the casbah!*

"We can talk about Jace's future plans later," Rob hastened to add. If early retirement was not in the family playbook, neither was conflict, so everyone was anxious to drop the subject and move on. Changing the topic with all the subtlety of a jackhammer, Rob asked, "How did the party go this afternoon?"

"It was perfect," Kate enthused, following his lead. "I can't thank you enough, Andie. And you, too, Celia."

"Oh, it was all Andie," Celia demurred.

"You helped," Andie protested.

"No, I didn't. Take the credit, Andie. You deserve it. You worked hard and you put on one terrific party."

"So, Andie," Jason began, staring right at her with that probing gaze. "How did you get to be a party planner when everyone else in the family is in the financial world? How did you come to make the leap into something so different?"

"I—I'm not a party planner," Andie returned quickly.

"Why would you think Andrea is a party planner?" her mother inquired, sounding a little miffed on Andie's behalf. She smiled fondly at her youngest daughter. "Andie is a rising star at Peacock and Sons, the high-end auction house. We expect her to be running the place any day now."

"Mum, let's not go overboard," Andie mumbled. Rising star? Running the place? Hardly.

"Oh, I'm sorry." Jace looked perplexed. "I mean, when I saw the things you were doing for the bridal shower, I just assumed you were a professional."

"No, not really. I like arranging parties, that's all. Just as a hobby." She smiled awkwardly. "Nothing serious."

"But nothing serious is the best kind of job to have," Jace commented.

"You're wonderful at it, Andie," Kate put in. "It's not just the shower. I know you worked hard on the engagement party, too. And every detail of the wedding, really. Andie's stepped in as my unofficial wedding planner and she's doing such an amazing job. Honestly, Rob and I would've been up a creek without Andie calling in connections."

Jace sipped from his wineglass. "Maybe you should think about making it your profession," he suggested. "You're clearly good at it, and it might be fun."

There was that word again, the one that struck terror in her parents' hearts.

"Andie does not need to become a party planner," Margaret Summerhill declared. "Of course she's wonderful at it. She's wonderful at anything she sets her mind to and always has been. But she's much too smart and ambitious to go into a field like that. Aren't you, Andie?''

"Well, I—''

"Of course you are.'' Her mother was quite adamant when she got rolling. "Party planning is, I'm sure, very rewarding for some people. But it's not good enough for our Andrea. I mean, hiring clowns and blowing up balloons? Rescuing brides and cakes and dresses from typhoons and natural disasters and crazy mothers-in-law? As a full-time occupation?'' She managed a laugh. "I don't think so.''

Jace's lips curved into a mischievous smile. He raised his glass toward Andie. "My company hosts a lot of functions, and we have event planners in the hotels. We could use someone like you. So if you decide you do want to look into it as a business venture, let me know. I might be in a position to hire you.'' He winked. "If you catch me before I retire.''

Andie's eyes widened. *He just winked at me.* But that was only the half of it. He really thought she was that good? After seeing her toss some dishes on a few tables and fold some napkins? He wasn't serious about the job offer, was he?

"She's *not* a party planner,'' her mother said again.

Andie took a sip of wine. "I actually was a party planner once,'' she said quietly. She gave Jace a determined smile. "How long was it for, Mum?

Three months?'' All water long under the bridge. "You see, Jace, I decided that college just wasn't my thing. So I dropped out.''

"Andie, you don't need to—'' Mum began, but Andie continued.

"It's all right, Mum. I don't mind if Jace knows about it.'' She widened her smile. "I didn't like whatever it was that I was studying at the time— I think it was pre-law then. It was so dull and so *not* me—so a friend and I dropped out and launched our own business. We used up all our money in about three months and planned exactly one party. We weren't very good at it,'' she confided. "In fact, we were awful.''

"But, Andie, you shouldn't have dropped out of school,'' her father said sensibly. "And you certainly shouldn't have started a business without thinking it through more clearly. Ninety percent of new businesses fail within the first year. You were, what, nineteen? No shame in that. It's behind you.''

"But you're older and wiser now,'' Jace offered. "Just because it didn't work then doesn't mean it wouldn't work now.''

"Andie, it's not a steady or reliable career,'' her mother insisted. "Too risky for you. I think you need something you can count on, with a paycheck every two weeks.''

"Absolutely right,'' her father declared, but Andie could see that Jace McKinley did not agree. His chocolate-brown eyes told her that quite clearly. *Taking risks, taking chances, never sitting still...* It was right there in his eyes.

But was event planning something she could think about doing again? Planning fund-raisers and soirees and weddings and bar mitzvahs, every day a new party... It sounded wonderful. Of course, it involved a lot of details, too, and a lot of sensible financial planning and contracts and taxes and billing and all the other things she'd screwed up the first time.

As her educational career had skipped over economics, art history, law, and accounting, as her professional life had tripped through banking, tax planning and the auction house, as she had gone from one thing to the next, looking for the right fit, she had studiously avoided considering event planning as a career again. It had hurt too much to fail the first time.

She glanced up at Jace. *Just because it didn't work then doesn't mean it wouldn't work now.* He'd tossed the comment into the conversation as if it were nothing. Did he know that his words had made such an impact on her? She had a feeling her mother knew. Of course, her mother also knew that Andie was reckless and impetuous. It would be just like her to latch onto his crazy idea and leap before she looked. Andie gazed down at her plate. Was it a crazy idea, just more of the patented impractical, impulsive Andie Summerhill repertoire? Or was it something more? Was she really different now?

After those two small contretemps, both involving Jason McKinley and the issue of work, the dinner proceeded smoothly, with everyone on their best behavior. Rob and Kate were swoony and in love, Mr. and Mrs. Summerhill went back to being the proud parents, Celia was as polished and serene as ever, judiciously offering a word here and there, and Jace... Well, he was Jace. He didn't say anything, didn't do anything, just sat there, dark and edgy. He smiled, he responded pleasantly, but he was different from the members of the Summerhill family, nonetheless. Night and day.

Andie gazed around the table. She had a deep and abiding love for her parents and her siblings, even her new sister-in-law-to-be. But she had never noticed until now that they all had similar coloring: light-brown hair and hazel eyes. Andie was the only redhead in the family, the only one with eyes more green than hazel. Why had she never noticed she stood out like a sore thumb?

And it wasn't just their physical features that were so alike. They all dressed in conservative, carefully chosen clothing, all ate with the right forks, no elbows on the table. They didn't raise their voices, never, ever made a mess... In fact, she thought, as the dessert was served, they might as well have been the crème brûlée family. Not that there was anything wrong with crème brûlée. She liked crème brûlée a lot. But still...

Her gaze was drawn to Jace. Was it her fault she was intrigued by Jace McKinley, the flaming cherries jubilee thrown onto the dessert cart?

Or maybe he was more like carrot cake. A little nutty, but rich and yummy. Or a hot fudge sundae, hot and cold at the same time, ever so much fun to eat, with a new sensation in every spoonful. Or...

"Andie?"

She jumped. "Yes, Mum. What is it?"

"If you're finished torturing that crème brûlée," she said with a smile, "I have some questions about the arrangements for the party. Do you mind coming with me to the ballroom?"

"No, of course not." She hastily dropped her spoon and her napkin and pushed away from the dinner table, following her mother, who was already out in the hall.

Why was Mum rushing like that? They had plenty of time. Was there some disaster with the party arrangements Andie wasn't aware of?

The minute she was inside the door of the ballroom, her mother whirled around. "So," she said pointedly. "What do you think of him?"

Andie felt a rush of heat to her cheeks. Was it that obvious she was fixated on him? "Jace, you mean?"

"Of course." Her mother frowned. "I don't know what to think, Andie. I'm the one who pushed Celia into finding someone, and now she has, and..." She shook her head. "I don't like him. At all."

"You don't? I—I do."

"You do?" She shook her head more vigorously. "He has a lot of charm, I'll give him that. And he does all right."

In mother-speak, that meant he had tons of money. Mum must have checked to make sure the minute she'd heard his name. Andie hid a small smile.

"And he's handsome," her mother went on. "Maybe too handsome."

"Good looks are a problem?"

"No, but…" Her mother broke off, looking quite upset for her. Margaret Summerhill was a very even-tempered woman, but the situation was obviously distressing her. "I want Celia to be happy, but I'm not sure he's the right man for her. He strikes me as arrogant. Cocky. Rash. That might be okay for someone else, but they're not the qualities I want in a man for Celia."

"All that bit about risk-taking and retiring and having fun, you mean?" Andie asked, her heart sinking. All the qualities she thought made him exciting and unique were the very things her mother disliked. "I wouldn't worry, Mum. I don't get the idea they're that serious, do you?"

"I don't know."

Andie had the definite impression that Celia and Jace didn't even like each other that much, considering how cool and distant they seemed around each other. She'd noticed it before the tea and again at dinner. No wistful glances or affectionate touches. No…anything. Or maybe that was just wishful thinking on her part. To her mother, she said, "I agree that he may not seem like the most logical choice for Cee, but it's up to her, don't you think?"

"I suppose." Her mother took her hand. "Keep an eye on him, will you?"

"What kind of eye?"

"Well, you know. This weekend. I just have this funny feeling that..." She glanced over Andie's shoulder at the catering personnel, who were clanking bottles as they set up the bars. Bending her head closer, she murmured, "I get the feeling that there is something Celia isn't telling us."

Andie had that exact same feeling. "Mum, enjoy the party. Rob and Kate are engaged, and that's what you should be focused on. Try to have..." She stopped herself before she said the f-word. *Fun.* "Try to have a good time, okay?"

"Of course." Her mother kissed her on the cheek. "And thank you again for making it all come off so beautifully."

"You're very welcome." Andie disengaged herself, ready to run upstairs and freshen up before the party started.

"Andie?"

She turned back. "What, Mum?"

"I'm sorry to be so unpleasant about Celia's boyfriend," she said quickly. "It's just that she's not as assured and confident as you are when it comes to men, and I feel more of a need to watch out for her." Margaret Summerhill shook her head again. "I just know in my heart Jason McKinley isn't the right man for Celia."

Andie had a funny feeling in the pit of her stomach. If she was honest with herself, she was pretty sure he wasn't the right man for Celia, either.

But what about for *her?*

CHAPTER FOUR

Almost midnight

"ANDIE, it's a great party—congrats to Rob and Kate." Stan Felding, a business associate of Andie's parents', had waylaid her as she wended her way through the candlelit ballroom.

"Thanks so much, Stan. Thanks for coming."

Earlier Andie had been tired, but the music and the company were giving her a boost. She was totally a people person, and seeing so many happy faces was really cheering her up. Joy, romance, all that good stuff. Andie hadn't been without a smile the entire evening.

She nabbed another glass of champagne from a passing tray, content that the food and drink and entertainment were flowing smoothly and didn't require anything from her. She needed to make a note that the caterers were excellent, and she should use them again if she got a chance.

Except, of course, the odds of her needing another caterer anytime soon were not that great. Once the wedding was over, she would go back to being Andrea Summerhill, lowly associate at the auction house of Peacock and Sons, who could be counted on in a pinch to step up and help rescue the canapés at the odd cocktail party, but was not in any official way associated with event planning. No choosing of the theme or the menu. No finding the clown or blowing up the balloons. That gloomy thought almost affected her mood, but she wouldn't let it.

Too bad none of her crowd was here. The party guests were mostly pals of Rob and Kate, of course, with a generous helping of her parents' friends. Not people Andie knew that well. Rob and Kate were busy tonight, being in love and trying to keep up with their social obligations as the guests of honor while Celia and her date…

Andie took a generous gulp of champagne. Yeah, right. The last thing she wanted to do was hang around and be a third wheel with Celia and her sexy boyfriend. Or not-boyfriend. Whatever Jace was, he was with Celia. She scanned the shadowy ballroom, looking for them. Were they dancing cheek-to-cheek, proving once and for all that they were a couple? Or were they enjoying a private moment in a corner somewhere?

Maybe Celia was off trying to convince him to give up his reckless and risky retirement plans. She probably hoped she could turn him into the man of her dreams, the one with the good looks and the money but a more practical approach to life.

And wouldn't that be a shame?

"Hey, wait a minute…" Andie blinked. Was that Celia?

Andie would've recognized her sister's sleek honey-brown bob and elegant carriage anywhere. Just as she'd imagined, Celia *was* tucked into a corner and she *was* enjoying a private conversation. In fact, she was talking with a great deal of animation, more animation than Andie had seen from her so far this weekend. But it wasn't Jace she was talking to. It was another man, someone Andie recognized as one of Kate's colleagues. A tax accountant, she recalled.

Andie peered at them. Yes, that was definitely Celia and definitely the accountant she remembered from Kate's guest list. Where was Celia's date of record while she was chatting away the night with some other guy? Should Andie say something to her sister? This was incredibly unlike Celia. No one ever had to tell Celia to mind her manners. So what the heck was going on?

It was none of her business, Andie decided after a moment. Besides, they were just talking. Nothing more.

"Maybe they broke up over that whole retirement thing," Andie mused as she traded her empty champagne flute for a full one.

"Did you say something, miss?" the waiter asked.

"No, no, I didn't." She put on her prettiest smile. This was a party, darn it. And she loved parties! She wasn't going to let anything or anyone dim her pleasure tonight. So what if she didn't have a date? She was wearing a beautiful dress— a simple black halter that was both classy and daring; she had arranged yet another smashing party; she was footloose and fancy-free; her feet didn't hurt even though her shoes were spectacular; and she loved the way her hair felt, floating around her shoulders. She also loved the way Jace had looked in his tuxedo when she'd seen him enter the ballroom with Celia. That had been hours ago, and yet the vision of him in stark black and white was burned into her brain.

Uh-oh. Bad thing to think about.

"There's still a lot on my list of good things," she told herself sternly, avoiding the sizzling mental image of Jace in the tuxedo. So what if Celia had two guys and she had none? So what if she was starting to think she wanted to be a party planner and her mother was going to hate it? So what if Mum despised Jace, while Andie thought he just might be one of the Seven Wonders of the World?

She took another sip of champagne, feeling tension begin to creep in around the edges of her good spirits. Not wanting to be a downer in the effervescent atmosphere of the ballroom, Andie decided to sneak out onto the terrace for just a second, to get some fresh air to fortify her for the rest of the night.

As she pushed open the French doors, she took a whiff of the cool night air and smiled up into the starry sky. Moonlight. Stars. Who could be grumpy in this kind of setting? Life was out there, just waiting to be lived. And tonight, it was sparkling.

"Andie?"

She spun around. She hadn't noticed him hiding in the shadows at the end of the terrace. "Jace? What are you doing out here?"

"Nothing." Hands in his pockets, he strode closer. "How about you?"

The moonlight above and the diffused light streaming through the glass doors from inside cast his features in stark relief. It looked as if you could cut glass on those cheekbones, on that hard jawline and straight, aquiline nose. Andie caught her breath. What in the world was Celia doing inside, chatting up some mild-mannered accountant, when Jace was out here?

"I, uh…" *I was thinking about you and it bummed me out, so…* "I needed some air," she said.

"Yeah, me, too." He turned away, resting his hands on the stone railing around the edge of the terrace, gazing out at the trees and the rolling lawn between the main house and the carriage house.

Andie knew it was foolish, but she came up right beside him, anyway. "Nice night, isn't it?"

"Beautiful." He moved aside enough to accommodate her. And then he edged around, glancing down at her beneath heavy-lidded eyes. His voice was low and a little rough when he whispered, "Not as beautiful as you are."

He spoke so softly Andie wasn't sure she'd

heard him right. But his dark eyes were alight with the same message, and she knew she had to believe it. She shivered. *He really thinks I'm beautiful?*

"Andie, I'm sorry," he continued in that same uneven, husky voice that wrapped around her and made her feel all warm and tingly. "I didn't mean for this to happen. But I'm feeling attracted to you, and I need to know if you feel the same way."

"Me?" Guilt warred with desire. All he had to do was look at her, melting into a puddle, and he would know his answer. But she avoided the issue as best she could. "I can't imagine there is any woman in this universe who doesn't find you attractive," she said breathlessly.

"That's not what I asked." He leaned in even closer, grazing a finger under her chin, tipping it up. It was one of the most sensual things she'd ever felt, that one finger, brushing her skin, bridging the gap between the two of them, and she held herself very still. "It's weird, because from the first moment I saw you, I was just…fascinated."

"Me, too," she murmured.

"I didn't expect to meet someone like you." He had his whole hand along the side of her face now, cupping her cheek, and it was so sweet, so tender, she couldn't quite break away. She found herself reaching up a finger to trace the intriguing dimple in his chin. Why was she so fascinated with that small cleft?

"When Celia asked me for the weekend," Jace went on, "I thought, sure, why not? Innocuous enough. I never expected anyone in her family to be like you. But there you were in that sunroom, barefoot, wearing shorts with a big streak of dust on your bottom, and for some reason—"

"I had dust on my butt?" She backed away from his hand. Not exactly a romantic image. Especially when he had just mentioned Celia, and they both knew that connection was standing between them like a brick wall.

"That's what I mean. With your butterfly napkins and the way you wrinkled your forehead with concentration while you rearranged those damn plates ten times—"

"Twice," she corrected.

"Twice." He was smiling now, and the flash of white teeth and gorgeous lips took her breath away. He took both her hands in his to pull her closer again. "The point is, I thought you were adorable. Fresh, funny, smart… And really good at the party thing."

Although she might be a romantic at heart, Andie had a healthy cynical streak to balance all that romanticism, and it kicked in now. Jace's date was inside, not paying him any attention, so he was out here with her. Yeah, she could add two and two. Andie drew her hands away. "You can't tell from one bridal shower how good I am. Do you know how many women in this world throw nifty showers? A lot of us. You're just trying to flatter me so I'll fall under your spell or whatever. Easy pickup. That's it, isn't it?"

He arched a dark eyebrow. "You think I figure you're an easy pickup? Aren't you kind of rushing things? I haven't even kissed you yet."

"I'm not stupid, Jace."

"Yes, you are, if you think I'm trying to seduce you with phony compliments just to get a one-nighter out of you." He sounded angry. "I wouldn't do that. I don't play those games."

"Could've fooled me," she returned. "Out here in the moonlight, telling me I'm beautiful—"

"You *are* beautiful. You have to know that," he scoffed. "Anyone who looks like you knows that she's beautiful. Especially in that dress."

Well, she thought she was okay, and it was a nice dress, but... She hazarded a glance back at him. He looked sincere, radiating all that heat and longing her way. Okay, so maybe he meant that part about her being beautiful. But the rest of it? Ha. "Jace, you barely know me. Yet you tossed out that job offer like it was the real thing."

"It *was* the real thing. Try me. Come work for me. Take a risk. It'd be good for you."

She hated people telling her what was good for her. Besides, for her whole life, everyone she trusted had told her that safe and steady was good, while rash and impetuous was wrong. And her hasty experiment as a college drop-out had proved them right. Why should she leap back to the other side now? She shook her head. "I'm untried, unproven," she argued. "What would the experienced event planners you already have on the payroll think of that?''

''I happen to be very good at what I do. And one part of that is assembling the best teams, no matter what the assignment.'' He rammed his hands in his pockets. ''I recognize talent. You may not believe me, but it's gotten me where I am today. As I said, it's a risk. So what? I believe in risks. Like...''

Like what? She narrowed her eyes at him, trying to read his mind. Unless she was way off the mark, it wasn't hard to figure out what was on his mind right now.

He was staring at her mouth as if the only thing that mattered to him was whether he could kiss her. And she wanted him to kiss her. She wanted it bad.

Andie licked her lip, trying to remember to breathe, to get some air in her lungs. ''Stop looking at me like that—like you're the Big Bad Wolf and I'm the granny.''

''I never thought for one minute you were my granny,'' he whispered, and the flicker of heat and fire intensified in his chocolate-brown eyes. He bent nearer. His lips were only about an inch away from hers, close enough that she could feel the warm puffs of his breath on her mouth. His hands slid over her bare shoulders, and Andie almost expired from the tantalizing feel of his hands on her skin.

''I—I can't do this,'' she managed to say. She was really, really proud of herself for hanging on at a moment like this, when self-control was awfully hard to come by.

He swore under his breath. "Why?"

"I don't trust you." She retreated a few more steps, safely out of range of his hands and his lips. "You're a guest of my family, you're a guest of my sister, and yet you're coming on to me. That's just wrong."

"Andie, there's nothing between me and Celia. You know that."

"I'm not sure I do," she countered. "And what about Celia?"

"I don't know." He ran a hasty hand through his short, sleek hair, rumpling it a little, marring his perfect appearance. Good. It was nice to see he could be rumpled, too.

"Why don't you get back to me when you're sure?" The skirt of her black halter dress swirled as she turned away from him.

"Andie!" he called out.

But she had no intention of letting him reel her back in with his hypnotic voice. Without looking back, Andie made a beeline for the safety of the ballroom.

JACE STAYED where he was for a few minutes, wondering how he had let things get so screwed up. He'd accepted an invitation for a simple weekend in the country, and suddenly he was knee-deep in women and champagne and moonlight and romance.

"How did I get to be here?" he asked out loud. It wasn't bad enough that he'd misunderstood the invitation. He'd seen it as a simple offer from a business acquaintance—Celia wasn't even close enough to be a friend—that would give him a chance to get out of the city on an otherwise empty weekend. Yes, walking into the Summerhill home and discovering immediately that the family thought he was Celia's new boyfriend was awkward, but only the tip of the big fat awkwardness iceberg. He hadn't said anything to anyone about the fact that he barely knew Celia, all the while she was presenting him as something akin to a boyfriend. He didn't want to be rude enough to out her little lie, but he sure felt like it.

Her family clearly disapproved of him, but he really didn't care; he wasn't romantically involved with Celia, after all.

But he might start to care, because he was definitely interested in Andie. She was the most maddening woman he had ever met, but her body kept sending messages to his body that just wouldn't quit. He wanted her. He wanted her with every breath he took.

It was absurd. And yet it was what it was.

And since she believed he was Celia's boyfriend, she wouldn't come near him. Not that he blamed her. In fact, he admired her loyalty. The weird thing was, he didn't think Celia was any more interested in him than he was in her. Sure, she was smart and pleasant and even pretty, but there was no spark between them and never had been. Which was probably why it hadn't occurred to him to think she might intend for him to be her *date* date for the engagement party. "So what did you think, Einstein?" he asked himself.

He considered that one for a second.

"I *didn't* think." And that was the problem.

Well, it was time to start thinking now. He was a man who went after what he wanted, come hell or high water, and he wasn't prepared to give up on Andie Summerhill over some silly misunderstanding. Not without a fight.

Pushing away from the stone railing, Jace stalked into the ballroom. The musicians had left, and the waiters were pouring the last of the champagne and clearing away the silver trays of hors d'oeuvres. The bars set up in the corners were now unmanned. It seemed as if Andie's party was winding down. So where was Andie? She hadn't left, had she?

Since her dress, like those of most of the other women in the room, was black, he didn't see her at first glance. But Celia... Her dress was a creamy beige that stood out in the darkened ballroom. Jace spotted her sitting in front of one of the bars. Now that he looked closer, he could see that Andie was with her, tipping her beautiful fiery red head toward her sister.

"Aw, Andie..."

He loved the way her hair spilled over her shoulders, the way the black halter dress cupped her

breasts and swirled around her hips. He'd already
been intrigued by her when he saw her in shorts
and a T-shirt, her hair scooped up into a sloppy
ponytail. But in the halter dress, with no other jewelry but a diamond bracelet around her wrist, her
glorious red hair tumbling over her bare white
shoulders… His mouth went dry just looking at
her.

"And she thinks she's not beautiful." It was
laughable.

Right now, the sisters had their heads together,
talking intently about something, and they didn't
notice him as he circled around behind the bar,
sliding along the wall, shamelessly eavesdropping.
A handy potted palm gave him plenty of cover. He
knew it was kind of conniving to hover in a dark
corner behind a palm tree, but he didn't care.

All's fair in love and war, he thought. If they
were talking about him, he had every right in the
world to know what was being said.

CHAPTER FIVE

After midnight

"CEE, I CAN'T BELIEVE you lied to me," he heard Andie murmur. "And to him."

"I didn't lie, exactly."

"Yes," Andie said more distinctly. "You did. You looked me right in the face and told me he had possibilities, that he was your date for the weekend. But now you've admitted there's nothing at all between you—there never was, and you never intended that there would be. I mean, this isn't even a try-out, let alone a real date. Plus, you've admitted you didn't tell him what he was walking into. The poor thing."

"But—"

"No buts," Andie responded tersely. "And now we're all in a mess. It's so not like you to be hitting on other guys while your date is out of the room. I can't even believe you did that. What's happened to you all of a sudden? And what would you have done if Mum had caught you?"

"She didn't. And I wasn't hitting on David,"

Celia insisted. "How was I supposed to know that I would meet someone I really liked at the exact wrong time? I could hardly pass up the chance to talk to him."

Andie murmured something Jace couldn't catch.

"I was only trying to make Mum happy," Celia said in a defensive tone. "Was that so much to ask? On paper, Jason seemed like the perfect choice. He's obviously presentable—"

"Presentable?" Andie repeated with a laugh. "That's the understatement of the century. The man is gorgeous. Drool-in-your-breakfast-cereal, trip-over-your-shoelaces gorgeous."

Behind the bar, Jace grinned. That was what he called a positive endorsement.

"Well, he's too good-looking, if you ask me," Celia argued.

"Mum said the same thing and I just don't understand it. How can he be too good-looking?"

Yeah, Jace thought to himself. *You go, Andie!*

"When someone's that good-looking, you have to wonder if he's trustworthy." Celia's voice was so matter-of-fact, Jace was wounded. Why did everybody in this family think he was untrustworthy?

"That's ridiculous," Andie scoffed. "You said yourself you pretty much duped him into coming here this weekend. He had all kinds of chances to tell me or Mum or anyone else that he doesn't even know you that well. He could've jumped up at the first sign of disapproval and told us to bug off. But he didn't. I mean, what a great guy! Did he rat you out? Did he leave in a huff once he figured out that you were using him to keep Mum happy?''

"I'm not altogether clear he knows that,'' Celia said delicately.

Oh, yes, he does, Jace thought to himself.

"I still say he has integrity.'' Andie's voice rose a little, and she sounded as if she was on a roll. "Not only that, but he's polite. And nice. I mean, you dumped him on me and he didn't complain. And I made him try to fold napkins and he actually tried, even though he was hopeless. What guy lets himself look ridiculous without telling you to jump off a cliff?''

"But, Andie, I just don't think he has, well, enough gravitas.''

"*Gravitas?* If by that you mean he's not boring, then I agree.'' Andie sat up straighter. "He's smart and funny and…''

Jace was enjoying this. He couldn't wait to see what compliment Andie came up with next.

"And caring,'' she finished smartly. "Did you notice how he stood up for me with the party-planning thing, because he thinks I might like it, even though Mum thinks it's stupid? He's amazing. That's all there is to it.''

"Okay, okay, I'm convinced,'' Celia muttered. "He's a great guy, all right?''

Andie's voice dropped. "I'm sorry, Cee. I don't know why I'm pushing this so hard. It's not like I want you to want him.''

Why don't you just admit that you're the one who wants me? Jace wanted to shout.

"It hardly matters." Celia stood up, and Jace ducked even lower. "He'll be leaving tomorrow after brunch. So let's just get through the rest of the weekend in one piece, all right?"

"But..."

"But what?"

"But don't you want to tell Mum and Dad that he isn't really with you, in the sense of, you know, *with* you?"

"Andie, Mum would never forgive me for lying to her. I let her think he was a real prospect. She was pushing me so hard to bring someone home, and I told her this one might be serious. I actually told her that!" Celia's voice took on a panicky edge. "Promise me you won't tell her I lied."

"Cee, this is so unlike you. You're never in trouble. You never lie. I just don't know what to think."

"It's easier for you, Andie. For whatever reason, Mum decided she couldn't push you around a long time ago, and she gave up trying. But with me... Things are different. I don't want to disappoint her," she murmured. "Just this one weekend. A little white lie for one weekend isn't so much to ask, is it?"

Tell her no, Andie, he ordered silently. *Tell her you have a stake in this and you want her to come across with the truth and put it all out in the open.*

But she grumbled, "Okay, just for this weekend. But no longer than that."

"You're a doll, Andie." Celia bent to kiss her sister. "Just the weekend, and then he and I will drive back into the city, and I'll apologize to him on the way. I swear. And next week or something, I'll call and tell Mum that it just didn't work out, and everyone will be happy."

"Cee, you know Mum and Dad will still love you, even if you never find the perfect man. Mum just wants you to be happy, and you want her to be happy, and you've both made a real hash of this." Andie let out a long sigh. "Which just goes to show we should tell Mum the truth next time. Even if she doesn't like it to start out with, it'll still be better in the long run."

He had the feeling she wasn't talking only about Celia's faux love life now, but her own choices as well. He knew he was right about that party-planning thing. He knew it.

As the sisters left the ballroom, still murmuring together, Jace lingered behind, musing over what he'd just heard.

Andie might have agreed to keep the secret for the rest of the weekend, but he hadn't. He smiled. Now that he knew how she felt about him, he had no compunctions about going after what *he* wanted. And that was Andie Summerhill.

ANDIE SLIPPED OUT of her dress, letting the black silk pool on the floor. She was too tired to hang it up now. "In the morning," she mumbled.

Wearing nothing but her bikini panties and her fabulous high heels, she stumbled over to the bed. She knew she had to rouse herself at least enough to take off the shoes, but she was exhausted. Two parties, one dinner, a lot of smiling, and a boatload of emotional turmoil...

Yeah, well, there were times when you just had to do what you had to do. Andie sat down and took off the shoes.

She managed to scrounge up pajamas with fluffy white sheep all over them. Well, the top, anyway. But it was still soothing. And then she crawled into bed, determined to stay there for a good long time. If she slept in, Jace and Celia might be gone by the time she got up and she wouldn't have to see him at all. That would be a relief.

"Maybe I can call him sometime, after Cee tells Mum she's not seeing him anymore," she whispered, her words muffled by her pillow. Maybe if they let this whole thing die down for a few weeks, her mother wouldn't care if Andie asked him out. Or maybe he would ask her out. Maybe he would call or drop by and they could sort everything out like rational adults.

She frowned, flipping over onto her back and staring at the ceiling. But her mother *would* care. Mum didn't like him.

Andie punched her pillow. "How can they not like him?" she said out loud. "I love him. I mean, I don't *love* love him. But maybe I could if I got to go out with him.'' She smiled into her shadowy bedroom. "He thought I was beautiful.''

And she thought he was one fine specimen himself. She loved that dimple in his chin, and the way his deep-brown eyes were lit from within. And the way his jaw could look so sharp and hard one minute, but soft and touchable the next. Touchable…

This time she groaned, pulling the pillow over her head. The thought of touching him reminded her of the moonlight on the terrace and how hot his gaze had been, how much she'd been hoping in some guilty little corner of her heart that he would just cover her mouth with his and kiss her till she melted into a puddle of desire.

All she could think about now was that Jace McKinley and his bedroom eyes were alone somewhere in the house at this very moment, that things could have been quite different if only she hadn't run away from him on the terrace.

"No, no and no,'' she told herself fiercely, sitting up in bed. She'd thought he was with Celia, even if Celia was hiding inside with that other guy, David the accountant. But Andie had been loyal. No way would she be hitting on Jace when she thought he was involved with her sister.

But he wasn't involved with Celia, was he? Not by any stretch of the imagination. It didn't help, though, since Andie had come right out and insulted him on the trust issue, accused him of lying to her about his assessment of her professional abilities, and then suggested he was trying to seduce her for a quick one-nighter.

Not exactly destined to make him feel all warm and toasty.

She slumped back into the bed, trying to get herself into a comfy position. But all she did was toss and turn and then toss and turn again. Her bed was usually so comfortable she went straight to Dreamland. But not tonight. As she lay there, kicking around her sheets, rearranging the pillows, she felt the pangs of a headache, probably from too much champagne. But could she blame the after-effects of champagne for making her feel all tingly from head to foot? For making her skin ache so that even her loose pajama top felt too tight and confining?

Knowing Jace was in the house, she couldn't sit still. Her body was trembling with the need to be touched. And it was making her miserable.

First she tried opening the window, hoping for a breeze. No such luck. The air outside felt sticky and humid.

She flapped her pajama top up and down, but that was no help. Finally, she shut the window.

Sliding to the floor, Andie sat under the window for several moments. She was so tired and yet she knew she wouldn't be able to sleep. Not now.

She needed something cool, something soothing. She needed ice cream. But ice cream was downstairs in the kitchen and she was up here, wearing only a pajama top and a pair of bikini underwear.

The chances that she would run into another family member while taking a midnight stroll down to the kitchen were pretty slim. This was a conservative household where people just didn't make nocturnal ice-cream runs. Except for her.

Better to be safe than sorry, however, especially with someone like Jace on the loose. "Oh, please," she said out loud. That was ridiculous. Her mother had probably stuck him in the outer reaches of the guest wing, and he wouldn't be able to find his way to the front door without a guide dog.

Andie stood up and walked into the closet. It took her several minutes of rooting around, but finally she found a robe. It was a deep, garnet-red silk that didn't go with the fluffy cotton sheep on her pajama top, but she didn't care. The robe covered her up enough to get her downstairs to the kitchen without incident, even if she should happen to trip over, oh, Rob or Kate or Aunt Linda, who were all staying overnight.

She didn't wait to find slippers, but padded barefoot out into the dark hall. No one there. Of course not. Everyone else had fallen asleep hours ago, just as she'd assumed.

Cautiously she crept to the main stairs. She was peering into the shadows, ready to take that first step, when she felt a hand on her shoulder.

Whirling around, she grabbed on to the railing, her heart pounding. A dark, tall shape loomed before her. But when she inhaled, she knew that scent immediately. A clean male scent with just a hint of sweat and night air. She sagged with relief. "Jace, you scared me."

"I need to talk to you," he said in an urgent undertone.

"And you expected to run into me in the middle of the night on the stairs to have this conversation?" she demanded, trying to get rid of the raspy squeak that took away the punch in her words.

She was trying to sound indignant and cranky, but it wasn't easy when it was so late and she was so tired, and he looked so yummy, standing there barefoot, wearing a pair of faded jeans and a black T-shirt. She hadn't seen Jace in jeans before. It was a sight, all right. She hoped it was dim enough that he couldn't see her lick her lips.

"I had a feeling you wouldn't be able to sleep any more than I could," he said darkly.

"So you waited around at the top of the stairs till I showed up?"

"Not exactly."

She waved a hand, not ready to hear the whole explanation. "It doesn't matter. I was on my way down to get some ice cream in the kitchen. Do you want to come with me? We can talk there."

"No," he said roughly. And then he reached for her. She had started to move past him, but he caught her hand and reeled her in.

This time she didn't have a chance to resist. His lips slanted across hers, his mouth devoured her, and all she could do to stay upright was tangle her arms around him and hold on tight.

His hands framed her face, and he nibbled her bottom lip, kissing her soft and slow, then taking it deeper, hotter, and she heard herself moan into his mouth. He tasted like wine and moonlight, like heady desire and intoxicating secrets. In the middle of the night, everything seemed more tempting and provocative. Forbidden.

The kiss was absolutely luscious. Crème brûlée, cherries jubilee, carrot cake, hot fudge sundae… Way better than any of that.

She couldn't get enough of him. His mouth and his tongue were so warm and delicious, and she pressed into him with every ounce of longing she'd been holding back. Tiny shivers shimmied through her veins, making her dizzy with desire. It was all she could do not to rip off his clothes and jump him right there in the hall. The hall! Oh, heavens.

He was breathing hard when he broke away. So was she. She welcomed the respite, hoping to get some oxygen to her brain so she could think again. But she felt bereft, too. She wanted to start all over again. She touched her tongue to her tender lip. Oh, man, he tasted good. And she was hungry again.

Jace said softly, "I really did plan to talk, not get sidetracked this way. But I'm not sorry I did."

"Me, either." Her legs felt shaky, and she had the absurd desire just to sit down on the hard wood in the upstairs hall. Luckily, Jace's strong embrace kept her steady and on her feet. "Jace, we're in the hall," she whispered. "We can't stay out here. Someone could come by and see us."

"Where's your room?" he asked quickly.

That was such a bad idea. Her hot room with Jace in it? Uh, no.

"Where's yours? And what are you doing in this hall, anyway? Aren't you staying in the guest wing?" She was growing more confused by the minute. Was she so tired that she had imagined this whole thing? Had she really just fallen into Jace on the stairs and started kissing him like there was no tomorrow?

His tongue. His lips. That hadn't been a fantasy. She could still feel the reverberations of his kiss all the way down to her core.

"Your mother put me in this wing, next to Celia. Pushing for romance, I guess," he noted grimly.

"Celia," Andie repeated. "Oh, dear."

"Andie, you have to know that there is not now, and never has been, anything romantic between me and Celia," he vowed. He kept his hands on her face, forcing her to look at him and focus on his words. "That was one of the things I wanted to talk to you about, to make it perfectly clear. Celia is a business colleague. She invited me here for the weekend, never saying it was as her date."

"I know, Jace. I'm sorry." She rested her hands flat on his soft black T-shirt. "Celia got caught up in this insane plot to make my mother happy and keep her off her back for a while. Mum's been checking the portfolios of every eligible man from Wisconsin to Indiana, trying to find someone for my sister, and I guess Cee decided to make a counter-move. It's really weird, because it's so unlike her to..." She stopped, twisting her head. "Did you hear something? Is someone coming?"

But there was only silence.

"Let's get out of the hall," he told her, leaning down to kiss her again, quick and sweet.

"All right." Taking him by the hand, she led him back to her room. She still thought it was a terrible idea, but where else could they go? "But only to talk," she said severely.

"Uh-huh."

He didn't sound convincing.

Once inside the door, it took him about a second to gather her into his arms, swoop down on her mouth, and navigate them both toward the bed. They fell backward into the fluffy, heaped-up pillows and bedclothes with a whoosh.

Andie's eyes widened. Was Jace McKinley really in her bed?

CHAPTER SIX

Early hours of morning

"WE SHOULDN'T be doing this," she mumbled. But his mouth was on hers again, his hands were roaming over the curve of her bottom inside her silk robe, and she couldn't form a coherent thought. Not with so many different sensations of intense pleasure flooding her brain.

Somehow her robe opened, her pajama top and his T-shirt became scrunched up until their bellies were skin to skin. It didn't take much for him to slip his hand up, capturing her breast in one smooth motion. He tweaked her nipple ever so slightly before cupping her again, making her moan. Had she ever felt on fire? She sighed into his mouth, sliding her own fingers to trace his hard ribs and flat stomach, to dance around the waist of his jeans.

He sucked in his breath, but he didn't stop her. Andie's eager hand grazed the hard ridge in his jeans. She couldn't believe how greedy she felt for all of him when she knew he was a luxury she absolutely shouldn't have.

"Jace, we shouldn't be—" she tried again.

"Shh," he murmured, brushing kisses over her cheeks and her ear, pressing his lips to the pulse on the slope of her neck.

He'd managed to peel off her robe by now, and there she was, under his long, lean body, wearing nothing but a pair of skimpy black bikini pants and a short pajama top scattered with fluffy sheep, unbuttoned all the way down the front.

As Jace gazed down at her, his eyes so dark they were practically black, every part of her felt hot and moist. She was glazed with sweat. And then his hands and mouth seemed to be everywhere, rocketing her higher at the speed of light. If she didn't stop this soon, they would be tangled in her sheets with nothing but skin between them. But Andie was so turned on, she thought she might die if she even paused, let alone stopped. She wanted him. She wanted all of him.

So why in hell did some stupid little voice keep whining at her that this was wrong?

You're insane. Go for it! "I can't." She pulled the two sides of her top together. "Jace," she said, attempting to steady her voice and failing miserably, "I thought we were going to talk."

He pulled back immediately. "What? You seriously would rather...?" With a muttered oath, he rolled away and groaned, covering his face with his hands. "What is it, Andie? Do you expect me to believe you don't want this as much as I do?"

"No, of course not. I do want it." She crawled over closer. "It's just... I'm sorry, Jace, but this is my parents' house. I've never brought a man here. Never."

"You're kidding."

"No. I mean, I haven't been here that long. Well, sort of in and out..." Why was she talking about this now? He didn't need her whole résumé. "Okay, long story short—I've had a lot of jobs in the past couple of years. I've been a big, fat failure, okay? I didn't have any money and the economy was awful and...I moved back home last year. I hate it, but there it is."

"Do you really think your parents expect you to be celibate under their roof?" he asked, looking utterly confused.

"No, but... Well, yes, actually, I think they do. And it feels creepy to be making love under their roof when they still think you're dating my sister."

"But I told you—"

"Yes, I know. And Cee told me, too. But still..." She buttoned her pajama jacket quickly, looking around for something else to put on. She still felt awfully naked. "My mother thinks you're with Cee. And she—my mum, I mean—has a habit of barging in and waking me up in the mornings. What would she think if she saw you here?"

He looked bemused. "Have you ever thought of locking your door?"

"That wouldn't work. She'd just knock and keep knocking till I answered." Andie shook her head. "It's their house and I feel like I have to abide by their rules because I'm the misfit who came home and threw myself on their mercy. If they knew... Oh, I can't even think about it."

"Why don't you get an apartment of your own that you can afford?" he asked with a shade more impatience. "I mean, you have a job. You must be able to afford something."

She couldn't believe he'd just said that. "That is really unkind."

"And also true."

"Apartments are expensive!" she shot back, outraged.

"This is ridiculous." Jace rammed a hand through his hair, making it stick up in little spikes. "I get the idea you think you're this rebel, refusing to be in the family biz, playing your party games on the side, but you won't grow up or move out. How much of a rebel are you really?"

"I never said I was a rebel." Of course she had. She joked about it all the time. Not in front of Jace, though.

"Oh, I've got you pegged all right," he said under his breath.

"You think you're so smart. You barely know me. You know nothing about me." She pushed his legs out of her way as she scrambled out of the bed, still searching for her robe.

"Andie, listen to me. It's for your own good that I'm telling you this."

For your own good. Those words always pushed her buttons and made her furious.

"This has nothing to do with sex," he continued in that same infuriating, know-it-all tone. "It has to do with you being afraid to make your own decisions because your mom and dad are watching."

"That's ridiculous. And insulting." She pounced on the robe and started to shove her arms into the sleeves. "I also think it has everything to do with sex. I've turned you down twice now, and the great and powerful Jason McKinley doesn't like being turned down, does he?"

"Now *that* is insulting," he said slowly.

Andie turned around and looked at him. She couldn't help but weaken when she saw his smoky eyes and adorable cleft chin and sweet, soft lips. She shivered again. What kind of crazy woman was she, jumping out of bed when he was in it?

"I'm not denying we have chemistry," she whispered. How could she? "But I don't think that necessarily make us right for each other."

"How do we know that yet?"

Andie was starting to feel really frustrated. And she was not a nice person when she was frustrated. Oh well. At least it afforded her the opportunity to give free rein to her temper, to let herself get all bent out of shape and stop looking at his handsome face and to-die-for chest and those long, strong legs in those pale, worn jeans...

"You are driving me nuts!" she accused. *You and your chin!* "You're pushy and way too sure of yourself. You're like a steamroller or something. You think I should be a party planner, so damn the torpedoes, Andrea Summerhill *will* be a party planner! You think we have this chemistry thing going, so damn the torpedoes, we *will* jump into bed and spontaneously combust!"

"Steamrollers and torpedoes are different things," he interjected coolly.

Okay, now she really wanted to grind him under the heel of one of her fabulous party shoes. "Let me make this plain. I don't appreciate you telling me what to do any more than I appreciate that coming from my parents. At least they've known me my whole life. How do you know I should be an event planner? You don't!"

"We both know that's what you want," Jace returned, deadpan. "You want it almost as much as you want me."

"Baloney!" She didn't stop to consider the ambiguity of that retort. Did it mean she wanted him more? Or that she didn't want either? It was too late and she was too confused to figure that out right now.

But Jace just shook his head. "There is a serious issue on the table here, Andie," he maintained. "I can see who you are, who you really are. You're fresh and funny and exciting. You're dying to take some chances and make your own path. But you're afraid. Well, stop being afraid and grab what you

want. Whether that's me or a job or just moving
out of this palace—do it! So what if you screw up?
At least you'll be alive.''

Once again, he was insulting her, implying that
she wasn't alive at the moment. Yeah, well, she'd
felt her pulse pounding pretty good there for a
while. And so had he. ''You know,'' she said with
a thin smile, ''you really are a lot like the rest of
my family. You are every bit as domineering, and
every bit as goal-oriented. You just have different
goals, that's all.''

''Nothing wrong with a few goals.'' Jace rose
from the bed, striding right past her on his way to
the door.

So he was just going to leave in midargument?
Stung, Andie tossed out, ''I still say this is because
I turned you down. Twice.''

''And in this case, two strikes and you're out.''
He opened the door a crack. ''I'm not hanging
around to let you pick fights with me just to save
your pride. As far as I'm concerned, this is the end
of it. I'm not an idiot and I don't line up to be
knocked down again and again. I usually don't
even give second chances. I sure as hell don't give
thirds.''

''I'm not asking.''

''Yeah, well…'' But he stopped himself. She
could see that she had gotten under his skin, that
he was just as angry as she was, but he hid it better.
Damn him and his self-control. ''You think about

one thing, Andie. What is it that you're so afraid of?''

She really would have thrown her shoes at the door if she hadn't thought it would make a big enough ruckus to wake up half the house.

After he had gone, after she had crawled back into the bed to stare once more at the ceiling, she pondered the question. What was she afraid of?

"Of a whole heck of a lot of things," she whispered into her empty room. And Mr. Steamroller McKinley was at the top of the list.

"ANDIE? Don't tell me you're still in bed." Her mother threw open the curtains, letting sun flood into the bedroom.

Andie groaned and hid under her pillow.

"Andie? Get up. We have something very important to… Ouch!"

That got Andie to lift her head. "What?" she mumbled.

Her mother had a disgusted expression on her face and was brandishing a shoe in her hand. It was Andie's beautiful Manolo Blahnik from last night. "What was this doing in the middle of the floor? I could've fallen over it and broken my leg."

"Or broken my four-hundred-dollar shoe," Andie said grumpily.

"Andie!" Mrs. Summerhill's look of disgust turned to horror. With a rustle of silk, she stooped and picked up the black dress. Now she had a shoe in one hand and Andie's dress in the other. "What in the world is going on?"

Suddenly frantic, Andie sat up, scanning the floor. What if Jace had left one of his shoes behind? Or worse, his pants? What would her mother think about *that?* She didn't see anything, but...

With a sigh of relief, Andie remembered that Jace hadn't been wearing shoes last night, and he'd kept his clothes on. Phew.

"What is wrong with you, Andie?"

"I'm just..." She knew she was in a bad mood because of what had transpired between her and that rotten Jace McKinley last night. That and the fact that she'd had so little sleep. But still, she couldn't hold back the words. "Mum, I love you. You know that. But you shouldn't come blasting into my room without knocking. What if I..." She broke off, trying to patch together her courage. This was not something she and her mother normally discussed. "What if I had brought a man in here last night? And you waltzed right in to wake me up?"

Her mother's eyes widened. "Well, I..." She looked quite befuddled. "I never thought about it. I mean, I don't ask what you do or with whom, but I guess I assume it isn't... Andie, where is this coming from?"

"I don't know." She sank back into her bedclothes, feeling miserable. "I want to sleep in, okay, Mum? I'm going to skip brunch."

"Oh, no, you're not. Rise and shine, Andie. I

don't care about brunch, but you and Celia and I are due for a talk.'' She gave Andie her patented no-nonsense look, the one that made mere mortals quiver in her path. ''An important mother-daughter talk.''

''You and me and Celia?'' Andie inquired, hoping to verify that Jace would not be there.

''Yes, you and me and Celia.''

''No one else?''

Her mother gave her the no-nonsense look again. ''No one else. Now, get out of bed, will you? I'll collect Celia and meet you in the library.''

''All right, all right.'' Andie managed to get herself out of the bed and into the shower, but she was filled with a sense of doom. What was this all about? Why did her mother sound so ominous? And where was Jace this morning?

''Get a grip,'' she told herself firmly as she dressed. She grabbed a sunshine-yellow top and some white capris. Maybe the bright color of the linen shell would improve her outlook. Or blind her. She moved on to makeup. ''Mum doesn't know anything about you and Jace last night,'' she told her reflection. ''If she did, she wouldn't have been so shocked when you fussed about her coming in and finding a man in your bed.''

A man in her bed. Oh, Lord. She almost stuck the eyeliner right in her eye, and she had to set it down while she recovered. A man in her bed... here...at home? What had she been thinking?

Then again, why not?

"Andrea Summerhill, you are twenty-six years old, and if you want a man in your bed, even here, you should be able to have one." All of a sudden, the thought of laying down some rules with her mother, locking her door, or even spending every last dime on finding a place of her own didn't seem so unreasonable. Was it just because she was in a bad mood? Or was Jace right?

For the past year, she'd told herself that living at home was such a good idea. It was so easy, so safe, so comfortable.

"You're twenty-six and living at home again. Maybe that's a little too comfortable," she said out loud. And maybe Jace was partly right. Not totally or completely right—he didn't need to be such a know-it-all about *her* life—but maybe he had a point. Or two.

Andie finished up her makeup with a flourish. Frowning at herself in the mirror, she realized that she had no idea why she was bothering with makeup this morning, anyway. Jace wasn't supposed to be at this confab her mother had set up.

"You never know," she muttered as she slipped down the stairs to the library. "You just never know who you might run into."

Her mother and Celia were already there, and neither one looked happy. With her sleek light-brown bob and a beige linen shift, Celia looked as immaculate and pulled-together as always. She had her arms crossed over her chest and was wearing a grim expression, but she had nothing on their mother's forbidding face.

As usual, it was left to Andie to be the cheerful, chipper, devil-may-care one of the bunch. Although that was not exactly how she was feeling, she assumed the familiar role. Somebody had to. Especially if that somebody was about to be dressed down for engaging in inappropriate activities last night.

I didn't do anything, she argued with herself. Why was she so apprehensive about what her mother wanted to discuss? Mum wasn't psychic. She couldn't know that Andie had felt lust in her heart late last night. Could she?

"Here I am," she announced brightly, tossing herself into a leather wing chair and dangling her legs over the arm. "So, what are we up to this morning?"

"I need your support," her mother declared. "Celia, sit down. Andie and I need to talk to you."

Andie sat up. This was about Celia?

"What did I do?" her sister asked glumly. But she did take a seat in the wing chair opposite Andie.

"It's Jason McKinley, Celia." Mrs. Summerhill paced back and forth between her daughters. "At dinner last night, I started to think that he is not a good choice for you, Celia. Andie agreed with me—"

"No, I didn't," Andrea interrupted quickly.

"In principle, Andie agreed with me that Jason

McKinley was a bad choice for you," her mother continued, brooking no objections. "I'm sorry to have to be the one to tell you, but sometimes, well, the truth has to come out. And if it saves you hurt later, then you need to know now."

"What are you saying?" Celia inquired, looking confused.

"That he's the wrong man." Her mother lifted her chin. "He already left this morning, did you know that? Left a note for me and then just drove away."

So he was gone. Well, that was good news, wasn't it?

"I'm sure if he left, he had good reasons," Celia murmured.

"Still defending him? Oh, Celia, I didn't want to have to tell you this, but I think I'm going to have to. Aunt Linda told me that she saw him last night…" Mrs. Summerhill paused. If Andie hadn't known better, she would've sworn it was for dramatic effect. "…kissing another woman."

Andie's heart stopped beating for a moment. Was it possible that Aunt Linda had been roaming around the house in the wee hours, too, and she'd caught sight of her and Jace at the top of the stairs? Could her luck really be that terrible?

Celia put a hand over her eyes. "Oh, dear."

"I know, sweetie. But it's better you know. Aunt Linda saw him through the French doors at the party. At Rob and Kate's engagement party, can you imagine?" She shook her head. "He and this woman—Linda wasn't close enough to see who it was, but she could tell she was wearing black, so I know it wasn't you, Celia—well, they were all over each other. They were doing this on the terrace, while you were right inside.''

On the terrace? Before she could stop herself, Andie objected, ''But I didn't kiss him on the terrace! I absolutely did not. We were standing close together, just talking, and he told me I was beautiful and I backed off. Aunt Linda is wrong, Mum. I swear!''

Both heads turned. ''It was *you?*'' her mother demanded. ''You were kissing your sister's boyfriend?''

''You and Jason?'' Celia echoed. ''Oh, good grief. I should've known.''

''I told you, I didn't kiss him.'' Andie was overcome with guilt. ''Not then, anyway. Not at the party.''

''Not then? What are you trying to say, that you *did* kiss him later? When? The middle of the night?'' Their mom stopped in her tracks. ''So that's why you were asking me what I would do if there was a man in your room? You had Jason McKinley in your room last night?''

''It doesn't matter, Mum,'' Celia cut in. ''Don't yell at Andie.'' She rose from her chair, squaring her shoulders as if she were ready to face a firing squad. Andie had never known the members of her family to be so melodramatic. ''If he was with Andie last night,'' Celia announced, ''then she must really care about him. And it's only a mess because of me. I'm sorry, Andie.''

"I don't understand any of this," their mother grumbled. "Why should I be angry with you if Andie is bringing your boyfriend back to her room for…" She blinked. "…for heaven knows what."

This time, it was Celia who began to pace. "Because it was all a stupid game and Andie knew it. He was never my boyfriend, not even my date, really. I think Jason is an interesting and very eligible man, but I only brought him to get you off my back for the weekend, Mum. I couldn't take any more matchmaking. So I lied."

"What?" Their mother sat down in a wing chair with a thump. "Celia is suddenly lying and Andie is seducing her sister's boyfriend. My daughters have both lost their minds."

"Look, Mum, I'm the one who screwed up," Celia continued. Andie tried to break in to explain, but her sister wasn't having any of it. "It was stupid of me, and not fair to anyone, especially to Andie. But I did it and I will own up to it. Andie found out and called me on it, and we were all clear by whatever time it was she, uh…" She bit her lip. "…made out with Jason."

Made out with Jason. Andie decided to keep her mouth shut. Better part of valor and all that.

"Honestly, Mum," Celia said. "I wouldn't have cared if he'd been fooling around with an entire squad of Chicago Bulls cheerleaders out on the terrace."

"They're called Embraceable Ewes," Andie said quietly, "and he doesn't like basketball. He prefers baseball. Home runs, that sort of thing."

"How do you know all this?" her mother asked. "Exactly how much time did you spend with the man?"

"Not that much. Cee left him with me yesterday afternoon while she finished up some work, and we got to talking, that's all." Andie threw up her hands. "I like him, okay? I was interested."

She left out the part about how every word that dropped from his yummy lips sounded like a double entendre.

"I want you to know," her mother declared, "that I am completely shocked by all of this. I feel as though I don't know either of you. Celia suddenly turns into some girl from a soap opera, pretending this poor man is her boyfriend..."

"I know," Celia murmured, contrite.

But Mrs. Summerhill kept up her lecture. "And Andie, you should've known better than to fall for him while he was still attached to your sister, even if it was all a ruse."

"I know," she mumbled, also contrite. "I did try, Mum. It's just... There's this weird spark between us."

"Oh, dear." Her mother's tone softened. "You know, I think I noticed that yesterday. The way he looked at you over dinner... I have to admit, it was part of the reason I thought he was so wrong for Celia."

"How come I didn't notice?" Celia asked.

"I don't know," Andie said. "I did my best not to get all entangled, but he's so adorable and sweet and smart and…"

"And perfect for you," their mother finished. Her tone was odd, confused, as if she couldn't quite believe it herself. "It's really strange, Andie, but all the things that make him a terrible choice for Celia…might mean he's perfect for you."

Andie narrowed her gaze at her mother. "You're kidding, right? I thought you hated him."

"I admit that I think he's arrogant and kind of pushy," her mother allowed. "And I know that all that business about retiring and playing on his yacht would've driven Celia insane. But you, Andie, well, you might be exactly the right person to cut him down to size. Besides, I think you match up pretty well with him. If you thought his ideas were ridiculous, you'd tell him so. And vice versa. He might be the right person to challenge you, to get you off your comfy cushion here so you'll start looking for the things you want." Her voice took on a huskier edge when she whispered, "Plus, of course, he certainly is nice to look at."

Okay, now Andie knew she'd entered the Twilight Zone. Her *mother* recognized the hotness factor?

"I'm still upset with both of you," their mother said, recovering nicely.

"We're sorry," Celia offered. "Can we at least tell Andie she can pursue the guy if she wants to?"

"Oh, all right. Pursue away, Andie."

"Wait a second." Andie shook her head. "For starters, if I want somebody, I don't sit around asking for permission from my mother."

Her mother smiled as she sent her daughter a shrewd glance. "You know, Andie, I just realized that's the first time you've sounded like yourself since you moved back home last year after you lost the third job in a row. You've been acting so compliant, I almost forgot what you're really like. But suddenly, my rebel daughter is back."

"Celia tried to take my place there for a while, but I think I'm stepping back in," Andie noted dryly.

"Look, I had a bad weekend, okay?" Celia groused. "Maybe I'm asserting my independence just like Andie."

"Two rebellious daughters? Oh, dear. I suppose I'm just going to have to get used to this." But Margaret didn't really sound convinced.

"Well, I know one thing," Andie returned, trying to juggle too many thoughts at once. "I know I'm not as sure as you both seem to be that Jace is right for me. And for another, I have way too much to do in the next three weeks to have any time for any man, let alone one who requires as much attention as he does. I want everything to be perfect for Kate and Rob. They deserve a beautiful day, and I'm going to make sure they get it."

"Oh, that's right. The wedding planning." Mrs.

Summerhill gazed pensively at Andie. "Andie, I do think... No, I'm not going to say it."

"What?"

"Well, I don't know. It's just... You seem to love it so much, and I think if nothing else, this weekend has taught me not to make assumptions about my daughters." She sighed. "I hate to say it, but maybe Jason was right about that, too. Just because it didn't work once doesn't mean it won't ever work." She shrugged. "Maybe you ought to give the party-planning thing another try."

CHAPTER SEVEN

Three weeks later

"ANDIE, are you ready?" Celia peeked into the anteroom at the church, where they'd all dressed.

"Almost," Andie responded quickly. "Almost."

The bride, her maid of honor and one bridesmaid were ready, but Andie had needed to sneak away to doublecheck the candles and flowers in the church, so she was the last to finish. She had an assistant helping her today so that she could be a bridesmaid first and a wedding planner second, but there were some things she didn't trust Lindsay, as capable as she was, to handle.

"Hurry up, will you?"

"Coming." She smoothed her hair, done up in a sleek chignon, gave herself one last scan up and down, and decided everything was where it needed to be. The blush-colored dresses were understated, but flattering to each of them, and the clean lines matched up nicely with Kate's simple and elegant white silk gown. Left to her own devices, Andie had given all three attendants the same straight skirt, but slightly different bodices. Hers had fitted three-quarter sleeves and a little lace and seed pearls scattered around a rather dramatic décolletage, while Celia's was sleeveless with a square, unadorned neckline, and the maid of honor, Mary Beth, a college friend of Kate's, had chosen short sleeves and a round neck with pearls.

Andie had to admit she liked her dress the best of the three, but hey, if she had to pick them out and harangue the seamstress into extra-speedy service to get the gowns done on time, then she deserved the prettiest one, right? She beamed at her own image. She really did love weddings.

"Come on, Andie," Celia urged her. "Quit wasting the smiles on yourself. The photographer is waiting. He's already done everything else, so all he needs is the full complement of bridesmaids." Carrying both their bouquets, she tugged at her sister's hand. "That means you. Get a move on."

"Coming, coming." Lifting her skirt, Andie followed Celia out into the rose garden behind the Little Chapel on the Knoll, an exquisite white church she'd found for the wedding service. It wasn't grand, but it fitted Kate and Rob's plans, and better yet, was available on short notice.

Celia handed over Andie's bouquet of pale peach and pink roses, and Andie slid into her place in the line-up, smiling broadly on cue. As the photographer gave them orders, Celia whispered, "Did you call him?"

Without moving her lips or marring her smile, Andie managed to say, "Who?"

"You know who. Jace. Did you talk to him? Is he coming?"

"To the wedding?"

"Of course to the wedding." Celia turned her head and glared at her sister. "Stop being coy. Did you talk to him or not?"

"First bridesmaid, move your head back to the left, please—and look at me," the photographer commanded. Celia had no choice but to comply.

"I left him three messages, but no, we haven't talked," Andie murmured.

"I think he's been out of town," Celia told her, keeping her smile wide for the camera.

"Now the bride and just her three attendants, please," he called out, waving his arm. "Gentlemen, you can step aside for now."

They rotated obediently as Celia added, "I sent him some figures he needed on that hotel deal and he hasn't gotten back to me. His assistant said he was out of town, so I'm sure that's why he hasn't called."

"Celia," Andie muttered, "drop it, okay? I tried. He didn't call back. It's been three weeks. If he wanted to see me or talk to me, he would. He's a big boy."

A very big boy. But Jason McKinley was really

the last thing she wanted to discuss on her brother's wedding day.

When the photographer decided to pose a few more shots with only the bride and the maid of honor, Celia took Andie's arm, pulling her aside. "For one thing, I know you didn't call him right away, so it hasn't been three weeks."

Trust her sister to be precise, Andie thought. But, yes, she had stewed for at least ten days after the engagement party, burying herself in wedding details and trying not to stare at the phone or think about Jace. "Okay, so he's had a week and a half," she amended. "It's still plenty of time."

"I saw him at a meeting the Thursday after the engagement party and he was grumpy and wouldn't discuss you—*very* grumpy," Celia told her. "That seems like good evidence to me that he was smitten."

"Smitten? I hardly think so."

"I think he really fell for you, Andie. He asked me how you were and I could see it in his eyes."

Andie sent her sister a suspicious glance. Celia, reading mysterious messages in people's eyes? That was something new. But then she hadn't been herself since the weekend of the engagement party. These days, Celia was doing crazy things like skipping around, humming to herself. It was bizarre. "What do you mean, he asked you how I was? What did you say?"

Celia lifted her narrow shoulders in a shrug. "I said you were doing okay."

"Did you tell him I was smitten, too?" she demanded.

"Of course not." She frowned. "What do you take me for? If you want him to know you're smitten, you're going to have to tell him yourself. The point is, that was two weeks ago. You can't blame him if he's been out of town since then."

"Yes, but—"

"No buts. Call him again."

"I called him three times. I left three messages." Picking up her skirt, Andie went back inside the chapel, with Celia trailing close behind. "I swallowed my pride, Cee, and I didn't want to. But I felt it was the right thing to do, to let him know that after I'd had some time to think about it, I did decide he'd made some good points. So, you know, I caved. I gave in. I let him win."

Celia's lips curved into a knowing smile. "I'll bet you left some pretty funny messages. Message number one: 'Hello, Jason. I hate you. Don't call me.' Message number two: 'Jason, it's me again. Maybe you were, you know, sort of, kind of right about some things. Because I am a better person than you are, I'm willing to admit that. But I still don't want you to call me.' And message number three: 'Okay, it's me. Why haven't you called yet? What is wrong with you?' Allowed by a clunk on his machine when you hung up. That's what I think, Andie. Am I close?"

"No, you're not close at all," Andie snapped. "I said I was sorry about some things, but that he was wrong, too, for pushing so hard. I told him I was launching my event-planning business and getting an apartment in the city, and maybe I would see him sometime. Perfectly nice. Perfectly reasonable.''

"So you didn't ask him to the wedding?''

"No," she said flatly, "but it's not like he doesn't know when it is or where it is. I, uh, sent him an invitation." She shrugged. "I had some left over. So I sent him one a couple of weeks ago. Just so he knows.''

"I think he'll be here.''

"I don't.''

Lindsay, Andie's assistant, murmured, "Ladies, guests are starting to arrive. You'll need to go back to the bride's room and get ready.''

"Of course.'' Andie refused to discuss the matter any further. "This is Kate's day," she reminded Celia. "Let's concentrate on that, okay?''

"Okay,'' her sister agreed reluctantly.

Andie could tell Kate was getting nervous, so she did her best to be cheerful and helpful and soothing, checking on the old and the new and the borrowed and the blue, peeking her head around the corner to make sure the music had started, waiting for the cue. Kate's anxiety must be spilling over onto her.

But when it was finally time to march down the aisle, Andie knew the butterflies were not just about the wedding. It wasn't about the last-minute details, either, because the chapel looked beautiful, with candles and white roses everywhere. It was the most romantic setting she'd ever seen. She felt like bursting into tears herself.

Her heart was beating too quickly, and she felt too warm. And some strange, persistent voice was whispering in her ear. *Is he here? Is that him at the end of the third pew? No? Not here then?*

"No," she whispered to herself. "Not here."

But her smile stayed, plastered to her face as she clutched her flowers in a death-grip and sailed straight ahead toward the altar.

Things were a blur after that. She heard the minister, she listened to the vows, and when she saw that Kate was starting to cry as she got to the "I, Katharine, take you, Robert..." part, Andie automatically passed a lace hanky along to Celia, who gave it to Mary Beth, who offered it to Kate.

"I do," Rob said, and his deep voice was just as shaky and emotional as Kate's had been earlier.

My brother is getting married, she realized with a kind of awe. *Married. He's pledging his whole heart to someone else, and his life will never be the same.*

Was she brave enough to do that when her turn came? Was she willing to take the kind of risk that Rob and Kate were leaping into?

She had no idea.

"I now pronounce you husband and wife," the minister intoned. "I am very happy to present to you, Mr. and Mrs. Robert Summerhill."

As everyone clapped, Kate and Rob waltzed

back down the aisle, beaming with joy, and Andie turned, too, ready to take the groomsman's arm and bring up the rear. It was only when she made the complete turn, facing the back of the chapel, that she saw him.

Jace.

Her knees went weak, and she had to hang on to the poor groomsman for dear life. Jace was lounging at the back, as if he'd arrived at the very last minute and hadn't even had time to find a seat. He looked wonderful, wearing a black suit with a bright white shirt and a dark silk tie. Of course he looked wonderful. The man was gorgeous.

His eyes met hers, and Andie's heart leapt in her chest. He was here. That had to mean he wanted to see her, right? That had to mean he was making the effort because he was…smitten. A small smile started to play around her lips. It broke into a full grin when he began to smile, too.

She wasn't sure she could keep walking all the way down that endless aisle, but she did, putting one foot in front of the other, trying to stay calm and failing miserably, until finally she was there.

"Hi," she said breathlessly, disengaging her arm from her escort and letting him join the receiving line without her. Awkward and unsure, she stood in front of Jace, twisting the ribbons from her bouquet between her fingers.

"You look beautiful," he told her. His chocolate-brown eyes, framed with thick lashes, were warm as his gaze swept over her. "Amazing."

"Thank you." Her pulse was racing. All it took was a look, and she melted right before his eyes. "I, uh, wasn't sure you were going to make it."

"I was invited," he noted with a hint of sardonic humor. "I don't really know the bride and groom all that well, but somehow I got an invitation. It was a little late, but hey, I got one."

"Imagine that."

Wedding guests were starting to file out of the sanctuary into the foyer, and they had to shuffle to the side, over by the wall, to stay out of the way. Jace bent closer, pulling on one of her ribbons. "Yeah, I'm not sure why I was invited, but I guess it helps when you have an in with the wedding planner."

"Oh? You have an in?"

"I'm not sure."

"But you're here," she said lightly, searching his eyes for clues. She couldn't stop smiling. It was very strange. "I guess that means you must think you have a shot."

"Maybe a shot." He pulled her right hand away from the flowers, bringing it up to his lips. As his mouth brushed her fingers, sending tingles down her arm, she found she was having trouble standing up again. "I'm hoping," he whispered.

"Oh, I think you have a shot." Andie's voice came out husky and low. She cleared her throat. "I did call. You didn't call back, though."

He didn't answer the implied question, but he didn't give up her hand, either. "Congratulations on the new business and the new apartment. Sounds like you're taking steps.''

''Yeah, who'd a thunk it?'' she joked. ''The Summerhills' youngest—you know, the one who thinks she's a free spirit and a rebel but couldn't seem to leave the nest. Well, she's finally moved out. Will wonders never cease?''

''Did you think any more about my job offer?''

''Actually, no.'' Was that why he was here? Surely, with the bedroom eyes and the seductively soft words and the hand-kissing, he wasn't here just to make a job offer?

''I noticed that you left me messages about your foray into party planning and city living, but you didn't say anything about...'' A long pause kept her hanging on his words.

''About?'' she prompted.

''About me. Personally.'' Now he dropped her hand and slid his own into the pocket of his expensive pants, dipping a shoulder back to negligently balance against the wall. ''I didn't want to seem too pushy or assume too much.''

''Oh.'' In other words, the next move was hers. She could handle that. ''Let me show you what I think about you personally, Jace.''

In heels, she was tall enough to reach him easily, and she smiled as she fastened both arms around his neck, bouquet and all. She gazed at him for a long moment, enjoying the close-up view. His dark, deep eyes, his soft lips, his hard jaw... So lovely to look at. Why was she so fascinated with that tiny indentation in his chin, anyway? With one finger, she traced the cleft.

"The thing is, Jace..." She did what she'd wanted to do forever. She touched her tongue to that mysterious line in his chin, enjoying the way the tiny gesture made him jump. Quietly, she murmured, "The thing is, I haven't known you for very long, but I think I might be in love with you."

"Oh, Andie..."

"No, don't say anything just yet." She put her finger to his lips. "I like you. I'm really..." She shivered. "I'm *really* attracted to you. I'd like to see where this could go between us. What do you think?"

"Yes," he whispered, but still he didn't move.

A bit shaky but determined to finish what she had started, Andie tipped her head up far enough to graze her lips against his, trying to tell him all the things with her kiss that she hadn't managed to say yet. Her mouth met his, barely, but he wasn't exactly kissing her back. She pushed harder.

He resisted a little at first, but then he seemed to give in, to shift and accommodate, his warm, wet, insistent mouth slanting sideways across hers, delving deeper, fiercer, sweeter. His arms wrapped around her so tightly she could barely breathe, but she didn't care. The bouquet slipped out of her hands, tumbling to the floor behind him with a soft thud, and they stood there for some time, caught up in the moment and in each other.

"Wow." Andie broke away, gasping for air. She was sizzling down to the pointy toes of her pumps. How long had that kiss lasted? Her body had come alive so fast, she wasn't quite sure how to handle it. She glanced down at the deep vee of her neckline, where her heart was beating so rapidly that her breasts threatened to surge right out of her gown. All she could manage to say was another "Wow."

"How fast can we get out of here?" Jace asked urgently, his arm around her waist still clasping her close.

"Out? But the receiving line…"

"Skip it," he ordered.

"I—I don't think I can," she stammered.

"It's probably over already. What were there, thirty people in there? I mean, it's a small wedding." He abandoned her long enough to peer around the corner. "There's just a few people left. Not worth going back for."

She'd missed the receiving line because she was making out with Jace? Well, no one had said anything. It couldn't have been that terrible, could it?

"How long till the reception?" he asked, pulling her back into his embrace, dropping a quick kiss on her lips.

"I don't know. What time is it?" She was disoriented, and her brain only got fuzzier the more he kept kissing her. She was the wedding planner, damn it. And a bridesmaid. She shouldn't be experiencing this mental meltdown.

"Andie?" It was Celia, looking very shy as she edged around the corner into the sanctuary. Her new beau, David the accountant, was visible behind her. Celia murmured, "Hello, Jason. Good to see you. It seems the two of you have reached some sort of, um, compromise."

Andie knew her lipstick was smeared and tendrils of hair were escaping the chignon, and that any missing lipstick had shown up on Jace's mouth. As surreptitiously as possible, she reached up and wiped some of it away with her finger. She knew what they looked like. But what could she say? *Jace and I have this problem—we can't keep our hands off each other, even at inopportune moments.* Yeah, that would do it.

"We're doing fine," Jace commented. "Fine. Celia, what would you say if I told you I think I'm falling in love with your sister?"

Andie swallowed. Had he just said what she thought he'd said? He gripped her hand tightly and she squeezed right back, grinning like a fool.

"Oh, well, that's...nice." Celia brightened. "Congratulations."

"It is nice, isn't it?" Andie returned. She nodded her head. "Very nice."

"Okay, well, listen, I wanted to let you know that we're leaving. Andie, you rode with me. You don't need to ride back with me, do you?" She waved a finger in the air, pointing in the general direction of the door. "We'll just see you at the hotel tonight for the reception. Eight o'clock, right?''

"Eight o'clock?" Jace repeated.

"Uh-huh." Already backing away, Celia seemed to be waiting for Andie to explain. When she didn't, Celia jumped in. "The wedding itself was tiny because the church is so small, but the reception will have a larger guest list. Dinner, dancing, that sort of thing. Back downtown. Andie booked the ballroom at one of your new hotels. Didn't she tell you?"

"No, she didn't," he murmured.

"Okay, well, now you know. We're off," Celia called out. "See you later."

But Andie wasn't really paying attention. Gazing at Jace, she knew exactly what he was thinking. And it had nothing to do with the fact that she'd chosen his hotel for the reception. It had to do with eight o'clock, which was at least five hours away. Plenty of time. A smile curved her lips, and at the same time a spark of anticipation appeared in Jace's eyes.

"What did you just say to Celia? That you think you're falling in love with me? Was that serious?" she asked, feeling warmth and joy begin to seep through her whole body.

"Oh, yeah." He bent to kiss her again, taking his time, getting her all warm and toasty.

"You know, with the reception not till eight, we have plenty of time," she whispered. "Plenty of time."

"Plenty." He was sort of half-carrying, half-guiding her to the front door of the church, nibbling on her the whole way. "I have a limo. Where should we go?"

"I don't care," she told him, giving a small gasp as he swept her up into his arms and strode toward the waiting car. Andie tightened her grip around his neck, going along for the ride.

His driver scurried to open the door as Jace bent to tuck her inside. "Which hotel?" he asked impatiently.

"Uh. For what?"

"The reception. Which of my hotels is it at?"

Clear your head, Andie. Don't be such a goon.
"The Sullivan."

He grinned at her. "Good choice." Quickly, he instructed the driver where to go, and then slid in beside her. He snapped shut the smoked glass between them and the front seat, drawing her over into his lap before they'd even left the curb.

She'd forgotten just how forceful and overwhelming he could be. "So we're going to the hotel? Are we, um, getting a room?" she asked delicately.

It was hard to be delicate when he was licking the slope of her neck and had one hand under her dress, skating up her calf, swooshing the heavy fabric out of his way. She couldn't help tilting back her head and giving in to whatever he wanted. Because she wanted it more.

"Yeah," he murmured into her ear. "Don't

worry. I have connections. And the Sullivan has a great presidential suite.''

"I'm sure it does, but—"

"Don't worry," he said again. He drew back and gave her a rakish grin. "That'll give us a place to freshen up. In case you're worried we're wrinkling your dress.''

"Oh, I hadn't thought about it.'' Honestly, her gown had never crossed her mind. His hand was up to her knee now, and she began to wiggle, unable to sit still while little flames licked at her knee and her neck and her thigh. Ohhh. He was up to her thigh. She was melting into his lap. Her voice was as shivery as her spine when she whispered, "Jace?"

"Mm-hmmm?" He shrugged out of his jacket and started to work on his tie.

"We're not going to make it to the hotel, are we?"

"Depends on what you mean by make it," he said sweetly. He pitched down far enough to kiss her again as he stripped off the tie. "We'll get there all right. But…''

"But we may make it in this limo first, right?"

His grin lit up the whole back seat. "Is that what you want?"

She reached for his shirt, unbuttoning like mad. "Oh, yeah, that's what I want.''

"Good." But he stilled, smoothing her hair away from her face with one hand and gazing at her with tenderness and desire and something that almost looked like awe. "I love you, Andie. I think we're perfect together."

She giggled. His sweet words shouldn't have made her laugh, but they did. "You're crazy, Jace. You do realize that, right?" Settling next to him on the wide leather seat, ready for the ride of a lifetime, Andie relaxed into the perfection that was the two of them together. "I love you, too. We are going to have so much fun."

"Your family hates me," he warned. "You ready for that?"

"They don't hate you." She snuggled closer, slipping her hands inside his open shirt, reaching for his belt buckle. "You have to understand. It's taken them all these years to get used to me, the round peg in their square household. And now we're adding a corkscrew to the mix."

"That's me?" His fingers danced higher, palming her bottom, as he fitted her whole leg around him. "I'm not sure I want to be a corkscrew."

"Too late. You're with me now. Your fate is sealed."

"I'm with you now." Jace grinned. "I like the sound of that."

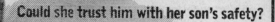
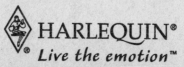

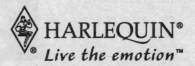

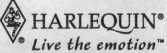